THE SUGAR QUEEN

EMERSON PASS CONTEMPORARIES, BOOK ONE

TESS THOMPSON

Blue Midnight:

"This is a beautiful book with an unexpected twist that takes the story from romance to mystery and back again. I've already started the 2nd book in the series!" - *Mama O*

"This beautiful book captured my attention and never let it go. I did not want it to end and so very much look forward to reading the next book." - *Pris Shartle*

"I enjoyed this new book cover to cover. I read it on my long flight home from Ireland and it helped the time fly by, I wish it had been longer so my whole flight could have been lost to this lovely novel about second chances and finding the truth. Written with wisdom and humor this novel shares the raw emotions a new divorce can leave behind." - *J. Sorenson*

"Tess Thompson is definitely one of my auto-buy authors! I love her writing style. Her characters are so real to life that you just can't put the book down once you start! Blue Midnight makes you believe in second chances. It makes you believe that everyone deserves an HEA. I loved the twists and turns in this book, the mystery and suspense, the family dynamics and the restoration of trust and security." - *Angela MacIntyre*

"Tess writes books with real characters in them, characters with flaws and baggage and gives them a second chance. (Real people, some remind me of myself and my girlfriends.) Then she cleverly and thoroughly develops those characters and makes you feel deeply for them. Characters are complex and multi-faceted, and the plot seems to unfold naturally, and never feels contrived." - *K. Lescinsky*

Caramel and Magnolias:

"Nobody writes characters like Tess Thompson. It's like she looks into our lives and creates her characters based on our best friends, our lovers, and our neighbors. Caramel and Magnolias, and the authors debut novel Riversong, have some of the best characters I've ever had a chance to fall in love with. I don't like leaving spoilers in reviews so just trust me, Nicholas Sparks has nothing on Tess Thompson, her writing flows so smoothly you can't help but to want to read on!" - *T. M. Frazier*

"I love Tess Thompson's books because I love good writing. Her prose is clean and tight, which are increasingly rare qualities, and manages to evoke a full range of emotions with both subtlety and power. Her fiction goes well beyond art imitating life. Thompson's characters are alive and fully-realized, the action is believable, and the story unfolds with the right balance of tension and exuberance. CARAMEL AND MAGNOLIAS is a pleasure to read." - *Tsuruoka*

"The author has an incredible way of painting an image with her words. Her storytelling is beautiful, and leaves you wanting more! I love that the story is about friendship (2 best friends) and love. The characters are richly drawn and I found myself rooting for them from the very beginning. I think you will, too!" - *Fogvision*

"I got swept off my feet, my heartstrings were pulled, I held my breath, and tightened my muscles in suspense. Tess paints stunning scenery with her words and draws you in to the lives of her characters."- *T. Bean*

Duet For Three Hands:
"Tears trickled down the side of my face when I reached the end of this road. Not because the story left me feeling sad or disappointed, no. Rather, because I already missed them. My friends. Though it isn't goodbye, but see you later. And so I will sit impatiently waiting, with desperate eagerness to hear where life has taken you, what burdens have you downtrodden, and

what triumphs warm your heart. And in the meantime, I will go out and live, keeping your lessons and friendship and love close, the light to guide me through any darkness. And to the author I say thank you. My heart, my soul -all of me - needed these words, these friends, this love. I am forever changed by the beauty of your talent." - *Lisa M.Gott*

"I am a great fan of Tess Thompson's books and this new one definitely shows her branching out with an engaging enjoyable historical drama/love story. She is a true pro in the way she weaves her storyline, develops true to life characters that you love! The background and setting is so picturesque and visible just from her words. Each book shows her expanding, growing and excelling in her art. Yet another one not to miss. Buy it you won't be disappointed. The ONLY disappointment is when it ends!!!" - *Sparky's Last*

"There are some definite villains in this book. Ohhhh, how I loved to hate them. But I have to give Thompson credit because they never came off as caricatures or one dimensional. They all felt authentic to me and (sadly) I could easily picture them. I loved to love some and loved to hate others." - *The Baking Bookworm*

"I stayed up the entire night reading Duet For Three Hands and unbeknownst to myself, I fell asleep in the middle of reading the book. I literally woke up the next morning with Tyler the Kindle beside me (thankfully, still safe and intact) with no ounce of battery left. I shouldn't have worried about deadlines because, guess what? Duet For Three Hands was the epitome of unputdownable." - *The Bookish Owl*

Miller's Secret
"From the very first page, I was captivated by this wonderful tale. The cast of characters amazing - very fleshed out and multi-

dimensional. The descriptions were perfect - just enough to make you feel like you were transported back to the 20's and 40's.... This book was the perfect escape, filled with so many twists and turns I was on the edge of my seat for the entire read." - *Hilary Grossman*

"The sad story of a freezing-cold orphan looking out the window at his rich benefactors on Christmas Eve started me off with Horatio-Alger expectations for this book. But I quickly got pulled into a completely different world--the complex five-character braid that the plot weaves. The three men and two women characters are so alive I felt I could walk up and start talking to any one of them, and I'd love to have lunch with Henry. Then the plot quickly turned sinister enough to keep me turning the pages.
Class is set against class, poor and rich struggle for happiness and security, yet it is love all but one of them are hungry for. ......Where does love come from? What do you do about it? The story kept me going, and gave me hope. For a little bonus, there are Thompson's delightful observations, like: "You'd never know we could make something this good out of the milk from an animal who eats hats." A really good read!" - *Kay in Seattle*

"She paints vivid word pictures such that I could smell the ocean and hear the doves. Then there are the stories within a story that twist and turn until they all come together in the end. I really had a hard time putting it down. Five stars aren't enough!"
- *M.R. Williams*

ALSO BY TESS THOMPSON

CLIFFSIDE BAY

BLUE MOUNTAIN SERIES

EMERSON PASS

The School Mistress of Emerson Pass

The Sugar Queen of Emerson Pass

RIVER VALLEY

Riversong

Riverbend

Riverstar

Riversnow

Riverstorm

Tommy's Wish

River Valley Bundle, Books 1-4

LEGLEY BAY

Caramel and Magnolias

Tea and Primroses

STANDALONES

The Santa Trial

Duet for Three Hands

Miller's Secret

THE SUGAR QUEEN

EMERSON PASS CONTEMPORARIES, BOOK ONE

TESS THOMPSON

For my brother Adam and my sister-in-law Rochelle - and to the memory of their beautiful baby Miles, who we forever hold in our hearts.

THE SUGAR QUEEN

A WARNING TO READERS

The Sugar Queen deals with the stillbirth of an infant. My intention is never to trigger someone's memories and personal loss in any way. If this is the case, please do not read.

B randi

THE GHOSTS OF EMERSON PASS HAUNT ME. NOT THE SPIRITS OF those who built this town from bricks and dreams. They're all resting in peace, probably sitting around a table eating my great-great-great-grandmother Lizzie's chicken stew. No, these apparitions are the loves of my life.

They're only memories now, replaced by gaping holes of grief. One is a secret buried in the town cemetery under a gravestone with no name. The other is Trapper Barnes, professional athlete and descendant of the infamous Alexander Barnes. The boy who left and never returned. The boy who chose hockey over me.

The boy I sent away.

Until he returned on an ordinary afternoon in August.

The bells over the front door of my bakery jingled as I was about to close for the day. I looked up, surprised to have a new customer. Emerson Pass was a small town. Everyone knew my sandwiches, muffins, cookies, and cakes were gone by three. By four, I had only a few sad scones begging for a buyer.

My heart stopped for at least three seconds. Trapper Barnes stood before me.

I blinked three times to make sure I wasn't seeing things. But no, it was him. Tall and tanned with the same thick brown hair and big brown eyes.

"Hey, Brandi." A deep voice, masculine yet soft. He smiled, showing his straight white teeth. Other than his dimples, all youthful roundness had disappeared, leaving chiseled cheekbones and a defined chin. The years had broadened his shoulders and chest. He was even better-looking than he'd been when we were kids. Of course he was. This was Trapper Barnes. Town hero. Hockey star. Love of my life.

I'd seen him on television and magazines over the years. Not often, as I avoided anything to do with professional hockey. If I accidentally caught a glimpse of him, the wound opened fresh, and I was wrecked for days. None of those photographs did him justice. The man was sinfully beautiful.

I couldn't utter a sound. Instead, I stared at him. Could he see the way my chest ripped open and bled onto my counter? I stole a glance at his left hand. No ring. Thank God, nothing but one long, gorgeous finger. I'd accepted long ago that he would never be mine, but belonging to someone else? The weight of that pain would crush me.

"It smells fantastic in here." His brown eyes sparkled as if he were on the brink of laughter. "Now that I'm no longer training, I can have a treat every once in a while. I'll take the pumpkin one."

I grabbed the last pumpkin from the platters. No longer training? What did that mean? I set the scone on a plate and slid it across the wide counter. God help me, I could smell his cologne. He smelled the same as the last day I'd ever spent with him.

"How much?" he asked.

I shook my head. "On the house. The scone's dry by this time of day."

His mouth lifted in that same drowsy smile he'd had since we were kids. "You speak. I thought maybe you'd gone mute since I left."

"Yes, sorry. You surprised me." The understatement of the century.

"The Sugar Queen." He gestured toward the doors. "It's perfect."

"Thanks." I'm never a woman of many words, but my dry mouth made elegant oratory even more difficult.

"Mama tells me this is the best bakery in town," he said.

I glanced around, wondering what it looked like through his eyes. Industrial lights hung over the counter. Round bistro-style tables and chairs looked out to the street. A silver espresso machine and a refrigerator with premade items took up one side, with the register and counter on the other. A chalkboard with the menu hung on the wall, written in my neat handwriting. Every morning I set out the day's offerings on various platters and boards in an attractive display on the counter.

"It's the *only* bakery in town," I said.

He smiled again and lifted one thick eyebrow. "Probably because no one dares compete with you."

Trapper. Always kind and encouraging to everyone he ever met. Lifting people up was like a mission with him. He could find the best part of a person, no matter who they were. He never missed an opportunity to inspire or encourage. I'd almost forgotten what it was like to bask in the glow of his compliment. Back in the day it had been the only antidote to my mother's criticism. And there it was. I ached with wanting him, as if no time had passed. *No,* I screamed silently. *Don't let him break you. Not again.*

"What're you doing here?" I asked. "I mean, here in town."

"I've moved home. Didn't Breck and Huck tell you?"

Breck and Huck and Trapper were best friends from childhood. And no, they had not mentioned that Trapper was moving home permanently. *Oh God.* How could this be happening? I couldn't have him here. Not living and breathing and stopping in for a damn scone. How would I look him in the eye, knowing what I'd done? The secret I'd kept from him.

"They don't come by often." I came out from behind the counter and turned the Open sign to Closed. "Anyway, it's none of my business what you do."

As I turned to face him, he placed his hand over his heart and smiled. "Ouch."

Damn that smile. Still melted me like butter over a biscuit.

"You look beautiful," he said. "More so than ever."

"Not really." I wondered if I had any flour on my face. When I was in the zone I didn't think twice about my appearance. In the shop, I wore my long blond hair in a braid and usually didn't bother with more than mascara and blush, always promising myself to remember lipstick but never quite managing. Truth is, I didn't care about what I looked like. Everyone in this town had already seen me. I wasn't interested in romance. The only Friday night date I wanted was a television show and a glass of wine.

The only man I'd ever cared about looking pretty for had left a long time ago.

"I always knew you'd do something spectacular," he said.

"Baking bread is hardly spectacular," I said.

"Tell that to the customers lined up out your door every morning."

"How do you know that?" I asked.

His chiseled features softened. I saw a hint of the vulnerable, sensitive boy I'd loved instead of the giant, confident man before me. "I've been by a few times. I didn't know if you'd want to see me, so I just kept walking."

"Why today then?" I kept my words clipped, unemotional. All I wanted was for him to leave so I could sort through what to do. I didn't want him here. Not in my shop or my town.

"I couldn't stop myself," he said. "I wanted to see you."

My stomach churned. "I would've thought Emerson Pass was a little small for you these days. Did you get hurt? Is that why you're retiring?"

"That's right. Bad knee. I lasted longer than most. It was time to come home and start a new chapter. I got some advice from my friend Brody Mullen. After my injury, he said to move back home. Start a new chapter with no regrets."

I had no idea who that was. "I don't follow hockey."

His eyes widened. "Brody Mullen's a former football quarterback. Some say the best there ever was. You don't watch sports anymore?"

"No time. The world of professional sports is irrelevant to my life." I motioned toward the back where my ovens resided. "Common people like me are just trying to make our rent."

"There's nothing common about you. Never has been."

I ignored the praise. I'd be damned if he was going to suck me in with his effortless charm. Had I not evolved from a lovesick teenager? *Remember your secret,* I reminded myself. *Remember what you kept from him.*

"You used to love hockey," he said. "If I recall correctly, you never missed a game."

"I loved watching *you.* When you left, hockey lost its appeal."

"Oh, okay." He glanced down at the counter. "Guess that answers that question."

"What's that?" I asked, then silently cursed myself. *Stop engaging. Tell him to leave.*

"Sometimes when I played, I wondered if you were watching me on television."

"I wasn't."

He flinched. "Got it."

"What did you expect? That I was here pining for you?"

"Jeez, Brandi, you don't have to be mean."

The hurt in his eyes nearly undid my resolve to remain cold. "I'm sorry. I didn't mean to sound that way. You had the life you dreamed of, and I'm glad for you." His dreams had come true.

I'd wanted that for him. *Remember that*, I reminded myself. "I'm just surprised you ever thought of me at all."

"Do I need to remind you how it all went down?" he asked softly. "You're the one who ended things. You're the one who made the rules. No contact, remember? *You* made it so I couldn't come home."

"How's that exactly?" My voice cracked. "Your family owns most of this town. It's yours more than mine."

"Because I couldn't come home and risk seeing you. It hurt too much."

His words nearly knocked me across the room. I gripped the edge of the counter to stay in place. He didn't mean it, I reminded myself. He chose hockey. Not me. "From what I could tell, you made up for it by dating a plethora of actresses and models."

His mouth lifted in a sad smile. "You didn't watch my games, but you read tabloids about me?"

"It's hard to avoid. I stand in grocery store lines." I wiped crumbs from the counter into my apron and tossed them into the garbage.

"Most of that stuff is lies. I only dated half the women they said I did."

An arrow pierced my chest. *Half the women.* Women who were not me. My lunch continued to churn in my stomach. A drop of perspiration slid down my lower back. "You were a girl magnet in high school. Some things never change." I looked past him to the street. The wind had come up, shaking the leaves of the aspens that lined Barnes Avenue.

"I never noticed anyone but you," he said. "I never wanted anyone but you. Surely you remember that accurately?"

I avoided eye contact by reaching under the counter for a cloth I had soaking in bleach. "Where are you living?" I wiped the counter with short, furious strokes.

"I had a house built on my dad's property. You didn't know?"

"I don't exactly get updates about your life. Neither of your parents has ever set foot in this place."

He shoved his hands in his pockets and rocked back on his heels. "Yeah, about that. What happened between our mothers? Do you know? Mama said your mom shut her out after we broke up. Refused to answer her calls or emails. They were such good friends."

How could I explain this without telling him the truth? "After we broke up, my mom thought it would be best if they were no longer friends. Less messy that way, I guess."

"That's sad," he said. "The whole thing was sad."

"I'm sorry I hurt you, Trapper." I hadn't planned to say that, but somehow it slipped out of my mouth.

He shrugged one muscular shoulder. "You did. Bad."

"We were young," I said. "I wasn't ready."

"I remember your reasons." His jaw clenched as he looked down at the floor. "Didn't make it any easier to lose you, though."

I fiddled with my apron strings as waves of pain slapped me. "Have you been happy?" I asked through clenched teeth. "All your dreams came true—just like you planned." My chest ached as I waited for him to tell me. *Please*, I thought, *say yes. Please let one of us have had the life we wanted.*

"Yeah, all my hockey dreams did come true." He ran a hand over the top of his head. "They didn't make me as happy as I figured they would."

"What do you mean?"

"I loved playing, don't get me wrong. But as the years went on, I started to understand it was simply a job. Not family. Not friendship. Not love. When the docs said my knee was shot, I figured it was time to find some of what I gave up when I left. So I came home. Back to the place where I left my heart."

I almost reached over the counter to touch him but pushed my hands into my apron pockets to stop myself. How could I still love him this much? "Not much has changed here." Lame, I thought. What a stupid thing to say after he poured his heart out to me.

"Can I ask you something?" He shifted weight from one leg to the other.

"Sure."

"Did you ever have any intention of going with me to University of Michigan like we'd talked about, or did you know all along you wanted to stay here?" He asked this as if the words were being yanked out of him by an invisible rope.

"I'd planned on going, but I changed my mind," I said.

"What did I do wrong?" His voice softened. He shoved his hands into the pockets of his jeans. I swear to God, he looked like the little boy I'd met on the first day of grade school. "I'd like to know that. For peace of mind."

"Nothing. Trapper, it was never you." The back of my throat ached. I swallowed, trying to keep my composure. "We were young. It was a high school thing—not meant to last." *Liar, liar, liar.*

"I never thought it was just a high school romance. I thought we were forever. I've never been able to move on." He rubbed the heel of his hand on his forehead. "I should probably stop talking now."

We were more than high school sweethearts. I'd known it then, and I knew it now. "I haven't either." The words were out before I could stop them.

"Why haven't you ever reached out to me?" His eyes filled. "I would've been so happy to hear from you. There's not a day that's gone by that I haven't thought about you."

"It would've been wrong of me. You and I just weren't meant to be. For so many reasons."

"I can't think of one." He swiped at his eyes.

I knew one. Her name was Ava Elizabeth, and she was buried in the town cemetery. Our baby. Our stillborn baby.

"I didn't get into Michigan," I said. "That's why I couldn't go with you."

He rocked back on his heels, as if I'd smacked him. "What? How come you didn't tell me that?"

"I was ashamed."

He studied me for a few seconds before speaking. "If you'd gotten in, would you have gone with me?"

"It doesn't matter. I didn't get in. I couldn't just follow you and make your life my life. Eventually, you would've come to resent me."

"I don't think so."

"Think about it, Trapper. What was I supposed to do? Live in your dorm room and work at a fast-food place? Michigan was your dream, not mine."

"I wish you'd have told me the truth," he said. "You owed me that at least."

"What good would that have done?" The truth? My rejection from Michigan was nothing compared to the other lie.

His cheeks reddened. "Because it would've helped me understand what the hell happened between us. One day we're in love and the next day you're breaking up with me. None of it made sense to me. It still doesn't."

"Do you remember the fight we had the week before we broke up?" I asked.

He nodded and shifted his gaze to the floor. "When you asked me if a circumstance demanded it, would I choose you or hockey—and I said hockey."

After all these years, I could still feel the way those words had knocked a hole right through my middle. "That's right." I'd known I was pregnant by then. I hadn't yet told my parents or Trapper. I'd planned to tell Trapper that night and see if we could come up with a plan together. However, the moment he'd said those words, I knew what I had to do.

Let go. Send him away to begin the rest of his life. At least one of us would have all our dreams come true.

He looked up at me. "That answer is the biggest regret of my life. I should never have said something so cruel."

"It was hard to hear but necessary," I said. "You were eighteen years old, and your whole career was in front of you. I was just the girl in high school you thought you loved."

"I *did* love you. Not *thought* I loved you," he said.

"No eighteen-year-old boy with the kind of drive and talent you had should ever pick a teenage romance over a college that would lead to a professional career. That would simply be stupid. Do you hear me? Don't regret your honesty. It saved us both a lot of heartache in the end."

"Did it? Or did it drive you away? I always felt like it was some kind of test and I failed and ruined everything between us."

It was and it did.

"We were kids." This wasn't how I'd wanted this conversation to go. I needed him to leave. "What did we know about love? High school love never lasts. I was just a blip on your life. You know that."

"I never knew that. In fact, I thought the opposite. Until you sent me away, I thought we'd get married. I thought we'd have a few kids by now." His face twisted in obvious pain. "And then I ruined it by telling you hockey was more important than you."

"Trapper, listen to me." My chest hurt so much I could hardly breathe. "If I'd tagged along, you would've outgrown me."

"I disagree."

"What does it matter now?" I asked.

His voice rose in pitch. Tears dripped from his eyes. "I thought we were in love. Like epic love. The kind that lasts forever. Did you ever love me? I thought you did, and then you didn't. I've never understood what happened."

I looked at him too long. His expression changed from sad to expectant. The truth must have leaked out of my eyes along with the tears that suddenly blurred my vision. "I loved you enough to let you go."

"That makes no sense."

"What I needed from you was more than you could give." My careless mistake would have cost him everything. Two nights in a row I'd forgotten to take my birth control pills. Instead of telling him, I kept it to myself. The first of the secrets I'd kept from him.

"What did you need?"

"I needed you to want to stay here and have a simple life. In the end, we simply didn't fit together. I couldn't leave here. I never have, you know."

He watched me with those eyes that still drew me in like no one else's ever had. "Well, I'm back now for good. Does that mean anything to you?"

"Too much time has passed, Trapper. We don't even know each other anymore."

"Fair enough." The corners of his mouth twitched into a smile that did nothing to hide his sadness. "But we could get to know each other again."

"I...I can't," I said.

"Are you seeing someone?"

My first instinct was to lie. However, this town was too small for yet more deceit. "I'm not. I don't want a relationship. I'm too busy."

He picked up a napkin from the counter and wiped his eyes. "Right. Got it. I feel like an idiot coming in here and talking about this stuff. If it means anything, my intention was to come in and say hello to an old friend. I didn't plan for us to get into the past to this extent."

"You know what they say about best intentions." I smiled, hoping to lighten the mood.

"I guess so," he said. "I'm still trying to find a way to move on."

"I'm fine. You're fine. Everything's fine." I couldn't keep my voice from cracking like a burned, brittle cookie. "There's no reason to hold on to the past."

"I guess I should go, then." He turned toward the door.

"Don't forget your scone. I can bag it up for you." Why had I put it on a plate in the first place?

"Nah, I lost my appetite. See you around."

I watched him walk out the door. He looked left, then right, as if deciding which way to go. In the end, he crossed Barnes Avenue and hopped into a shiny black truck and drove away, just as he'd done ten years earlier.

Find a way to move on. He'd never been able to move on or get over me? As hard as this was to believe, I knew it to be true. Trapper had never lied to me. I was the liar.

If I'd gone to him back then and told him about the pregnancy, would the course of our lives have been altered but not ruined? Did my grief kill our baby? I'd never know now. Trapper could never be mine. Not after the secret I kept from him.

I sank to the floor behind the counter and cried.

***

THIRTY MINUTES LATER, I DROVE OUT TO THE CEMETERY AND PARKED in my usual spot. I walked down the winding cement path to the Strom family plot where my baby rested. I sat on the grass next to her. My mother had not allowed me to have her name or dates etched into the simple headstone. Only a simple outline of a bird carved into the granite marked her existence. Ava meant bird. My little bird.

I traced my fingers over the etching. "He came back. And it turns out I still love him. I know, not surprising. I never stopped. All his dreams came true. At least I was able to give him that."

I'd had to lie to him, pretend I didn't love him, and hide my pregnancy so that he might have the life he deserved. Hockey was his destiny. "When he was a little boy, all he ever cared about was hockey. You should've seen him on the ice. He was a sight. I couldn't hold him back from his dreams."

I knew if it came down to it, he'd choose the game over me. He proved me right when I asked him. *Which would you choose?*

Me or hockey? We'd been sitting in lawn chairs at his Grammie and Pa's house on the first warm day of spring.

"I don't have to choose. I can have both," he'd said, flashing me that confident grin.

"In this game, you have to choose." I'd turned away, afraid to show him my reaction.

"Hockey. I mean, for now anyway. If I'm to give you a great life, it has to start with me playing hockey."

There it was. The answer. I knew what I had to do.

Now I spoke to my daughter as if she were there. "When he moved away to college, I thought I might die without him."

I didn't, obviously. It was just my heart that had died. The rest of me was intact. After he left, I told my parents I was pregnant. My mother hatched a plan. A secret pregnancy. Adoption. No one would know, including Trapper and his parents. "I'll be damned if I let a baby wreck your life like it did mine."

It? "It" was me. I was her baby. And I was still here, ruining all her plans.

She'd wanted everything for me that she'd had to give up when she became pregnant at seventeen. She'd wanted a college education. She'd wanted a life with intellectuals and professionals. Instead, she'd gotten pregnant and married my dad. What had been a summer camp counselor fling had created a baby. Dad had brought her home to his mountain town in Colorado. As far as I could tell, she'd hated every moment of her life here.

Everyone seemed to understand that I lacked the brains to pursue academics except my mother. She couldn't see me as I was, refusing to have me tested for learning disabilities, berating me that if I only tried harder my grades would be better.

In the end, it didn't matter what she wanted for me. I was a disappointment. Even my compassionate father, who loved me more than anything in the world, was crestfallen at my failure to get into college. Then I broke his heart further when I got pregnant.

My mother had located a wonderful couple who desperately

wanted a child. He was a doctor. She was a professor. The family my mother wished we'd been. Little did she know, I'd had no intention of giving my baby to anyone.

I'd been confined to the house as the baby grew inside me. To keep occupied, I'd baked bread in my mother's kitchen. Loaves and loaves. Sourdough, wheat, oat, pumpernickel. I'd kneaded and measured and watched the yeast rise day after day. After I conquered bread, I'd moved on to cakes and cookies and muffins from the recipes from my great-great-great-grandmother Lizzie.

All the while I'd tried to work out how I was going to escape with my baby. I was a young woman with no skills and no family support unless I did exactly what they wanted. Still, I'd been determined that somehow, I would find a way to raise her on my own.

Finally, in desperation, I'd called my friend Crystal Whalen. She'd lived in Seattle during the school year and visited her grandparents during the summers. Descendants of Harley and Merry Depaul, her grandparents had continued the family's horse breeding farm in Emerson Pass. However, her mother, Jennifer, had had different ideas. She'd chosen pottery over horses and had moved to Seattle, where she'd opened her own studio. When I told Crystal about the baby and my parents' wishes, Jennifer had offered the baby and me a room in her home. I could stay with them until l got on my feet. She, too, had been a single mother, raising Crystal by herself. By choice, she assured me. "Who needs a man?"

Me, I'd thought. I wasn't independent or progressive thinking like Jennifer. I had no talents or ambitions.

Sweet little Brandi Vargas. Blonde and cute in my high school cheerleader uniform, but without an ounce of brains. I'd wanted Trapper and babies and to bake bread on Sunday afternoons in my kitchen. No woman in this day and age was supposed to want such a simple life. Despite that, I had.

When it came time for the baby's arrival, my parents had driven me to Denver, not wanting the local doctors to know about my pregnancy. In triage, the doctor's face had blanched. He hadn't looked me in the eye. I'd known something was wrong.

"What is it?"

"I'm not getting a heartbeat."

No words strung together in the English language had ever been as cruel.

I'd given birth to a baby girl. A baby girl who'd died in my womb.

I'd begged my parents to let me take her home and bury her in the plot with Lizzie and Jasper and the rest of our family. They'd agreed, as long as I kept her name and dates off the headstone. We'd asked the funeral director to please keep it quiet.

For months afterward, I'd barely left the house except to go to the cemetery. I'd bring a blanket and stay for hours. Other than that, I kept to my room watching television or staring out the window. An entire season went by, then another. Finally, one day, my father perched on the side of my bed and proposed an idea.

"There's going to be a farmers' market in town on Wednesdays," he'd said. "How about you bake some bread and sweets to sell?"

I'd agreed, mostly to quell the look of worry in his eyes. The very first Wednesday, I'd sold out of every loaf of bread, all the cookies, and most of the muffins. News of my delicious baked items spread, and people started stopping by the house, asking if I had anything to sell. People referred to me as the Sugar Queen.

When my mother couldn't stand the flour on her kitchen floor one more minute, Dad encouraged me to take out a loan and open my own shop. He owned the building that used to be the Johnsons' dry goods store back in the day. The former tenants had used it for a frozen yogurt shop that went under. I'd blamed the cold winters. Who wanted frozen yogurt when icicles hung from the rafters?

From the moment I'd walked in, even before Dad and I had

installed the industrial ovens and painted the walls a cream color, the voices of the Johnson family seemed to speak to us. *Offer a good product and service, and customers will come.* Dad had suggested I use my nickname for the shop. He'd painted the doors red, then we hung a sign: The Sugar Queen.

I'd practically heard the Johnson sisters cheering me on as Dad and I'd given a face-lift to the front of the building. Cherry siding and tall windows with hanging baskets of bright flowers brought the storefront into this century. I'd decorated the inside with bistro tables and a wide counter made of repurposed wood from the original floors.

From that day forward, I started work every morning at 4:00 a.m. and opened the doors at 7:00 a.m. The inside always smelled of sugar, butter, and fresh coffee. Customers flocked to my little place. A hit, despite my deficiencies.

Our guidance counselor had once advised me to use my pretty face and sweet disposition to my advantage, implying I didn't have much else going for me. Didn't I get the last laugh? I *did* have a talent. A talent for which I was admired and adored. Or my products were, anyway. Notwithstanding the tears that sometimes fell in the batter, I was the Sugar Queen.

Most days, I worked so hard proving everyone wrong I didn't have time or energy to think of all I'd lost. I made a good living doing what I loved. Crystal moved to Emerson Pass after her husband's death and opened a kitchen shop next door to my bakery. Mom and I came to a distant truce. Dad was still my biggest fan.

A happy ending, of sorts. Until the day Trapper came home and I had to face the past, my lies piling up like sticky, messy muffins on a platter.

"What do I do, little bird?"

But my little bird didn't answer. She never did.

2

T rapper

AN HOUR AFTER I SAW BRANDI, I WALKED UNDER THE MELODIC rustle of the aspens that lined Barnes Avenue. Not much had changed in our quaint tourist town since I'd lived here as a child. Baskets with vibrant displays of begonias, lobelia, petunias, and creeping Jenny hung from the retro streetlamps. Higgins Meat Shop, Puck's Bar and Grill, and Al's Diner remained in the same brick buildings they'd been in all my life. A high-end grocery store that sold fancy cheese and organic produce had replaced the more pedestrian one of my youth. One of the original brick buildings had become Emerson Pass Brewery. A French bistro and a pizza joint shared another. Next to Brandi's bakery, a kitchen shop, new since I was last home, had a sign in the window advertising gourmet cooking classes.

Emerson Pass was built in the valley between two mountains. The northern sister, as we called her, was brown and bare in patches where ski paths had been cleared. Once ski season arrived, it would be covered in snow. Our southern sister remained wooded, other than roads and a peppering of homes.

I stopped in the town square, a grassy area where a statue of Alexander Barnes and his wife, Quinn, hinted at the influence my family had had on Emerson Pass for over a hundred years. Alexander had built the town in brick on his own dime after a fire destroyed it in the latter part of the nineteenth century. They stood strong and proud to this day. I ran my fingers down the bronze rendition of the man I'd come from. When I was a kid I'd often come here to stare into the image of his face, wondering if I would ever be the leader and man he had been.

Today, as I looked into those lifeless eyes, the weight of my failures haunted me. Alexander had believed in love, family, and community. Legend said he fell in love with the beautiful school-teacher Quinn Cooper the first moment he set eyes upon her. He spent his life making sure she knew she was loved. Alexander would never have told his Quinn that he would choose something over her.

Her question that day had been a test. She'd needed me to say I would choose her and instead I'd blurted out the words of a selfish young man. Brandi would not have asked me to choose. She simply needed to know that I would. I'd let her down, and she'd never forgiven me.

After seeing her today, I knew only one thing. I still loved her. As much as I'd wanted her to be someone I once loved—a fond memory of my high school sweetheart—it simply wasn't true. I loved her the same as I always had.

I'd had such plans for us. First, college together, and then a wedding before I was drafted onto a professional team. I'd play for however long my body lasted, and then we'd come back here together and start a family. Some of the guys I'd played with were the type to take advantage of the women who offered themselves. Many of the married ones slept around just because they could. That wasn't me. If I'd still had Brandi, I would have remained faithful to her despite the fame, money, and attention.

From the first time I kissed her, I'd known she was the one. I'd never loved anyone else. Would I ever be able to? God, I wanted to. I wanted someone to fill this hole she'd left in me. Was moving back here a mistake? This was a small town. I was sure to run into her frequently. Would it be too painful? I'd never be able to see her without this awful ache in my gut and a craving to touch her, be with her, make her laugh.

I turned to Quinn's statue. The artist had carved her famous thick blond hair under a jaunty hat. She'd been good to Alexander and his five children, rescuing them from the heartache of losing a wife and mother. I knew from reading her journals how much she'd loved them all. Maybe that was my mistake. Reading those journals had made me too much of a romantic. Not everyone wins the one they love. Some of us are too stupid to keep them.

I'd thought from the time we had our first kiss that she and I were a love story like the one Quinn and Alexander had shared. For whatever reasons, we were not. Would I ever find anyone who would push aside her memory? I wanted that more than anything. At the moment it felt like a farfetched dream.

My phone buzzed from my pocket with a message from my real estate broker.

The ice rink and property are officially yours. We just closed.

Temporarily cheered by this great news, I sat on a bench and typed back a response.

Fantastic. Can't wait to get started.

MY BROKER, BILL SCHAEFER, HANDED ME A RING OF KEYS. "IT'S ALL yours. For better or worse." A good friend of my father's, Bill handled all our real estate deals. My mother called him a "silver fox" and was endlessly trying to fix him up with eligible widows.

We stood in what used to be the lobby of the ice rink.

Remnants of the old carpet remained in shaggy sections of hideous red and blue. Paint peeled from the walls. The place smelled of mildew and decaying wood.

I peered through the clear plastic that separated the actual skating area from the lobby. What had once been covered in ice was now rotting floorboards. "I can't believe they let this place get this bad," I said.

"The Morrison family couldn't afford to keep it up and running," Bill said. "They shut it down about eight years ago. No one's touched it since."

"I'll make it shine," I said. "This town needs its rink back."

When I'd learned the old place where I'd learned to skate was in foreclosure, I'd made an offer a few months before I moved home. I'd gotten it for a steal and planned to completely renovate. I'd restore the inside rink and add an outdoor one for the winter months. Not only would it be ideal for recreation, I wanted to create a youth hockey training program here. Boys and girls with the talent and drive but not necessarily the funds would be invited to participate in camps.

For years I'd thought Emerson Pass should have an outdoor rink for recreational purposes, like the one that used to be here downtown back in Alexander's days. I'd grown up hearing stories of my forefathers wooing their women while skating. Now that we were a tourist town, I planned to bring that pastime back with a seasonal outdoor rink.

My great-great-grandfather Flynn had loved to skate and ski. Like me, he loved competition. My father says I must have inherited his love of sports and competition, because I came out kicking. After World War I, Flynn had become obsessed with skiing for recreation. While overseas, he and his twin, Theo, had seen the ski mountains in Europe and had been inspired to bring the sport home to Colorado.

The Barnes family cleared the mountain of trees, creating downhill ski routes. Using the logs, they built the first lodge, securing our fate as a ski town. Without that industry, I suspected the town would have died a natural death. People need commerce to thrive. Since then, every Barnes generation had run the mountain. My sister, Fiona, still at college, would someday come home to take over from my dad. Her passion, like his, was skiing. Skating and hockey, though, had my heart. As Bill had said, for better or worse, I'd added the rink to our list of family enterprises.

I shook Bill's hand. "Thanks, Bill. I'll be sure to invite you to the opening."

"I'll look forward to it." He adjusted his blue tie as his forehead crinkled. "But don't tell your mother."

"Why's that?"

He shook his head slowly. "She means well, but last time I attended one of her parties, I was trapped in the corner with one of her female friends who apparently had been encouraged by Rose to pursue me." He shuddered. "She was scary."

"My mother or the woman?"

"I was referring to the woman, but same goes for your mother."

"I feel you. Trust me."

I SQUINTED INTO THE BRILLIANT BLUE AS I LEFT THE GROCERY STORE with a bouquet of flowers and a bottle of wine. Mama had invited me to dinner, and I knew better than to go empty-handed.

I rolled the windows down as I traveled the country road toward my parents' home. Wildflowers in purples, reds, and yellows peppered the meadows. Their sweet scents drifted through my open windows. I draped my right arm over the back of the seat the way I'd done in high school. Only then, Brandi had been next to me. What I wouldn't give to go back to those days.

I turned down the Barneses' gravel road. There were several

houses on the fifty acres, built by various offspring of Alexander and Quinn. Two years ago, long before retirement seemed a possibility, my parents had asked if I wanted to build a house somewhere on our land. I'd agreed, knowing that someday I would want a place of my own in Emerson Pass. After all, this place was part of my DNA. Five generations of Barneses had spent their lives here. I knew it was my ultimate destiny to return.

Mama had spent the better part of a year working with the architect and contractors on my house. We'd corresponded throughout the whole process via email and phone calls, but I'd trusted her to make decisions about furniture and paint colors. Mama was a woman of exquisite taste, which sadly had not been passed on to me. I could barely tell the difference in shades of blue she presented as possible wall colors for my bedroom. I'd asked her for a house filled with light and airy rooms, comfortable over formal. A home where family and friends could gather on the patio or in the kitchen for parties. She said I leaned toward a modern farmhouse feel and favored light colors and traditional lines. I had no idea what that meant. All I knew was the sanctuary she made for me was now my favorite place on earth. I guess it's true that no one knows you like your mama.

I hadn't expected to be back here full time by now, hoping to play for at least a few more years. After my knee injury, I knew it was time to come home. Mama's hard work had made sure I had an actual home to soften my landing. The house had been completed two winters ago, but I hadn't spent much time there until recently. I'd come home during a few of my breaks, but our team schedule kept me on the road. I'd made sure not to go into town for fear I'd run into Brandi. My instincts to stay away were right. I should have done so today.

Besides the master, my house had five bedrooms. Mom had decided it would be best if I had a place for out-of-town guests, like former teammates. Given the popularity of Emerson Pass as a ski destination, she said, it was best to have places for friends.

I'd agreed. In general, it wasn't wise to question Rose Barnes. She was always right in the end. When my dad brought her to Emerson Pass for the first time, she'd offended her future mother-in-law by suggesting that the decor of the lodge needed an update. Two years later, the entire place had been redecorated. Grammie Harriet was not one to stay mad for long and quickly forgave my bossy and energetic mother. Grandfather Normandy always said Grammie was the sweetest woman he'd ever met. She couldn't hold a grudge to save her life.

I parked in the gravel driveway and grabbed the wine and flowers. My parents lived in the original Barnes home, built around 1900. Over the years, it had been remodeled, bringing the kitchen upstairs from the basement to the main living floor. The original wood floors had been replaced, but the vaulted ceilings and large windows remained. Having inspected photos of earlier times, I knew the outside had remained pretty much the same as the original—red brick and beams of hardwood made from trees on the property. Family lore told us that Alexander Barnes took several years to build the house. Had he imagined it would remain over a hundred years later?

My father's roses were in full bloom. A slight breeze brought their scent as I headed across the yard and walked in through the unlocked front door. White wainscoting, put in by my mother, contrasted nicely with the original dark wood of the foyer and stairs. Off to the right of the entryway, what had once been called the library was now the primary family room with comfortable furniture and a large-screen television. The basement where the old kitchen and staff quarters were was now my dad's man cave. He'd installed a pool table and bar, where he entertained his buddies during sports events.

"Mama?"

"In here," she called from the back of the house.

I scurried down the hallway, passing family photos placed decoratively on the wall. Many were of my sister, Fiona, and me during every stage of our lives, as well as my parents' and grandparents' wedding photos. There were also a few of long-ago relatives, including one of Alexander and Quinn Barnes with their seven children. I stopped to look, drawn to it for some reason during times of uncertainty. Seeing Brandi had shaken me. I needed to look at the photo of a happy family.

This one had been taken in 1918 before Flynn and Theo had joined the army to fight in WWI. They'd been only seventeen and had lied about their ages. Josephine, a striking blonde and the eldest, was tall and slender and stared unsmiling into the camera with a fierce intelligence. Her sisters, Cymbeline and Fiona, both with dark curls and delicate beauty, smiled, but I could see the fear in their eyes as they contemplated the dangers of war. The two younger children, born to Quinn and Alexander after their marriage, were around five and seven in the photo. Both girls looked like their mother, with dark eyes and massive amounts of wavy blond hair. The beauty of the Barnes women was legendary in this town. One had only to look at the photographs to know it wasn't unfounded.

I poked my head into the library—we still called it that a hundred years later—to see if my father was there, but the room was empty. Often, during the off-season from the slopes, he spent time reading or watching sports in the early after-noons. I wandered over to a cabinet where Dad kept the jour-nals, letters, photographs, and marriage and death certificates of the Barnes family, dating back to Alexander. One of the leather-bound journals was on the chair next to the cabinet. Dad had been piecing together family stories for a few years now, hoping to compile everything into one volume for the family.

I picked up the journal. From the loopy handwriting, I knew this was one of Quinn's. She and Alexander had kept detailed notes about their family. This passage was from 1914.

It's been months since I've written here in the pages of this journal. The children keep me so busy that it's hard to find time for an entry. I promised myself when Alexander and I married that I would include passages at least once a month on the state of the children and any other news of our friends and family. Thus far, I'm failing miserably.

I told Alexander last week that we're going to have another baby. With Adelaide being almost three, I didn't think I would have another. Given how amorous we are at night, I didn't imagine this much time would stretch out before another pregnancy unless I was incapable of producing another. I thought perhaps, given the difficult birth of our Addie, that something had gone wrong inside me. Alexander was overjoyed, as I expected he would be, although not surprised. He said I have the same glow I had with Addie. I'm quite certain he's lying about the glow. I've been nauseated from morning until night for the past week. He would have had to be blind not to notice my green complexion.

Alexander seems to have no concerns over the number of children we have! Which causes me to love him even more than I did yesterday. I think often of the time before I came here. The hunger and worry seem from another time, another life.

We've agreed I will not go back to teaching in the fall. Handing over the school is harder than it probably should be. Many women dream of having the opportunity to simply run a house and raise children. I see myself, despite being the mother of six, as the schoolmistress of Emerson Pass. However, I know it's better for me to be home with our children. Luckily, Martha Johnson has returned from her time at university and is anxious to take over for me. She's grown into such a fine young lady, pretty, capable, and smart. I'm proud to have been her teacher. Her sister will begin her second year at university in a few months. Soon, perhaps, both the Johnson girls will teach together. Alexander wants to add another classroom to meet the needs of our growing town.

Mother saw our new doctor, Leo Neal, yesterday. He's a great deal better than Dr. Moore, understanding modern techniques and caring for his patients with compassion instead of as a nuisance who pull him from his chair at the bar. Dr. Neal is amazed at Mother's recovery and says it's the mountain air that's made it easier to breathe, not the powder Dr. Moore prescribed.

On another note, young Dr. Neal asked if Martha had a beau. I had to hide my amusement at the way his ears turned bright red when he asked. I wouldn't be surprised to see the two of them dancing together at our social this Friday evening. Seeing young love turn into marriages and families gives Alexander and me much satisfaction. We can't help but feel pride to see our little town grow and our young people blossom. I can remember clearly the first day of school when I looked out on the frightened faces of my class. To see how far they've come is nothing short of miraculous.

Josephine and Poppy have begged us to allow them to attend the dance this weekend. They're both seventeen now, so I suppose it's time. I'd rather keep them young for a while longer, but that's not my decision. God has a plan for each of them, I'm sure. Jo remains resolute about opening a library in town. Last week, she sent a letter to Mr. Carnegie. Bold, that one. Especially when it comes to books. Poppy wants to become a veterinarian and look after all the farm animals. I worry if either of them will be given a chance in this man's world. This is the crux of motherhood—this mixture of worry and love and pride until it seems my heart might explode with the enormity of it all.

The twins had their thirteenth birthday yesterday. They wanted a picnic down by the creek for their party. The weather's warm enough to swim, even in that frigid water, so we all dressed in our bathing clothes and headed across the meadow. Last summer, Flynn and Cymbeline managed to make a pool for swimming by damming up a section of the creek with rocks. They worked on their project steadily for a month. Keeping up with Flynn has given Cymbeline muscles like a boy. The spot is a good five feet deep and perfect for a refreshing swim.

For our picnic, Lizzie and Mrs. Wu made the boys' favorites: fried chicken, potato salad, and pound cake. Alexander and Jasper have a fascination with the new ice cream maker and made another batch to go with our cake. Even I managed to eat a little and keep it down. The Cole family, Li and Fai, and even Mrs. Wu joined us. Flynn is thick as thieves with Noah and Roman Cole. They run wild in the meadows and forest, creating worlds of make-believe. Li and Theo, the intellectuals of our clan, are inclined toward books and quiet games. They have an ongoing chess game here in the library. Since the Wu family came to live with us, Fai and Li have become as robust and lively as the rest of our enthusiastic bunch. Mrs. Wu has learned some English. She and Lizzie share duties in the kitchen, which has been a blessing since Florence came.

Harley and Merry have had their second son since I last wrote. Jack's a fat, happy baby and looks exactly like Harley. Henry just turned four and is his father's shadow. He loves horses like no child I've ever seen. Even more so than Flynn and Cymbeline, which I didn't think was possible. Alexander gave Harley two colts for Christmas a few years ago and they've bred them twice now, producing fine horses, which they've sold for a handsome profit.

Lizzie and Jasper's little Florence, born a month before Adelaide, has finally recovered from her fever and cold. We fretted for a week. I don't believe Lizzie or Jasper slept the entire time she was ill. Even Mrs. Wu's miraculous tea didn't work. Today, however, Florence is well and playing out in the barn with the others. They're all excited because we've had another litter of piglets. She's quite the character. As pretty and pink as a cherry blossom like Lizzie, but with the personality of her father. By that I mean wickedly smart with a propensity for dictatorship. The other day I observed Florence, Jack, and Addie playing with toys in the nursery. Florence had sorted the toys by type and had a system for who could play with what, like her father with the wine inventory. Lizzie and I had a good laugh over that one.

Rachel Cole has finally stopped wearing all black. It's been four years since her husband's death, and she seems to be ready to live again. We had a nice talk yesterday, just the two of us, with our feet in the creek. She insists she'll never remarry. I hope and pray that the right man will come along to give her a second chance for love. Her brother, Wilber, has gone back to Chicago, making it even more lonely out there by herself with just the children. Rachel says he's gone to find a woman. She suspects he'll show up one day with a bride by his side and stay for good.

Fiona's as bubbly and sweet as always and soaks up learning like a sponge. Her brothers call her the Sweetheart of Emerson Pass because wherever she goes, people flock to her. I suspect it's her positive and *loving character that attracts others to her. It's as if they feel her sunny presence will somehow rub off on them. Theo says she is magical. I have to agree. Of course, I think that about all my children.*

Cymbeline, albeit smart and good at her studies, has a temper and a competitiveness I worry will get her into trouble later in life. It never occurs to her that she's a girl and therefore not capable of doing anything a boy can do. That said, thus far, it seems she <u>can</u> do everything a boy can do. She's sassy and opinionated yet has a heart as vast as the Colorado sky. I pray for the man she marries. He will have to be a patient, good-natured fellow and willing to marry a woman with her own accomplishments and will. I imagine a man as strong as an ox, with the mind of a fox and a heart like the most loyal puppy.

Adelaide's had a growth spurt finally but will be small like me, I suspect. She's shy and reserved, like my father, and is the pet of the household. I was afraid she wouldn't learn to walk because the others carried her around for the first two years of her life. She worships Fiona and follows her all over the house begging to be included in whatever game her older sister is playing. Fiona, bless her, is patient and loving. Perhaps she remembers how she did the same with Cymbeline when they were younger. I can still remember her crestfallen face that first day we all went off to school.

My sister and Clive will marry in the spring. Mother has finally agreed that she's old enough. Poor Clive has worked awfully hard to win Mother over. I never knew the woman could be so stubborn. Meanwhile, Annabelle has been hired to sew five wedding dresses in as many weeks. She's working out of a room in Alexander's office in town, using the new sewing machine we bought for her last year. We were all surprised when she started getting orders from Louisville! Soon, she'll have a wedding dress empire.

Ah, well, this entry must come to a close. The children have all come in from outside, where they've been doing Saturday chores. I can smell them from the library! As it did with Adelaide, my sense of smell seems to have heightened during pregnancy. I'll have to send them all upstairs for their baths or toss them back outside.

· · ·

As was always the case when I picked up one of the journals from my relatives of long ago, I was transported back in time. It must have been peaceful to live in a simpler era. Children these days were always on their phones or computers rather than playing outside or being delighted by a litter of piglets. Sometimes I wished I'd been born in a different era. Then again, I wouldn't have been able to play hockey. I might be a frustrated competitor like Cymbeline.

I set aside the journal and headed down the hallway to the kitchen. Mama was chopping carrots and humming along to her favorite country station. I set the flowers on the counter and moved aside a section of blond hair to kiss her on the cheek. "Hi, Mama."

"Hello, doll." Mama had a Southern drawl that elongated every word with extra syllables. A former gymnast, she was short but strong. Dressed in yoga pants and a tank top, she darted around the kitchen. Mama had two speeds—full throttle or asleep.

"Open that wine. We can have a glass before dinner." She tossed the carrots into a salad bowl and wiped her hands on a towel.

I obeyed. Mama said what she wanted, and most people gave it to her without question. I both feared and adored her in equal measure.

She put the flowers in a vase, then reached into the cabinet for wine glasses.

I poured us both a generous glass of the red blend I'd found at the grocery store. "That new store is kind of fancy. I'm not sure I like it."

"Oh, you Barnes men and your insistence on keeping everything exactly as it was in the past is completely unrealistic."

"Grammie thinks so, too," I said.

"That's because she's from here, too."

"You like it here, don't you, Mama?"

"I wouldn't want to live anywhere else. Why do you ask?"

"I don't know. I wonder if you miss Georgia and your sister," I said as I handed her a glass of wine.

"My sister, yes. But I go home to Georgia twice a year, and my sister comes here often."

"I was thinking about what it's like to be from here—how it tugged at me the entire time I was away. I was wondering if it's that way for you."

"Not every place is like Emerson Pass that way," Mama said. "Anyway, when I agreed to marry your dad, I knew Emerson Pass came along with the package. In fact, how I feel about him is wrapped up in this place. Even this house. This became my new world the first time he brought me home to meet Grammie and Pa."

"I'm glad to be back, Mama."

She clinked my glass. "I can't believe you're really here. I've missed you more than you can know."

"I didn't think it would happen this fast. I'd hoped for a few more years, but now that I've accepted it, I'm at peace."

"For real?" She peered at me with bright green eyes almost too big in her small heart-shaped face.

"It's an adjustment to be without the routine of practice and games, but I'm actually all right. I knew this day would come eventually."

"I remember the first year after I was done with gymnastics felt strange and empty," Mama said. "At first I didn't know what to do with myself, but after a time my days were filled with new passions."

"Speaking of which, I closed on the rink today. We're starting the renovation next week."

Her face lit up as she smacked the counter. "Wonderful news. I'm proud of the way you've handled forced retirement. Jumping right in on the next season of life is exactly what you should do." She sipped from her glass before setting it aside to shred lettuce.

"You don't think it was impulsive?"

"I think you can be impulsive, but this one feels right. I'd say it's about time someone took the rink into the current decade. The carpet in there must be older than me."

"You'll have your decorating skills put to the test." I perched on one of the stools at the island and watched Mama season three steaks.

"I'm not worried as long as you don't insist on carpet with geometric shapes in psychedelic colors," she said. "Like they did the last time someone renovated the place."

I chuckled. "You have my word."

"What else did you do today?"

I hesitated to tell her I'd stopped by to see Brandi. My mother had loved her when we were dating but after she abruptly broke up with me, Mama's allegiance had vanished. She'd been the one who had to pick me off the floor the night I'd come home devastated.

"What is it?" she asked. "You have that look on your face that you used to get when you, Huck, and Breck had done something you weren't supposed to."

I laughed. "No, nothing like that. I went by to see Brandi today."

My father came in from the patio with a book in one hand and an empty beer bottle in the other. "Brandi, huh?" He set aside the book and tossed the bottle into the recycle bin. "How did it go?" Dad, tall and broad-shouldered, had skied and played hockey competitively in high school and now participated in triathlons for fun. We shared the same dark hair and eyes and olive complexion.

"I made an idiot out of myself." I dropped my forehead into one hand as I flushed with heat.

"How so?" Mama asked.

"I basically told her I'd never gotten over her," I said. "And then she dropped a bombshell. She didn't get into Michigan."

"Really?" Dad said. "Why didn't she tell you back then?"

"She was ashamed, I guess. She also said she wouldn't have

31

gone with me, even if she had gotten in, so it doesn't really matter. To her, we were just a high school thing. Not meant to last—I think those were words she used. Which is not how I experienced it." I rubbed my eyes with the back of my hand. "I guess I'm still trying to figure out what happened."

"What happened," Mama said, emphasizing every word, "is that she broke your heart."

"Now, Rose," Dad said, running a hand over the top of his salt-and-pepper hair. A gesture we shared. "It was all a long time ago, and they were young." He turned toward me. "Too young to have made a life decision to get married. You kids needed to grow up a little before you could be together."

"She could've done it in a kinder way," Mama said. "To break up with you before prom and never speak to you again was uncalled for. Especially given how close you were."

"Honey, I thought we talked about this," Dad said.

"About what?" Mama widened her eyes, as if she were completely innocent.

"Not to talk harshly about the girl he loved," Dad said. "I thought it was a good decision on her part. She couldn't just follow you wherever your path took you. She needed to find her own way."

I nodded, thinking through what he said and how it stacked up against what she'd shared with me this afternoon. What would she have done if she'd followed me to college with no skills or plan? She would have been miserable. I wiped the rim of my glass where my lip balm had made a smudge. "You're right, but damn, it hurt."

Mama reached into the cabinet for another glass and slid it over to my father. "I can see her point, I suppose. No woman wants to follow a man around."

"You came here when I asked you to," Dad said.

"We were already finished with college and had jobs," Mama said. "That's different."

"I don't understand why I've never gotten over her," I said. "It's been ten years."

"It's time to move on, honey," Mama said. "She made her choice a long time ago."

"You're right. I need to spend time finding the right woman instead of crying over the wrong one." I scratched the back of my neck. "The moment I saw her all the same old feelings rushed back. Being with her was like no time had passed."

"Well, it *has* passed," Mama said. "She was your high school sweetheart. Now maybe she can be an acquaintance you remember fondly. You have a beautiful home and a new passion."

I nodded. She was correct. However, my heart didn't seem to know what my head did. Brandi Vargas was not my past, present, or future. She was just a girl I used to date back in high school.

I looked up from my glass to find my dad watching me. "What's up, Dad?"

"What is it you're not telling us?" he asked.

I hesitated, embarrassed. "A week before she broke up with me, she asked me if the circumstances were such that I had to choose between her and hockey, which would it be."

"You answered hockey," Dad said.

"I did."

"Well, of course you did," Mama said. "You couldn't choose a girl over your career. Hockey was your focus, as it should have been when you were eighteen years old. Not a girl."

"I don't know. I've thought about it so many times since then. It wasn't like she was asking me to choose. The question was more hypothetical. Like a test."

"She knew by then she hadn't gotten into school," Mama said. "Maybe she wanted you to stay."

I shook my head. "I don't think so. She said today that it would have been foolish for me to give up my scholarship for her. In fact, she said she would never have asked me to."

"Which makes the question confusing," Dad said.

"Right," I said.

Mama tucked her hair behind her ears and glared at my father, then me. "What's confusing is why we're talking about this instead of grilling steaks. I'm telling you—let this go. Move on. There are plenty of nice, smart women in this town," Mama said. "One of them will be just right for you. As a matter of fact, the wedding planner we hired at the lodge is adorable. She's from Nebraska. Very pretty and sweet as sweet tea."

"Are you talking about Tiffany?" Dad asked.

"That's right," Mama said. "I'm certain she's single."

"I'm not sure she's Trapper's type." Dad narrowed his eyes and studied me, as if I were a stranger to him.

"Why's that?" I asked, chuckling. "Should I be offended?"

"She's very prim and proper," Dad said. "I don't think she'd been off her parents' farm until we hired her. She moved here for the job. I could see her with someone like Breck."

"What's Breck got that I don't?" I asked.

"He's gentle," Dad said. "Soft-spoken and considerate. You'd probably scare her to death."

"He's a veterinarian. She's not a cat or dog," I said. The way Breck held a kitten in his big hands was enough to break your heart.

"He's a special boy," Mama said. "Always has been."

"What about me?" I asked, feigning hurt. "I want to be special."

"You're special." Mama laughed as she rolled her eyes. "Just not in the same way."

"Might I remind you that I was a superstar in the world of hockey?" I asked.

"That's all fine and dandy, but you're home now." Mama pointed at me with a salad tong. "We all knew you before braces fixed your teeth."

"This is a rough crowd." I grinned at my mother.

Dad leaned closer and clinked his glass with mine. "We better grill those steaks before we get her any more fired up."

"Yes, sir." As I had so many times before, I followed my father out to the patio. Regardless of Brandi, it was good to be home. I'd made the right choice.

3

B randi

THAT EVENING I TURNED ONTO THE GRAVEL ROAD TOWARD Crystal's house. Driving slowly, I climbed in elevation, passing a driveway with a sign that read Welte. Garth Welte was new to town, having moved here to practice law and ski during his off-hours. He was a regular at the bakery, ordering a double latte and a muffin of the day every morning before he headed to his office. We chatted for a few minutes if I wasn't too busy. I'd learned he was a former Olympic downhill skier. Now he practiced family law.

I turned left into the next driveway. Crystal was on the wrap-around porch in a rocking chair when I pulled up to the house. Locals called her place the Lake House. Not because it was on a lake but because the Lake family had built it for their summer home years ago. Typical Emerson Pass. Folks here loved to give every person, place, or thing a nickname. I always thought it was born from a desire to have one over on the tourists. Only residents knew the clandestine language.

I grabbed the baguette and bottle of wine from the passenger seat. For a split second, I thought of Rose Barnes. She'd taught me, when invited for dinner or a party, to always bring a gift for the hostess. I pushed that memory away. Thinking of Rose and Fenton Barnes made my chest ache.

Crystal unfolded her long legs and rose to meet me as I walked up the steps. "You brought a baguette," she said. "I could kiss you." She was tall and slender with a natural grace and elegance, and the fact that she could eat bread and still look like a model defied logic. Another annoying fact about my best friend? She'd been an actual model in Europe to put herself through culinary school.

"I smell fresh bread," she said as she gave me a quick once-over. "And despair."

I laughed. "You're right on both counts."

She invited me inside so we could open the wine and grab a cheese platter she'd put together. "I thought we could sit out back and look at the pond while we talk. There are a pair of swans in love."

"I love swans." I sighed. "But they make me sad."

"Because they mate for life?"

"I guess so."

"Come on, let's open this and you can tell me all about it." Crystal took the wine from where I'd tucked it against my side.

The house was spectacular, with high rustic beams and floor-to-ceiling windows that looked out to a pond and small meadow. We passed through the door to the kitchen, which smelled of fresh flowers and a hint of rosemary. Dark counters gleamed. I coveted her large high-end cooktop and refrigerator.

Crystal opened the wine while I cut the bread into thin slices on a wooden board. Then, with our treats, we went out to the back porch.

We sat in lounge chairs with the food and wine on a table

between us. Wild grass and flowers in the meadow did not stir in the warm evening air. Fat bees flew from one flower to the next. Several dragonflies perched on the deck's railing. Ducks made ripples on the water. At the far end of the pond, a pair of swans canoodled.

"What's going on?" Crystal twisted her legs into a pretzel and turned toward me, fixing her light hazel eyes on me.

"Trapper's back. He came into the bakery today," I said, then took a large drink from my wineglass.

She raised both perfectly shaped eyebrows. "Crap."

"He's retired from hockey and has come home permanently."

"How was it to see him after all this time?" she asked.

"Upsetting. Kind of scary."

"You mean because of your secret."

"Yes. What if he finds out?" I asked.

"How would he?"

"Lying was easier when he lived thousands of miles away."

"You didn't lie to him," she said. "You just kept something from him."

"A big something. I didn't tell him about his own child. That's as bad as it gets."

"It was all a long time ago," she said. "And he made his choice back then."

"Without all the information," I said. "If he'd known I was pregnant, he would've stayed and given up everything."

She shook her head. "After all this time, you still talk about him like he was perfect."

"He was. He is."

"No one is perfect." Crystal's gaze wandered to the swans. "You just loved him very much." Her voice constricted. "Like I loved Patrick."

We grew silent, both absorbed in our own thoughts. The pair of swans swam together toward the middle of the pond.

"If the baby had lived, I wonder if I would've told him about her eventually?" I asked, breaking the silence. "I think about that sometimes."

She didn't say anything. What could she say, after all? The baby hadn't lived. I hadn't had to make the decision.

"He's still confused over what happened between us," I said. "He asked a bunch of questions. I had to tell him about Michigan. I gave him the whole story about how we were only high school sweethearts and not meant to last."

"What did he say to that?"

"He said he thought we had an epic love and that we'd get married and live happily ever after. And that he'd never been able to move on from me."

She squeezed my wrist. "How did that make you feel?"

"Sad. Guilty. Regretful. He's such a good person. So much better than me." I groaned and looked to the sky. "He's going to meet someone here in town, fall in love, and have beautiful babies, and I'm going to have to see them at freaking church every Sunday."

Crystal poured more wine into my glass. "What if you two fell in love again and that woman was you? The one at church with the beautiful family."

"Impossible. There's this terrible lie between us. He would never forgive me for not telling him I was pregnant."

"People meet their high school sweethearts at reunions and fall back in love all the time. You don't know what he's capable of forgiving and understanding now that he's a man, not a boy. If your love was true and strong, nothing can break it. Not even after they die on you."

"Oh, Crystal." It was my turn to touch her arm. "I'm sorry."

She stared out over the landscape. "I still dream of Patrick every night. Each morning, just for a split second before I open my eyes, I think he'll be there with his head on the pillow."

Patrick had died in a helicopter crash over two years ago, leaving Crystal his fortune. He'd been one of the richest men in the world at the time of his death, having invented several highly successful technology apps. She didn't talk about money, but I knew from the press that he'd been a billionaire. I couldn't fathom that kind of money. Apparently, neither could Crystal. Other than on her house and business, I'd never seen her spend any. She worked five days a week at the shop as if she needed the money. I understood work kept her from sinking into depression. It was one of many things we had in common.

"Here's what we know," Crystal said. "He came into the shop to see you and immediately confessed that he'd never gotten over you. To me that sounds like an old flame worth blowing on."

"That sounds kind of dirty," I said, giggling.

"Seriously," she said. "What would you do if he came after you for real?"

The idea made my heart beat faster. Would my lie kill any chance of reconciliation?

In addition to that complication, which was an enormous one, we had such different lives now. He was a sex symbol, for heaven's sake. Girls probably had posters of him hanging in their rooms. I made cookies for a living. These two things didn't go together. We'd changed. Time had moved on, leaving the ghost of the two lovebirds we'd once been to wander the banks of the river.

"I know what you're thinking," Crystal said. "And it's erroneous."

"What am I thinking?" I picked up a piece of cheese but then thought better of it and put it back on the platter. My stomach had been off since the moment my one and only love walked into my place of business. Damn him.

"That you're not the same people you used to be. And that he's all sophisticated and famous now and you're just a small-town girl who makes bread."

"Cookies were my initial thought, but yes, bread will do," I said, laughing.

Her eyes softened as she waved a piece of bread at me.

"Here's what I know about people. Our circumstances might change, for better or worse. We might have sudden wealth or fame or success but at the core, we remain the same. If prone to arrogance or selfishness, those qualities stay and are sometimes even heightened by good fortune. However, those who were born humble and curious aren't changed, other than their ability to help others. Patrick was, despite his billions of dollars, still the same geeky, shy boy who'd spent hours in his dad's garage working on a computer program. I'm still the same gawky girl I used to be, even though I've inherited all Patrick's wealth. My clothes may be more expensive, and I drive a better car, but I'm still the same girl on the inside. When you lose someone you love, you realize how all the outer trimmings of life mean nothing. I'd still trade every bit of the wealth and lifestyle for one more moment with Patrick."

"I wish I could give you that."

"I wish you could too," she said. "But there's something you *can* do."

"What? Anything."

"If there's an opportunity for the two of you to rekindle what was obviously a special love, please don't dismiss it because of pride or fear. Take the chance I'll never get. Tell him the truth about the baby. Give him the opportunity to forgive you."

"I don't know how."

"Let fate handle that part," she said. "However it turns out—whatever his reaction—telling him the truth will set you free of all the guilt and shame."

"It would almost be a relief if he knew," I said.

"Did you always know you loved him?"

I thought for a moment, allowing myself to drift into the past. I'd become deft at shutting down memories of Trapper, but for now I let the images of our times together flood my mind. Trapper on the ice. The two of us bent over homework in his mama's kitchen. The scent of the wildflowers in the field where we lay side by side on a blanket, watching the sky and talking about our dreams for the future. His face crumpling in grief the day I told him it was over. "The thing with Trap is that he was always my cheerleader. Not just me but all of our group of friends. Anytime someone felt down, all they needed was a pep talk from the town hero to get them back up again."

"I remember he was about the most gorgeous boy I'd ever seen," Crystal said. "Other than Breck, but he was my cousin so that was gross."

"Cousins once removed or three times removed or something like that," I said. Harley's sister, Poppy, the town's first female veterinarian, was Breck's great-grandmother.

"Well, anyway, Trapper was dreamy," she said.

I sighed. "He was. Every girl in this town wanted him, and he chose me."

"Why wouldn't he?" Crystal asked. "I remember you quite well from those summers. I'd been jealous when I first met you. All that shiny blond hair and tanned skin with those perfect white teeth. You were the girl next door I wished I could be. If you recall, I had glasses and braces, dishwater-blond hair, and was so tall and skinny the mean girls at my high school in Seattle had nicknamed me Giraffe."

"You were waiting to bloom into a runway model," I said. "So those girls can suck it."

"I used to dread going home to Seattle at the end of the summer," Crystal said. "My mother's a fantastic person, but her arty lifestyle was a little nerve-racking for a kid who craved the steady, old-fashioned household of my grandparents and their horses."

"Do you ever think of carrying on the family tradition and getting a few horses?" I asked.

"I might."

Her hesitation prompted the next question. "What's holding you back?"

"I don't know. My mother rejected all that, and it sort of bled into my thinking. She hated living here. Hated the horses and how they dictated her life when she was young." Crystal's grandparents had sold the horse farm before they passed away, knowing their only daughter wasn't interested in carrying on with what had once been the family business.

"You have the room," I said, gesturing toward the meadow and pond.

"Maybe. We'll see. For now, we're talking about you."

We were quiet for a few minutes as we sipped our wine. The sun, low in the sky, shot ribbons of light through the trees on the edge of the property. A duck quacked and another answered.

"I've been ashamed for so long," I said. "I'm not sure I have the courage to tell him the truth." I'd internalized that shame until it grew so large it pushed aside the parts of me that were brave and felt worthy of love. Was Crystal right? Was it time to tell the truth?

"You were a kid," Crystal said. "With a controlling mother who basically forced you to keep the pregnancy a secret. I don't know Trapper like you do, but I suspect he has enough grace to understand exactly how it happened."

I closed my eyes for a moment and let the image of his earnest, sweet face drift into my consciousness. He deserved to know what had really happened. I had to find the courage to tell him.

THE NEXT DAY, AFTER THE MORNING RUSH, I TOOK A MOMENT TO assess my inventory. All the muffins were gone. There were still plenty of sandwiches made from my fresh baguettes and French ham and butter or turkey and Havarti. Stacks of chocolate chunk cookies and peanut butter were half of what they'd been when I opened but would last us until the afternoon.

In addition to my sandwiches, I still had loaves of sourdough, French baguettes, and banana and pumpkin bread. We were between rushes, so I sent my assistant back for a break while I tidied the display cases and platters. I usually had another influx of customers around noon, who came in to buy something to take home or purchase one of the sandwiches for lunch.

My routine was fairly simple. I had two staff members. One for the bakery and one for the front of house. I baked the bread in the morning from dough I'd made the day before. The assistant baker used my tried-and-true recipes to make the pastries and cookies during the afternoons, filling the place with the scent of sugar and butter that wafted onto the street. No better advertising existed.

The staff showed up around 7:00 a.m. for the breakfast rush and stayed to finish baking and handling customers after I left in the afternoons. During ski season, I'd often do a couple of ski runs after work. In the other seasons, I'd go to the YMCA for a workout or take a walk down on the river boardwalk. On Sundays, my shop was closed. I went to church in the morning. In the afternoon, I drove out to the cemetery to put a single flower on my daughter's grave.

Today, I was tired, having slept fitfully and been in and out of dreams about Trapper and the baby. All it took was one fifteen-minute conversation and every feeling I'd ever had for him had returned in spades. And the guilt. It was back, too.

I was writing the list of tomorrow's muffins and scone choices in chalk on my display board when someone entered the shop. I looked up to see Fenton Barnes, otherwise known as Trapper's dad. My heart immediately sped up at the sight of him. In all the years since I'd opened, he'd never come inside.

"Morning, Brandi," he said. "Could I get one of those ham sandwiches I keep hearing about?"

"Warm or cold?"

"Cold, I think. Reminds me of Paris. Don't tell my wife. She doesn't approve of butter."

I smiled at him. "Whatever happens at the Sugar Queen stays at the Sugar Queen. Anything else?" I took one of the white bistro plates from the shelf behind me, then reached into the refrigerated case for the largest of the sandwiches.

"Double espresso sounds pretty darn good." He waved a rolled-up newspaper at me. "I think I'll sit and read the paper."

"Take a seat. I'll bring the coffee out to you."

"Appreciate it," he said as he scooped up the plate with his large hand.

The machine made its usual loud sound as it ground fresh beans, then squirted creamy espresso into a cup.

I took the drink out to him. He had the paper spread out on the table, opened to the sports section.

"You've never been in before," I said before I could stop myself. "Why now?"

His lifted his gaze from the paper and looked directly into my eyes. "I want to talk to you about Trap."

I fiddled with my apron strings. "Okay."

"I know it's none of my business, but when it comes to my son, I've never been able to keep my papa bear instincts at bay."

I smiled, remembering how he used to shout encouragement during Trapper's hockey matches.

"I'll just get right to the point. My son has loved you since he was fourteen years old. He's never gotten over you. I wondered how you felt about him."

"Respectfully, sir, that's really neither here nor there."

"Why would you say that?" He tilted his head and peered at me as if I he'd just asked me to sum up a science hypothesis.

"It's been a million years since high school." I crossed my arms over my chest.

"He told me you didn't get into Michigan. This is all conjecture on my part, of course, but I always suspected you broke it off so that he could pursue his dream without the weight of a girlfriend who wasn't yet sure of her own place in the world."

I stared at him, taken aback by his insight. If he only knew the full story. How about the weight of a child and teenage mother? How would that have hindered his career? "I knew it wasn't right for me to follow him. He needed a fresh start."

He leaned back in his chair, watching me. "You know what I think?" He didn't wait for an answer. "I think that's very noble and showed a maturity Trapper didn't yet have. You did the right thing, in my opinion."

I swallowed the lump in my throat. "Thank you, sir."

"However, now is now. You're both all grown up, and maybe it's time to see if there's anything still there between you. I know he wants that."

He won't. Not once I tell him what I did. "Mr. Barnes, there are things that have happened—things I can't undo—that make it impossible for us to ever be together again."

"I can't imagine what that would be," he said.

"It's complicated." I hated this. Being this evasive right to Fenton Barnes's face was as hard as it had been to cut them all off ten years ago. They'd been my second family.

"Complicated sounds like an excuse," he said. "Unless there's something you're not telling me?"

Goose bumps prickled my arms. He knew I was keeping something from them. "Sir, too much time has passed. That's all."

He picked up his sandwich. "If you're worried about Rose, don't be."

"Does she hate me?"

"She could never hate you. Rose is a little hung up on the past, that's all. Regardless, she'll come around if you and Trap get back together. She won't say so because she's so darned stubborn, but she loved you like a daughter, which is why it hurt her so much when you broke it off. I swear she moped around for six months like it was her that got broken up with."

"I'm sorry about that." I couldn't imagine Rose moping around. She never stopped moving from what I remembered.

"You did what you had to do. No one faults you for what

happened." He bit into his sandwich and made an appreciative grunt. "Goodness, this is good. Better than Paris."

I smiled at the compliment. "Thank you, sir." A group of teenagers walked by the windows. Waves of envy surged through me. I longed to be that carefree. Once upon a time, Trapper and I and our friends had walked that same sidewalk on a summer's day, giggling and teasing one another.

"One other thing I wanted to ask you." Fenton dotted at his mouth with a napkin. "Why did your mother suddenly cut Rose out of her life?"

I gripped the sides of the tall chair as if it were a shield. How could I explain my mother's behavior? Her disappearance from Rose's life must have been horribly confusing. "I guess she thought it was best if they parted ways after what happened between Trapper and me."

"Any chance she'd change her mind now?"

"I'm not sure. My mom's stubborn too," I said, as an excuse. She could never be friends with Rose Barnes. The secret we'd kept from them was too big. When she'd decided we should keep my pregnancy hidden, it had been impossible for us to ever have the relationships we once had. Lies ruined love.

"They'd been friends before you two started dating. Rose missed her very much. I think she still does."

I shivered at the memory of Rose ringing the doorbell shortly after Trapper had left town. My mother had refused to answer. Finally, Rose had given up and driven away.

Now I shifted nervously from foot to foot. There were gaps in the story that Fen, Rose, and Trapper would never understand unless I told them the truth. Did I have the courage to do so? What would it do to all of us? Make it better or worse?

As if he heard my thoughts, Fenton gave me an encouraging smile. "Don't worry. Everything's going to work out just fine."

If only he could predict the future, I thought. But he couldn't. There were too many factors for everything to turn out "just fine."

"Enjoy your sandwich," I said. "And it was really nice to see you."

"You too."

As I passed by him, he stopped me with a soft grip on my wrist. "Whatever it is that you're not telling us—have a little faith that Trapper will understand."

I bit the inside of my lip to keep the tears away. "I don't think so."

"You'll never know unless you tell him." He released my arm. "Whatever it is, Brandi, you'll never be able to live freely unless you tell him what really happened."

"Yes, sir." By this time, my assistant had returned from her break.

I walked to the back, holding it together until I reached the bathroom. I locked the door and began the second good cry in as many days.

AFTER I LEFT THE SHOP, I WENT UP TO MY APARTMENT AND showered the day's flour from my skin and hair. With my hair in a towel, I called Crystal and asked if she'd be willing to go to dinner at Puck's.

"Is there a reason?" she asked.

"I just need a night out." I shared with her the content of Fenton's visit.

"I'll come by your place first and we can walk over together," Crystal said.

We agreed on a time before hanging up from the call. I blew out my hair and put on a pretty dress, neither of which alleviated the weight on my chest.

I paced around the apartment for a few minutes, replaying the conversation with Fenton. For a distraction, I turned on the television but couldn't get interested in anything. An open book on the coffee table didn't tempt me, either. My mind was all over the place.

Instead, I went to the closet in my bedroom and fetched my special box from the top shelf. When I was around ten, my mother had found the vintage hatbox stashed away in the corner of the attic. We were delighted to find stacks of letters between Lizzie and her mother.

I took the box into my living room and curled up on the couch. When Alexander had come to America from England, his valet, Jasper Strom, had accompanied him. Later, they sent for Lizzie. As I had been with Trapper, Lizzie had been in love with Jasper all her life. It took him fifteen years to figure out that she was the woman for him. They'd married and had a baby, Florence. I suppose it was silly, but reading the letters and imagining a simpler time gave me peace, kind of like reading one's favorite book time and again.

I kept them in the original envelopes. Legend has it that after Lizzie's mother's death, the letters she'd sent to England were returned to her. As a kid, I'd sorted them into chronological stacks. I had them almost memorized, but I picked one from 1910 to read, carefully sliding the fragile paper from the envelope.

December 24, 1910

Dearest Mummy,

You won't believe my news. Jasper has asked me to marry him. The day I never thought would come has finally arrived. He asked me in front of the entire Barnes family, as well as Quinn and her mother and sister. I wish I could remember exactly what he said, but the buzzing between my ears drowned out his words. He pulled his mother's ring from his pocket and said he couldn't go on without admitting his feelings for me. It's been ingrained in him that servants like us do not marry, but somehow Lord Barnes convinced him otherwise.

I'm giggling as I write this because Quinn's idea may have also prompted Jasper into action. We pretended that Clive Higgins had come to call on me. This was ridiculous in several ways. For one, he's about ten years too young for me. He's a good friend, however, and agreed to the ruse. Jasper became so jealous he stormed around for days. We all thought it quite funny. I know, it wasn't nice, but all's fair in love and war. Isn't that what you always told me?

Anyway, I knew we'd gotten to him when the night after Clive "called" on me he came charging into the kitchen with those piercing blue eyes of his flashing like lightning. "What in the devil do you have going on with Higgins? He's a butcher, for heaven's sake."

"I'm a cook," I said. "A perfect match for a man who sells meat, don't you think?"

"I do not think. I'm horrified that anyone in this household would think him an appropriate suitor for you. You're an old maid and he's an illiterate butcher of cattle."

I took offense to the old maid comment, even though the entire exchange had me greatly amused. "I'm not an old maid. I'm currently weighing my options from several interested men." I made that part up. I'm sorry for fibbing, Mummy, but really, the man can be so aggravating.

"Who else?" His normally clipped speech came out like thunder to match the lightning in his eyes. In fact, his face was a thundercloud.

"None of your concern," I said. "But as you know there are many single men here and hardly any women. I'll have my pick."

"You'll make a fool of yourself. Not to mention embarrassing Lord Barnes by making a mockery of your position here."

The hairs on the back of my neck stood straight up, and I'd never wanted to smack anyone in my life, but I sure did now. How dare he say I'd make a fool of myself. The only fool I'd made was loving him for fifteen years with no reciprocations. I said as much, albeit it with less ease, as there was an inordinate amount of stuttering and a little spit. I was like one of those actors at the play festival. Never sit in the front row, Mummy, unless you want the actors' spit on you.

"And anyway," I added, "Lord Barnes gave me his blessing. Like me, he believes in love."

He stared at me with his mouth slightly ajar, then huffed like a child. "This entire household's gone mad." He turned on his heel. His *shoe squeaked and left a black mark on my clean floor. Then he stormed out of the kitchen and up the stairs. His usual light step as loud as the children when they're hungry and on their way down to me and a warm snack.*

Mrs. Wu, who apparently had been stuck in the pantry, poked her head out and said something in Chinese. We can't speak each other's languages, Mrs. Wu and me, yet we seemed to understand each other anyway. There was our shared language of cooking, which could be communicated by watching each other. There was also the universal language of women that consisted of exchanges without words. There are guttural noises of disgust, raised eyebrows, tutting, and shaking of heads. And of course, touch.

"I'm sorry," I said to her as I gestured for her to come out of the pantry. "He's gone now."

She came to where I stood at the island and patted my shoulder. Then, she tapped her chest and grimaced. I knew exactly what that meant. She was sorry for my broken heart.

I patted her small, weathered hand, knowing of the heartbreak she'd seen in her own life. The loss of her son, daughter-in-law, and husband. Now she was alone with two small children to raise in what should have been her old age.

"Don't worry, Mrs. Wu," I said. "You and I have courage and hope that things will get better. Women like us never give up."

She bobbed her head in obvious agreement and picked up the ball of dough I'd been kneading and began to work on it herself. I mixed sugar and cinnamon together. It's strange, because I had the sense as we worked together to roll out the dough that everything was going to be just fine.

That evening, Jasper got down on one knee and proposed. I guess Quinn was right. Even Jasper can succumb to jealousy.

I know what you're thinking. However, Mummy, this is a different world we live in now. One in which the mistress of the house can be friends with the cook, and a woman from England and another from China can work side by side to make sweet buns. Here the butler isn't really a butler but the confidant and best friend of the head of house-

hold. A man and woman can marry, regardless of their position. I hope you'll be happy for me. I love you. Please give Papa my best.

Love, Lizzie

Good old Jasper had come around finally. He'd been there for Lizzie after all the years she'd loved him from afar. If their love affair was possible, did it mean mine with Trapper had a chance? Whatever the answer, Fenton and Crystal were right. I had to tell him what really happened. Otherwise, I would carry this shame and guilt for the rest of my life.

I went back into the bathroom and applied some makeup and brushed my teeth. This life required both courage and hope. Sometimes a girl had to step away from the oven and into the fire.

4

T rapper

THE GUYS WERE WAITING FOR ME IN THE OUTSIDE AREA OF PUCK'S. Located in the building where the first saloon had been, Puck's served bar food and any kind of beverage a person could want. The interior had been gutted and made into an open, industrial-style space. They'd kept the brick and used wood from the original bar to make a new one.

I passed through to the patio, consisting of round tables with umbrellas and a small stage for live music.

Breck waved me over to where he and Huck were working through a pitcher of beer with two guys I didn't recognize. Breck Stokes and Huck Clifton had been my best friends since we started kindergarten together. If you go back far enough, most of us in town come from four families: Barnes, Depaul, Higgins, or Strom. Huck's great-great-grandmother Josephine Barnes and my great-great-grandfather Flynn Barnes were siblings, which made Huck and me distant cousins. Breck was a Depaul. Brandi

53

was a Strom. None of it mattered much to us, but the stories of the early settlers were infamous in Emerson Pass.

"About time," Huck said, glancing up at me with his intense dark eyes. He'd been a war correspondent for a big news organization before moving home to buy the local newspaper. I often felt as if he were about to interrogate me. Brown curls and a shadow of a beard added to his mysterious and dramatic appearance.

An empty glass and an empty chair waited for me. As I sat, Breck introduced me to the other guys at the table: Darby Devillier and Garth Welte.

"Nice to meet you guys." I took a seat next to Breck. He'd carried on his family's tradition and become a veterinarian. Last fall he'd finished his schooling and moved home to take over the practice from his mother.

"Sorry I'm late," I said. "I had some business over at the rink."

"I heard you closed on the deal," Huck said. "You're crazy to take on a dilapidated ice rink, but congratulations."

"You're one to talk," I said. "Last I checked, you'd bought the town newspaper. Didn't you get the memo that print journalism is dying?"

Huck gave me the finger. Since I'd been home, Huck seemed even grumpier than usual. Breck thought he'd suffered some kind of breakdown while covering the war in Afghanistan. If that was true, he wasn't ready to talk about it. Knowing him, he might not ever tell us what really happened over there.

Breck, on the other hand, had the personality of a puppy—friendly, loyal, and a fierce protector of those he loved. He punched me on the arm as he looked over at me with his eyes that were sometimes dark blue and sometimes gray, but always kind. "Damn, it's good to have you home."

"Good to be home." I fought the ache in my chest. This man was like a brother to me, and I'd missed him. "Can't believe we're finally back where we belong."

"Amen to that," Breck said.

Not wanting to exclude the others, I turned to Darby and Garth, who sat together on the opposite side of the table. "What brings you guys to Emerson Pass?"

"I'm heading up the English department at the high school." Darby's thick dark hair fell over his forehead but was cropped close on the sides. Black glasses gave him a hip, nerdy vibe. He played with a silver ring he wore on a chain around his neck.

Garth wrapped long fingers around his glass of beer. "I practice family law. Opened an office here in town when I moved here last year." *He has kind eyes*, I thought. Brown and soft, as was his hair. A little too pretty. I hoped Brandi didn't know him.

"Welcome, gents," I said.

"Breck's trying to convince me I need a rescue dog," Darby said.

"Everyone needs a rescue," Breck said. "All mankind needs at least one dog and two cats." Breck, in addition to taking over his family's vet practice, ran a dog rescue outside of town. At any given time, they'd have anywhere from a few dogs to twenty, depending on shipments from other places. There were always cats, as well.

"Maybe a cat?" I asked. "They're low-maintenance."

"A cat might be a better choice, given my small apartment," Darby said.

"Wait a minute," I said. "Back to your job, Darby. Does that mean Mrs. Williams finally retired?"

"Principal Douglas didn't say." Darby pushed his glasses farther up his nose. "All I know is the job came out of nowhere. One day I'm worried about rent in LA and licking my wounds over getting majorly dumped. Next thing I know I land a job here in the most beautiful town in America." He grinned, raising his well-defined cheekbones. "And my mom thought my Dickens PhD wouldn't pay off."

I chuckled. "Well, you've come to a good place to be a teacher. They're revered here. Traces back to the very first schoolteacher, Quinn Cooper. My great-great-great-grandfather Alexander Barnes hired her to be the town's first schoolteacher, then they fell in love."

"She refused to bow to convention and welcomed students of color," Huck said. "A trailblazer."

"She must have been important if they named the high school after her," Darby said.

"True enough," Breck said.

"I hope you'll be happy here," I said. As a Barnes, I couldn't help but feel responsible for the residents of Emerson Pass, as if we could influence people's contentment. "I've been away ten years, but this town doesn't change much. Dead quiet in the months without snow. The minute the slopes open, all hell breaks loose."

"Garth here is an Olympic skier," Breck said. "You might have competition for town hero for the first time in your life."

"I'm hardly a hero." I shoved Breck in the ribs.

"Tell that to your thousands of fans," Breck said as he shoved me back.

"Last season they didn't love me so much," I said.

"Shoot, fans are fickle," Garth said. "I sure learned that with my fifteen minutes of fame."

I studied Garth Welte for a moment. He was dressed in cargo shorts and a faded Luke Bryan T-shirt. With those brown curls and doe eyes, it was hard to imagine him speeding down the slopes or behind the desk in a law office. Add the country-boy drawl, muscular torso, and the cross he wore around his neck, I could imagine him on a ranch instead of the mountain.

"The Olympics, though," I said. "That is way cool."

"To clarify, I'm a *former* Olympic skier," Garth said. "Now I'm an attorney. I came here to ski and practice law on the side. I'm all grown up and boring with an ex-wife who'll tell you just how much. I moved here for the powder, fly-fishing, and some peace."

"Where are you living?" I asked Garth.

"Southern sister." Garth gestured toward the mountain. "Up a ways."

"He built a killer house near the Lake House," Breck said.

I shook my head as memories flooded my brain. "I haven't thought about the Lake House in years."

"Remember the parties Lake's son used to throw there?" The Lake kid had been a few years older than us and old enough to buy beer. Brandi and I had spent more than one night under the stars by their pond. My chest tightened, remembering how soft her skin had been under my hands. "Do they still live there?"

"Mrs. Lake died a while back," Breck said. "A woman bought the place last summer. What's her name again?" he asked Huck.

"Crystal Whalen," Huck said in his quiet way, then recited the facts as if he were reading from a newspaper article. The man never forgot a detail. His career choice was no surprise. "Her grandparents lived here—Joy and Marvin Whalen—descendants of the horse breeders Harley and Merry Depaul. Her mother was named Jennifer. My mother used to say she was quite a character and not in a good way. Don't you remember Crystal? She spent summers here. She and Brandi were tight."

"Was she the tall, super-skinny one?" I asked. "Didn't I hear she became a model?"

Huck flashed me a rueful smile that bordered on condescending. "She *did* become a model for a short time. Of further note, however, was her marriage to the billionaire tech guy, Patrick Wilder."

"No way," Darby said. "Wasn't he one of the richest guys in America?"

"His widow, Crystal, is one of the richest people in America," Huck said. "He died a couple years ago."

I snapped my fingers. "Right, yeah. The helicopter crash on some ski expedition."

"Sad thing," Garth said. "It shook up the ski community when it happened. The outfit did these intense ski experiences for amateurs. On their way out for the day, the helicopter burst

57

into flames and crashed over some mountain in Alaska. No survivors."

"I wonder why she came back here?" I asked.

"Same reason I did," Garth said. "To find some peace. She owns the kitchen shop next to the bakery."

"You know her?" I asked.

"Just to say hello to," Garth said. "I get the sense she isn't interested in company. Last winter I trekked over to her house after we lost power to make sure she was all right. She's a city girl, so I worried she might not have enough wood for her fireplace."

"Did she?" Huck asked.

"Yeah, man. Stacks of it in the woodshed. I felt like a fool. She made it quite clear she didn't need a man to check in on her. But heck, where I'm from that's just what a man does."

"Where are you from?" I asked.

"Montana." A shadow crossed his face. "Until my parents split up, that is."

Huck looked over at me. "Garth's agreed to an interview for the paper. Former Olympic star moves to Emerson Pass."

"You're a good sport," I said to Garth. "Not much happens here, as I'm sure you've already figured out. The good people of Emerson Pass will eat that stuff up. Olympic hero and all."

"I'm a has-been. You, on the other hand, are kind of a big deal," Garth said. "Not to sound like a kid, but I'm a huge fan."

"Thanks," I said, pleased. This good ol' boy was my type of guy. "As of the end of last season, I'm also a has-been."

"You going to be okay?" Garth asked. "The transition back to the normal world can be rough. It was for me, anyway."

I shrugged as I poured myself a beer from the pitcher. "We'll see." So far, I'd been home only a few days, and my heart felt newly battered all over again. "Have you met my parents?" I asked Garth. "They own the ski resort and slopes."

"Yeah, dude. Your mother introduced herself to me on the

sidewalk one day," Garth said, as he shifted in his seat. "She's what my mom would call a spitfire."

"Rose Barnes is that," I said. "And more." Often "more" meant a little too much.

"She asked if I wanted to become a part-time ski instructor," Garth said. "I had to politely decline."

"Mama has no sense of boundaries," I said. Why would she think a former Olympic athlete would want to teach children how to ski?

A group of three women came outside and took the table next to us. Three gorgeous women. "Who are they?" I asked Huck.

Huck raised an eyebrow. "I don't recognize the blonde. But the one with the short hair and bangs is a photographer—Stormi Collins. I use her occasionally at the paper." He made a face as if he'd tasted something bitter. "I'll simply say that her name suits her. The other one is your parents' new wedding planner over at the lodge, Tiffany Birt. Fresh from a farm in Nebraska."

So that was Tiffany. Mama was right. She did look as sweet as sweet tea.

I glanced at Breck. He was staring at Tiffany. Maybe my dad's instincts were right.

"Dude, stop staring at her," I whispered to him. "She'll catch you."

Breck blinked and turned to me. "But seriously. Look at her."

Before I could reply, I noticed that Darby had gone still and pale.

"This is bad. Very bad," Darby said, under his breath.

"What is it?" Garth asked.

"I know the blonde," Darby said. "I had the hottest sex of my life with her one night during a visit to Cliffside Bay. Not that I could tell you her name."

"How is that possible?" Huck asked.

"In my defense, earlier that night, I'd asked a girl to marry me in front of an entire restaurant—and she said no. Shortly thereafter, hot blonde sat next to me at the bar and we hit it off.

We went back to my hotel room, where she did many unspeakable things to me."

"A little something to soothe the pain of rejection," Breck said. "Totally understandable."

"Maybe she won't see me." Darby partially covered his face with his hand.

Too late. The girl without a name had her gaze locked on Darby. Clearly, she recognized him. I wonder if she knew *his* name?

"She's coming over here," I said under my breath. "Let's see if she knows your name."

The girl was a beauty, with honey-colored hair, bright blue eyes, and curves in all the right places. With a sure gait, she crossed over to us, then planted herself at the end of the table.

"Well, this is weird. It's the Dickens guru," she said. "Darby Devillier. What are the odds?"

She did know his name. From the flush that rose to her cheeks, I'd bet money the sex had been good for her too. Who would have thought nerdy Darby was a king in the sack?

"Hey," Darby said. "How you been?"

"Peachy. I just opened an inn on the river," she said. "It took me years to save the money, and I had to sell my soul to the devil to get a loan, but here I am." Perhaps responding to our silence, she laughed. "Just kidding about the devil."

"That's great," Darby said. By the blank stare, I could see he had no idea about her dream or otherwise. One of us needed to save him.

"What are you doing here?" she asked Darby.

"I took a job teaching English at the high school," he said.

"Right. Dickens. Very cool." She grinned as she placed her hands on her hips. "What are the odds of us both ending up here?"

"I'm not a math guy, but I'd say a billion to one," Darby said.

"Anyway, I'm Jamie Wattson." She stuck out her hand for me to shake. "I know you from hockey, Trapper Barnes. Big fan."

I thanked her as we shook, somewhat taken aback by her obvious self-confidence.

"Too bad about last season," she said. "I wanted you to make a comeback, but I guess your knee didn't agree."

"Something like that," I said, drily, before introducing Garth, Huck, and Breck.

"What's up with your names?" Jamie asked. "Do you have to have a weird name to join your group?"

Breck chuckled. The man was incapable of taking offense. "Yeah, weird name required."

Jamie tented her hands and narrowed her eyes, clearly thinking through this name thing in further detail. "Actually, you guys sound like heroes in a romantic movie. Well, maybe not Garth. That sounds more like a country star."

"My mother named me after Garth Brooks," Garth said.

"I love that," Jamie said. What she lacked in subtlety she made up for in enthusiasm. No question she was gorgeous, but her personality was a little over-the-top. She reminded me of my mother.

"And what do you do, Garth? You're not a singer, are you? Did your mom doom you to a life of a poor musician?"

Garth shook his head, smiling. "No, ma'am. I'm an attorney."

"A country-boy lawyer, given that accent," Jamie said.

"You got me there," Garth said.

"And you run the paper, right?" Jamie asked Huck.

"Correct," he said.

"Stormi works for you sometimes," Jamie said.

"Also correct," Huck said.

"What about you?" she asked Breck. "Wait, don't tell me. I'll guess. You own the bookstore?"

"Um, no," he said. "I'm the local vet."

"I thought the vet was a woman," Jamie said.

"That's my mother," Breck said. "Why did you guess bookstore owner?"

"You just seem like a guy who would be into books," she said. "Maybe it's your sensitive eyes."

"*I'm* the book guy," Darby said.

Her eyes darted to her former one-night stand. "Hell yeah you are. I mean, come on. You're named Darby. Anyway, that's not all you are, Darby Devillier, but I think I'll keep that secret to myself. There are quite a few single ladies in this town who would love to know what I know."

Darby flushed red and ducked his head, staring into his beer. I stifled a laugh. Score one for Jamie Wattson. If Darby played this game well, he was sure to have another night of hot sex. Maybe more.

She tossed her glossy hair behind her shoulders. "Okay, I've got to get back to the girls before they start to wonder what I'm doing."

"Invite them over to sit with us," I said, impulsively. "The more the merrier." I ignored Huck's death stare. This night was about to get interesting.

"Oh my gosh, they would love that." Jamie lowered her voice. "I have to warn you, though. Tiffany's super shy. So don't sit her next to him." She pointed at Huck. "Can we say awkward silence?"

Huck's eyebrows came together, but he didn't say anything.

She trotted off to the girls' table.

Huck, once again, shot daggers at me with his eyes. I further infuriated him by grinning. I've loved messing with him all my life. It was good to be home. Screw Brandi, I thought. I was out on a summer's evening with my best buddies. A group of beautiful women were about to join us. This was the reason I'd come home.

Darby took off his glasses and rubbed the lenses with a corner of his T-shirt. "Now what am I supposed to do?"

"Get super laid," I said.

"Yeah, she made that pretty darn clear," Breck said. "And now that you know her name, you're all set."

"Hilarious," Darby said before taking a draw on his beer.

"Come on, it'll be fun," I said to Huck. "When was the last time you talked to a woman?"

"I don't need to talk to women," Huck said. "Especially one named Stormi Collins."

"Given the way that Jamie chatters away, I don't think you have to worry about it," Brett said.

"What do you have against Stormi?" Garth asked in a voice just above a whisper.

"She thinks a lot of herself," Huck said.

"So do you," Breck said. "Match made in heaven."

"Very funny," Huck said.

They were upon us now. I stood to grab a few extra chairs, as did Garth.

That's when Brandi walked out to the patio. I froze, chair in hand. She was with a tall, slender woman with honey-colored hair. Did I know her? I placed her a second later—Crystal Whalen. Gangly and skinny had transformed into ethereal beauty. White shorts and a silky pink blouse draped effortlessly on her slender frame. High-heeled sandals showed off her long legs. I could easily imagine her walking down a runway in Paris in the latest couture summer wear. However, my glance her way was fleeting. I only had eyes for Brandi. As I always had.

She was dressed in a light blue halter dress and flat sandals, and her light blond hair hung in loose waves down the middle of her back. Womanly curves that had been hidden under her apron back at the shop were quite evident under the thin cotton material of her dress. The physical work at her bakery had sculpted her shoulders and arms.

We made eye contact as I stood there with the stupid chair in my hands. A flicker of irritation crossed her face. She didn't want me here. Not in this bar or this town. That fact cut me to the core. To hide my feelings, I simply nodded at her and focused back on my friends. Huck, who never missed a detail of human behavior, shot me a sympathetic look. He knew I still loved her. Would my hopeless feelings ever go away? Again, I wondered if I'd made a mistake to come back here. No. This was my home. My home as much as hers. My family was the heart of this town and had been for over a century. I had every right to be here. That said, could I live here with the pain of her rejection around every corner?

Jamie, Stormi, and Tiffany had settled in at our table. For the next few minutes, Jamie told us about how she'd renovated the old Higgins home down by the river into a small inn. I knew the spot well. Clive Higgins and his brother, Wayne, had opened the town's first butcher shop back in the days of Alexander Barnes and Quinn Cooper. Clive had married Quinn's sister, Annabelle, and they'd built the house on the river. She'd been a wedding dress seamstress, famous in these parts for her craft. Brides came from all over Colorado to have her make their gowns.

I asked Jamie if she knew the story of Clive and Annabelle. Her face lit up. "Oh yes. In fact, I named the master suite after them. It's the most romantic of the six rooms."

When I left ten years ago, an older couple had been living at the house. I remembered it seemed run-down the last time I drove past. "Did you have a lot of renovations?" I asked.

"I did," Jamie said. "But my brother's an interior designer and he works in a firm with a contractor and architect. They gave me their work for free. I just had to come up with the money for all the repairs. I took out a big loan. Now I just have to pray people will come. It's more of a romantic place, like for couples or honeymooners, than your parents' lodge. I'm hoping to attract those looking for an intimate experience."

"It has the good vibes of Annabelle and all those wedding dresses she made there," I said. "That has to mean something."

Jamie smiled at me. "That's what I told my brother."

"You know, my mom might have some old newspaper articles about Annabelle," I said. "She might even have some photographs of a few of the brides you could frame and hang on the walls."

"I would love that. Thank you," Jamie said, eyes sparkling. "The history in this town is one of the main reasons I fell in love with the house. The old brick buildings of downtown and your parents' lodge and the pretty white church with the red door are *the* best."

"My dad knows more about the history of this town than anyone. He has a whole display at the lodge with stories of the Barnes family. You should drop by there and offer to buy him a beer. He could regale you with stories."

"Is the old rope swing still there?" Breck asked Jamie. "We used to go out there and swim all the time when we were teenagers."

"Oh, totally," Jamie said. "I couldn't get rid of the rope swing. I about died from happiness the first time I ever drove up and saw it. In fact, if you guys ever want to come swim, just head on over. I put a few picnic tables on the grass there. When my brother and his buddies were out here helping earlier in the summer, they made good use of it. They acted like a bunch of thirteen-year-old boys, shouting as they dropped into the water."

"That sounds nice," Tiffany said, so quiet I almost missed it.

She started when we all turned toward her, as if she hadn't realized she'd spoken out loud.

"Did you have a place like that back in Nebraska where you're from?" Stormi asked.

Tiffany nodded, avoiding eye contact. She was an odd match with the other two. Jamie was outgoing and blunt and Stormi intense and unapologetic. I liked all three of them. Could I be interested in any of them? I wished. I had to physically restrain myself from turning around to see what Brandi was doing.

"We swam down at the lake." Tiffany tugged on her long ponytail and directed her large and remarkably light blue eyes toward Stormi. She had a soft, sweet voice that matched her shy demeanor. "It was our treat after helping with chores. All the kids in town would meet up down there. I wasn't allowed to go after dinner, though."

"Why not?" Breck asked, in his usual curious way that was so genuine, most people succumbed to his questions and spilled their innermost thoughts. Somehow, he'd never learned to hone that skill to get a girl.

"My daddy says nothing good ever happens after sundown." Tiffany's thick eyebrows knit together. Her dark hair and brows were in deep contrast to her ice-blue eyes.

"Oh, so it was like the make-out place?" Jamie asked.

Tiffany flushed pink and stared into her glass of pink bubbly. "I guess so."

"I'm from Brooklyn," Stormi said, obviously wanting to help her friend out by diverting the attention away. "We didn't have spots on the river to swim. The kids from my hood would've had their minds blown to think of such a thing."

"Did you guys open fire hydrants like they do on TV?" Jamie asked.

Stormi chuckled. "No, that's just on television."

"Damn, that's too bad. I always wanted to do that," Jamie said. "I grew up in San Diego and was lucky to have the beach, but there's something so cool about New York City."

Brett lifted his face toward the sky. "Is it just me or do you guys smell smoke?"

"There's a small fire on the other side of the southern sister," Huck said. "One of my reporters is up there covering the fire."

"Should we be worried?" Stormi asked.

"Will it come here?" Tiffany asked. "To the town?"

"We haven't had a fire in this town since 1890," I said. "The river protects us."

"They jump rivers," Huck said. "We've had a hot, dry summer."

"Climate change," Breck said.

The sound of a helicopter overhead distracted us momentarily.

"My guy said it's contained, but if the wind changes direction, it could head toward us," Huck said. "We should all be prepared for evacuation if that happens."

"Evacuate?" Tiffany's stared at him with wide, unblinking eyes. "Will that happen?"

"Hasn't before," Breck said. "But you never know."

"How do we get out of here all at once?" Stormi asked. "There's only one road out."

"The cops will keep order," I said. "Might be slow going, but if we get the call, don't hesitate. They'll tell you where to go."

"In California, we're accustomed to this," Darby said. "Have a bag packed with stuff, just in case."

"Good plan for here, too," I said. "In fact, if you have camping gear, have it handy."

"Camping?" Stormi asked. "Good God, are we in the wilderness?"

"Kind of," Darby said. "Isn't it awesome?"

"I'm not sure *awesome* is the word I'd use," Stormi said.

"I think it is," Jamie said to Darby.

Darby blushed again.

We continued talking and drinking. I enjoyed myself, but I never lost awareness of Brandi's presence across the patio. A sharp pain stabbed my chest very time she laughed.

Around nine, a guy with a guitar and a microphone began to play covers of seventies and eighties songs. Emerson Pass has always been a little stuck in the past.

A few people got up to dance. Breck was the first from our table to take the leap, asking Tiffany. She appeared so startled that I thought she'd refuse him. Instead, she held out her hand and he lifted her to her feet. Seconds later, they were dancing like two eight-year-olds at their aunt's wedding, stiff-armed with a good five inches between them. Jamie looked over at Darby, who was studying the saltshaker as though it had the code to unlock the secrets of the universe.

"Hey, Dickens, how about a dance for old times' sake?" Jamie asked.

"We've never danced before," Darby said. "Have we?"

"You don't remember?"

"No, no, I don't."

"I'm just messing with you." Jamie pushed back her chair and spread her hands on the table. "Come on, don't make me beg."

"I'm not a good dancer," he said. Regardless, like a lamb to slaughter, he followed her onto the dance floor. Unlike Breck and Tiffany, they danced close. I'm a guy and even I could see the heat between them. I wondered how long until they were making their one-night stand a regular thing.

That left Huck, Stormi, Garth, and me.

"Well, shoot, I think I'll ask my neighbor to dance," Garth said. "Break the ice so she knows I'm harmless. I worry about her living all alone in that big house."

"Would you worry about her the same if she were an old lady?" Huck lifted one wry eyebrow.

Garth smiled as he pushed out from the table. "I surely would. A neighbor's a neighbor. Where I'm from a man takes care of a woman, no matter if she's yours or not."

"Are you for real?" Stormi asked.

"Yes, ma'am. About as real as they come." He tipped his head toward her and traipsed across the wooden deck toward Crystal.

"Stormi, I know we just met, but would you like to dance?" I asked.

"Do hockey players know how to dance?" she asked, peering at me under her fringe of bangs and smiling. Those full lips of hers were as sassy as her mouth. She looked down at her feet. Her toes were painted a coral color and encased in low sandals. "I kind of like my feet."

"Skating *is* a dance," I said. "I promise to take good care and not break any of your bones."

"Fine, then. I accept."

We went out to the dance floor. Of average height, Stormi came up to my shoulders. She had one arm around my neck and the other in my hand, and we swayed easily to the music.

"Do you have places like this in Brooklyn?" I asked.

She shook her head. "Not really. This place is what we'd call rustic. I swear I can feel the ghosts of gold miners and cowboys in this place."

"Do you believe in ghosts?" I asked.

"Maybe." Her thin shoulders rose and fell in a quick shrug. "Ever since I arrived here, I've felt the presence of those who've come before. Not in a creepy way, but like they're supportive and encouraging."

"You like it here, then?" I asked.

"For sure. I'll never leave if I can help it. When I went to art school, I didn't think I'd be making my bread and butter from weddings, but it isn't too bad. At least I'm working, like I dreamed of. I can do my art photos for myself. Eating and paying rent have to take priority over creating art."

"Absolutely." Do not look in Brandi's direction, I ordered myself. This is how it will be from now on. You knew this moving back here. She will be everywhere, and you have to suck it up and deal with her.

I didn't listen. My gaze skittered to her anyway. She sat alone, staring into her glass of wine.

"I've heard a lot about you," Stormi said. "You're kind of a legend in this town."

"Only in my own mind," I said.

"Even Huck talks nicely about you, and he's pretty much a prick about everyone."

"He was always serious, but he's different now. Whatever he saw overseas changed him."

"He's a bear to work for. For some reason, he hates me."

"It's probably not personal. He's just a little rough around the edges."

"I think he enjoys sending me out to take pictures of the town Fourth of July festivities for the paper or whatever, as if it's a punishment. Little does he know, I love it. I'm all about this small-town vibe. What could be more joyful than taking pictures of people having fun? Don't tell him, though. He likes the idea that it's torture for me to report on something as mundane as a picnic. If he'd ever bothered to ask, he'd know that after the experiences of my childhood, I welcome anything that hints at happy, normal families."

"I'm not sure there's any true 'normal' families," I said.

"That's probably because you're from one," she said.

"Touché," I said.

"Do you and Huck go way back?" she asked.

"We're distant cousins," I said. "And best friends."

"I'll keep my opinions to myself then."

"In his defense, he's gone through a lot," I said.

"Haven't we all?"

Despite her obvious dislike for my friend, I liked her. She was refreshingly raw and honest. I sensed how much she'd overcome to get where she was, which I admired.

"I work with Brandi some, too," she said.

"That right?"

"I hear you guys have a past?"

"Something like that," I said.

"Good to know."

"Why's that?" I asked.

"In a small town, it's nice to know who is off-limits."

"We were together ten years ago. In high school. Does that mean all the women in this town are afraid to date me? For fear of losing rights to shop at her bakery?"

Stormi laughed. "Those cookies are serious, dude. No one with monthly PMS wants to be cut off."

"For the record, she broke up with me."

"That's the word on the street. But that was back in high school. Everyone breaks up before college. Now, however, is a whole new era. You're back. She's still here. Why don't you get in there and stoke that old flame?"

I shook my head. "I'm a simple guy with a soft heart. Getting it stomped on isn't my idea of fun."

"She hasn't taken her eyes off you since we walked onto this dance floor. You don't have to dig too deep to know what that means. I'd have to be an idiot to make a move on the hot hockey player newly returned to town when the Sugar Queen still has a thing for him."

"You think?" I asked.

"Trust me. I study faces for a living. That's a woman who still loves you."

"Should I ask her to dance?"

"If I were you, I'd dance with everyone but her. Get her jealous. Make her come to you."

"You're kind of a badass," I said.

"Brooklyn, baby. What can I say?"

I followed her advice, dancing with Jamie, who entertained me with stories about the inn's renovations, including the family of raccoons she'd found in the attic. "They scared me so bad I almost peed my pants," she said.

"They're scary, no doubt. Those claws."

"Right?"

Next, I danced with Tiffany. She avoided eye contact and stayed a good distance from me. Instead we talked about how she was adjusting to town and how much she enjoyed working for my mama. "She scares me, though," Tiffany said.

"She scares me too," I said. "Like one of those small dogs with supersharp teeth."

That made her giggle. "Is it true that you and the Sugar Queen were high school sweethearts?"

"Sure is." Did everyone know about us? Who was I kidding? This was Emerson Pass. Gossip was more entertaining than television.

"I had a high school sweetheart," she said.

"What happened?"

"He died the summer after we graduated. My whole life changed in an instant."

"I'm sorry." The pain in her voice made my heart ache.

"It's been eight years, but not a day goes by I don't think about him. We had our whole life planned out, and then in a blink of an eye he was gone. I had to find the will to go on without him."

"I felt the same after I lost Brandi," I said. "I thought until the day she broke up with me that we'd get married."

"I'm sorry," Tiffany said.

Before I could thank her, the song ended and Breck appeared. "One more with me?" he asked Tiffany.

She shook her head. "I'd best be going. I have a meeting with a bride and groom early tomorrow morning."

"Do you have a way home?" Breck asked her.

"I live in one of the apartments in the building behind the library," she said. "I'll walk."

"That's four blocks away," Breck said. "I'll walk you there."

"But you're not ready to go yet," Tiffany said. "It's still early."

"I've got dogs at home that need a bathroom break," Breck said. "I should go too. And I don't want you walking home alone."

That was a lie. His mother was at home. She could let the pooches out. Did Breck like her? I glanced at him. There was no way to tell. He had the same placid, benevolent expression he always had.

"If it's no trouble, I'd like that. Even though it's perfectly safe here, isn't it?" she asked, sounding nervous.

"Most likely," Breck said. "But why take chances?"

She scurried off to gather her purse. I nudged him in the ribs with my elbow. "Smooth, asking to walk her home."

"Just being a gentleman," he said under his breath.

"Why'd you lie about the dogs then?"

"You're annoying," Breck said. "She's really pretty, and I like how she's quiet and polite."

"Be gentle and don't push. I get the feeling she's a slow-burn type of girl."

"I'm the king of the slow burn," Breck said. "So slow it never ignites."

"You never know." I slapped him on the back. "When the right woman will appear."

"Wish me luck." He punched me lightly on the shoulder.

"Always."

CLOSING TIME CAME TOO SOON. I HADN'T BEEN OUT LATE VERY often. Hockey meant a strict training regimen and curfews. Not that I'd needed any outside edict to keep me focused. The game had been my sole purpose since I left Emerson Pass. A professional therapist might say I hadn't had the proper balance in my life, but I hadn't cared. I'd understood that hockey was a season in my life. Like everything that matters to me, I gave it my all. Now that I was home, I planned to put effort into the rink but also to spend time with friends and family, making memories and having a heck of a good time. I had plenty of money to last me the rest of my life, especially since my family owned land and buildings in town that generated income without any of us lifting a finger. Still, the work ethic of Barnes men and women ran thick in our blood. We lived to serve others and to give back to our community. I was clear about my new purpose.

The aspect I hadn't factored in was how much Brandi's presence would shake me.

Case in point? Now, as I hit the button to unlock my truck where it was parked in front of the bar, I saw her and Crystal on the sidewalk. The very sight of her unnerved me. My pulse quickened. She wakened my libido as no woman ever had. I imagined scooping her up and hauling her into the cab of my truck the way I had when we were in high school and kissing her until our lips were bruised. Back then, she'd wanted me. Present day was a different story, and it hurt more than it should. For heaven's sake, it had been ten damn years.

I got into the truck and watched as she left Crystal at her car and headed toward her apartment above the bakery. I should have driven away, but the old protective instinct kicked in like a yoke on a stubborn mule. I couldn't leave until she was safely inside.

To my surprise, she stopped at the side entrance to her building and turned her head in my direction. I immediately went hot. Totally busted.

5

B randi

I was about to unlock the side door that led up to my apartment when I saw him. There he was, just sitting in that shiny black truck watching me. As though he was supposed to protect me or something. As though he had any right. After ignoring me all night and dancing with every woman in the bar except me, he had the nerve to make sure I got home safely? This was no coincidence. Waiting until I was securely inside before driving away was such a Trapper thing to do. I should be pleased, right? I mean, he was the same sweet, overly protective Trapper, doing what he'd always done. That was just it, though. Time had moved on. I wasn't a blissed-out teenager with hearts for pupils any longer. I was a grown woman with a business. I could stumble home from the bar without his help.

The street wasn't even dark. Those vintage lights that made Barnes Avenue look like a postcard were all lit up.

That's it. He's going to get a major talking-to. I marched across the street ready for a fight. He rolled down his window before I reached him, wearing a sheepish expression.

"What do you think you're doing, Trapper Barnes?" I shouted this, pitchy, which made me even angrier. Why did this man get to me this way?

He blinked and lifted that ridiculous mouth into one of his sexy smiles. "Just making sure you get home safe. Is that a crime?"

"I don't need you to look after me. I've been doing just fine for ten years all on my own."

"My apologies," he said. "I thought being a gentleman never went out of style."

"There were about half dozen other women who would've welcomed your escort home."

He raised his eyebrows. "Are you jealous?"

"You really are the most arrogant man this town has ever produced. Not every woman in the world wants you."

A flicker of hurt showed in his eyes. I should've taken it back, but I was too frustrated. My skin itched and burned. I wished I could scratch a layer or two off in exchange for some peace. Or maybe I just wanted to slide through that window and straddle him as I used to back in the days when he drove a truck in need of a new paint job instead of this shiny black one that represented all the ways he'd moved on without me.

"Brandi, I'm sorry, okay? I didn't mean any harm."

All the bluster left me. I turned into a saggy balloon emptied of all its helium. "Never mind. I've overreacted. It's weird to have you back here."

"Okay." He drew out the word. "Not sure what to say now."

"You danced with every single woman in the bar tonight. Was that necessary?" Why the heck had I said that? If it hadn't been totally obvious how jealous I'd been, it certainly was now. Bless him, he didn't rub it in or tease me. Not Trapper. The guy didn't have one mean streak in him. He was always kind. Considerate. A gentleman. Dammit.

"I didn't realize it would bother you. I'd have sat them all out had I known. Anyway, they're all just new friends. I didn't have much of a chance for a social life when I was playing, so this is all kind of new to me." He rubbed the stubble on his face. "You could've asked me to dance, you know."

"I didn't have a chance."

"I'm sorry."

"Don't be. I'm a big girl." I crossed my arms over my chest and glared at him.

"I meant, I'm sorry that my presence bothers you so much." His eyes were as sad and soft as a kicked puppy's. "I guess this town isn't big enough for the both of us."

The nicer he was, the meaner I became. I hated feeling like the bad one, but it was true. "You've been back only a few days, and I can't seem to step out of my apartment without seeing you." I'd meant this to sound apologetic, but instead it came out snappish and tart. To be fair, I'd only seen him twice, and once had been when he came into my shop.

"I'll stay away as best I can. If that's what you want." He shifted in his seat, and he pushed the button to start the truck's engine.

"Your dad came to see me today," I blurted out.

He turned the engine off and slowly turned toward me. "He did what?"

"He stopped by the bakery for a sandwich and espresso and to talk about you and me and what happened between our mothers."

"Why would he do that?" Trapper looked out the front window and tapped his fingertips against the steering wheel.

"I'm not sure." Liar. I knew exactly. He wanted me to fess up to the truth.

"What did you tell him?' he asked.

"Nothing really." My voice wavered as I tried not to cry.

He reached through the open window to brush my bare

shoulder. "Brandi, are you okay? You can talk to me. No matter what, I'm always here for you. I'll always listen."

I jerked away from him, stepping back from the truck. My skin tingled where he'd touched me. "I'm fine. In case you were wondering, Stormi is great. Very smart and artistic. I mean, she's exactly the kind of girl I figured you'd be interested in."

"I'm sorry, what are you talking about?"

"You're obviously into her. She's perfect for you. A New Yorker. All sophisticated and everything, just like you. I've been here and I'm still the same old silly, stupid Brandi. You've been off having this big life, and I can see it all over you."

He lifted his head to look at me. "You can see what all over me?"

"The city."

He threw his head back and laughed. "Brandi Vargas, have you lost your mind?"

"What's that mean?"

"I hardly know Stormi. She's a new friend, that's all."

"She made you laugh tonight. That used to be my job." I placed my hands over the window frame.

The tiny muscles around his eyes twitched as he gazed at me. "You did a great job of it back then." He rubbed his hand over his closely cropped hair. How many times had I seen him do that? The gesture had always told me when he was worried or stressed. "Brandi, there's only one woman in this town for me. I thought I made it pretty clear yesterday how I feel about you."

"Feel? Present tense?" This was wrong. I knew it was wrong. But I couldn't stop myself. I needed him, wanted him. One more night in his arms. Then I'd let him go. I chastised myself. *Who are you kidding? You're just making this worse. Leading him on, acting jealous.*

"Yes. The moment I saw you, I knew." He stroked one of my hands with his thumb.

"Knew what?" I fixed my gaze on his thumb.

"That I'll always love you. There's no hope for me. I'll never get over you."

Do the right thing. Either tell him or walk away. This isn't fair. Yet if I told him, it would truly be the end. I didn't know if I could watch him drive away another time.

My eyes filled as I lifted my chin to look at his face. "Don't you see? We were doomed. I would've held you back, Trapper. You know that as much as I do. Can you imagine taking me to one of your fancy parties?" I tried to smile through my tears. "I was never in your league."

"You're wrong. All these years, I've hardly dated. I had no interest in the women who made themselves only too available to me and the other guys. I've only ever loved one woman, and that's you. I would've been loyal. As far as taking you to a fancy party, I don't know what you've imagined my life was like, but there isn't a woman on the planet prettier or sweeter or smarter than you. You are the *only* league I've ever wanted to play in. No one has ever come close to you." He placed his hands on the sides of my face. "Listen to me carefully. I would've been proud to have you by my side. Don't ever doubt that for one second. You gave me strength and challenged me to be a better man."

"Is that really true?"

"Yes, it's true. Still, I understand. You had your own life to figure out, not just traipse after mine. I'm sorry I didn't see that at the time. I'm sorry I said I'd choose hockey over you."

"The question wasn't fair. I should never have asked you that way." My head drooped, as if it were suddenly too heavy.

"I've missed you every single day." He swiped the tears from my cheeks. "You're the only girl I ever wanted to dance with."

He played with my hair, wrapping it around one of his long fingers. "Do you know how much I've missed you?"

"How could you? With all those women falling all over you and living the high life? I hated those pictures in the magazines. Every time I saw one, I felt sick to my stomach."

"The thought of you with someone else did the same to me."

79

I allowed myself to touch his face, taking in his finely formed bone structure under my fingers as if I were reading braille. The curve of his cheekbone and hard jawline that had once been boyish were now all man, but his dimples were the same. I took in every ounce of him as if I might never see him again. I placed a finger in the dimple on his left cheek, then touched his mouth. "I used to know every inch of you.

"And you crushed it just like I knew you would. Even though I missed you like crazy, I was always proud. I know better than anyone how hard you worked to catch that dream."

"I'm proud of you too, baby," he said.

"What do you want, Trap?" I whispered. "What do you want from me?"

His words broke into the night, untethered. "Same thing I've always wanted. For you to be my wife."

My breath caught. I strained to see his expression in the dark. Tears flooded my eyes at the sweetness in his voice. "Trap, do you mean that?"

"You know I always say what I mean."

He put one of his large hands over mine and lifted my chin with the other. "There's something I need to ask you. Is there a piece I'm missing? Did something happen to you that spring? Something besides the rejection from Michigan?"

"Yes, something happened," I whispered. "Something I didn't know how to deal with."

"What was it? Please, you can tell me anything."

"Not like this. Not tonight." Why had I come over here? I should have just waved and walked inside.

"I won't push you," he said softly. "Whatever it is will not change how I feel about you."

"I'm not sure about that."

He turned the power on without the engine running and switched on the radio. "I'll tell you what, let's get a dance in right now."

He lifted the door handle. I moved aside as he unfolded

himself from the truck. "You and I never got our prom. How about you make at least one of those up tonight?" The street was empty. No one stayed up past closing time in Emerson Pass. Lights from the trees twinkled at us. The town council had voted two years ago to have them up all year.

"Right here? In the street?" I asked.

The song, ironically, was Miranda Lambert's "The House that Built Me." We could have easily replaced the word *house* with *town* to describe our own experiences growing up.

I moved into his arms. He held me close as we swayed to the music. I rested my damp cheek against his hard chest and breathed in his scent. Overhead, the stars were bright in the black sky. Another song came on, but we stayed together, hardly moving.

"What're we doing, Trapper?"

"Dancing."

"This is dangerous." This was wrong. He was getting carried away, thinking that it would be as simple as all this. Just a dance in the street.

"No, not dangerous. This is right. I don't care how much time has passed."

"We should be careful."

"That's not really how I do things," he said. "Give me a chance to remind you how good we were together."

"I remember," I said. Alarm bells rang loud. I was falling into a hole I wouldn't be able to get out of.

"Let me court you like in the days of Alexander and Quinn," he said. "We can go nice and slow. Get to know each other again. I'll prove to you how worthy I am."

"That was never the problem," I said under my breath.

"May I kiss you?" he said into my ear.

The second song ended. In the silence between songs, the leaves of the aspens that lined the street rustled in the breeze, making a soft swishing sound. And then, the hoot of an owl way off in the distance somewhere introduced the next song.

"Yes, you may kiss me." I lifted my face and closed my eyes. His lips brushed mine, gently and for no longer than a few seconds. In that small moment, a lifetime.

"You're so beautiful." He grabbed my hand and held it against his chest, then swooped down to capture my mouth in another kiss. Time stopped. It was the past and the present and the future all there in the feel of his lips moving against mine.

And just like that, I was in too deep.

6

T rapper

THE NEXT MORNING, I WOKE LATE. DISORIENTED, I RUBBED MY EYES and focused on the abstract painting on the wall next to the bed. It was painted with bright yellows, reds, and oranges, and I'd bought it at an auction a few years back because it reminded me of Emerson Pass in the fall. This was my bedroom in my new house. I was home.

For most of my adult life, I'd awakened in strange hotel rooms, sometimes uncertain which city I was in until I remembered who we were to play that day. The travel had grown tiresome quickly. I yearned to be in one place, close to the people I loved. Don't get me wrong, I'd loved every moment of the game. I lived for the feel of the ice under me as I slammed a puck into the goal.

I got out of bed and headed down to my home gym for a workout. As I lifted weights, I thought about the conversation I'd had with Brandi. Was she correct? Would her love have distracted me from the craving for competition, to push myself to the edge of my limits as an athlete? Did she make the ultimate sacrifice when she sent me off to capture my dreams?

I felt certain now that Brandi had loved me when we were young. She might be able to love me again, if I did things right. Still, doubt nagged at me. What was it she needed to tell me? Was she correct in assuming it would keep us apart?

Then there were my romantic notions. I was afraid to let them get away from me, but I swear I'd already gone down the path of a wedding and babies before I'd even stepped into the shower. I decided to go into town and buy Brandi some flowers and ask her out for dinner.

Outside, the air smelled of smoke. I scanned the horizon and detected smoke from the south. The fire must have worsened overnight. While standing in line at the checkout stand a few minutes later, I learned the fire that had started in the southern mountain from lightning had indeed grown during the night. Winds had picked up and caused the fire to spread across the heavily forested mountain. The houses were in jeopardy. If it jumped the river, so was my rink and the high school.

I left my truck in the grocery store parking lot and walked down to Brandi's bakery. She was behind the counter helping customers. I got in line like the rest of them, waiting my turn to order one of the delicacies stacked on platters.

"What're you doing here?" Brandi asked under her breath, while staring at the flowers in my arms. I'd gone all out with a huge bouquet of lilies and roses.

"I brought you these." I matched her volume.

She leaned closer and spoke through her teeth. "Do not hand me those or the whole town will be talking."

"Oh, these? They're not for you," I said just as quietly.

She flushed, then smiled. "All right, good."

"I'd like the turkey and cheese baguette, please," I said in my normal voice. "What do you think of these flowers? I'm taking them to my mama."

Someone sniggered behind me, and I turned to see Breck standing two people back in the line. "Mama's boy," he called out.

"Guilty." I raised a hand toward heaven as if testifying.

"Take your pick from the stack," Brandi said.

I chose the largest one. "This will do."

"That's eight dollars, please." Brandi's cheeks had pinkened to match the roses in the bouquet.

"Eight dollars?" I asked. "That's a city price for a sandwich."

One half of her mouth raised in a sassy smirk. "You may have been gone too long, Mr. Barnes. There's nothing this good where you've been."

"The sandwich and the owner," I whispered.

"Enjoy your sandwich, Mr. Barnes." Brandi pointed toward the window. "Preferably outside."

"Yes, ma'am."

Breck winked at me as I headed toward the door.

So much for thinking it was a good idea to see her at work. I didn't want to examine too closely why she was so obviously embarrassed by me. Hopefully she just wanted to avoid gossip.

Breck joined me outside at one of the little tables in front of the windows. Wind fluttered our paper napkins. I stuck one between my legs and looked up at the sky, which had turned an eerie orange hue.

I unwrapped my sandwich and took a bite. How could bread be this good? The Havarti melted in my mouth like butter. "This is the best sandwich I've ever had."

"I'd say you're biased but I have to agree," Breck said. "Brandi knows what she's doing."

"I heard a rumor that a certain someone was dancing with another certain someone on the street last night," Breck said.

I gaped at him. "Who told you?"

"One of the girls at my office," Breck said. "Who heard it from her boyfriend who's a dishwasher at Puck's."

"Great. Now it'll be all over town," I said. "No wonder she didn't want the flowers."

"Who cares who knows?" Breck asked.

"Not me, but I'm afraid Brandi might."

"Tell me everything." Today, his eyes matched the color of his denim shirt.

"Sometimes you act like a girl," I said.

"I love women, so I'll take that as a compliment."

I didn't have the chance to tell him anything because just then my mother appeared, spotted us, and came running over.

"Boys," she said as we both stood, each of us giving her a dutiful kiss on the cheek. "What's this I hear about Brandi and Trapper?"

Breck laughed. "Have a seat, Rose. Trapper was just about to tell me all about it."

"Would you like some flowers?" I gestured toward the bouquet on the table.

"I'll pretend that I don't know those weren't really for me," she said as she reached for half of my sandwich. "Is it true you two were dancing in the street?"

I groaned.

"It didn't take long, I'll say that," Breck said.

"Do I need to worry?" Mama asked as she studied the sandwich.

"About?" I asked.

"Your heart being broken by the same woman twice." Mama opened her sandwich and rearranged the lettuce, then put aside the cheese.

I bit into my sandwich as an answer.

"You know, timing's everything," Breck said. "Maybe it's time."

Mama held her stolen sandwich aloft as if contemplating whether or not to eat it. "I told you to move on, but apparently now that you're a big shot, you don't listen to your mama."

"Mama, I listen to you."

"But not in equal measure to how much you love that girl," Mama said.

"I'm powerless against these feelings. I can't help myself. If last night was any indication, she still has feelings for me, too. Or, at least dormant ones I can bring out with my charm."

"Dancing in the street is charming and romantic," Mama said. "Something your father would've done."

"They kissed, too," Breck said.

"How do you know *that*?" I asked.

"Apparently the dishwasher at Puck's has a good view of the street while working," Breck said, clearly delighted by this piece of gossip. I made a mental note to throttle him later.

"We talked a little, too." I winced as the image of her face crumpling into tears came to mind. "She wanted me to have all my dreams come true and thought she'd hold me back."

"That's so Brandi," Breck said. "She always wanted everything for you."

"And not enough for herself," I said.

Mama nodded. "What are you going to do now?"

"I'm going to court her like I'm Alexander Barnes," I said. "Old-school, with flowers and gifts and nice dates."

Mama rolled her eyes. "You Barnes men and this adulation of Alexander borders on ridiculous."

"It's legendary, Mama. All Barnes men have an obligation to live as he lived and keep the Barnes spirit of romance alive."

Breck shook his head. "You inherited those qualities. All I got from Poppy was a terrible devotion to animals."

"You have your family's spirit and kind heart," Mama said. "Your mother has to be one of the best women ever to grace this planet."

"I know." Breck's eyes clouded as he pushed away his plate. "I worry about her. She's been lonely. I didn't realize how much until I moved home."

"She was devoted to your father," Mama said. "When we lost him, she vowed to never love another man. I can understand that sentiment, given how I feel about Fenton. Regardless, I sure wish she'd be open to the idea."

"It's been long enough," Breck said. "I was fifteen when he passed."

"Thirteen years," Mama said. "Hard to believe it's been that long. I can remember the first time I met them like it was yesterday. We went to dinner, and I was a hot mess. Your father and Fenton were as tight as you two, and I knew if they didn't like me, I was done for."

"But they did," Breck said.

We'd both heard this story many times, but neither of us ever minded when our parents told us of the times when they were all young.

"Your father made me a martini. I'd never had one, and it went straight to my head. I got so dizzy I had to lie down in the guest room. I've never been so mortified in my life. Daniel teased me about it for the next seventeen years. Every time we went over to your house, he had a martini waiting for me. The joke never got old. However, I never drank another one. I learned my lesson. My, how I miss him."

"Me too," Breck said.

Mama patted his hand. "You're so much like him. Thoughtful and gentle. He's looking down from above, so proud of you."

"Thanks, Rose." Breck's eyes reddened. "I'm glad to be back here where people knew him."

"Anytime you want to talk about him, just let me know," Mama said.

A sparrow landed on our table. "Hey, little one," Breck said. "Aren't you brave?"

"They come for the crumbs, I bet," Mama said.

The sparrow pecked at the remnants of Breck's sandwich before hopping away.

"I've never seen one do that," I said. "Even the birds know Brandi's food is the best."

"If you're going to pursue Brandi, what am I going to do

about her mother?" Mama asked, as if we'd been talking about her. "Should I reach out to Malinda?" She tapped her nail against the metal table. "It's been ten years."

"I'm not sure it's a good idea," I said.

"An invitation to dinner is a nice olive branch," Breck said. "At least that's what my mom always says. No one can stay angry while breaking bread together."

"She's the one who wouldn't speak to me after what happened between you and Brandi," Mama said. "An olive branch might not be well-received."

I was about to comment when I noticed Breck's gaze wander. I turned to see that his attention had drifted toward Tiffany, who was walking down the street carrying a wide three-ring binder.

"It's Tiffany," Breck said.

Just to torture him, I waved and called out to her. "Hey, Tiffany."

She smiled and waved back, then scurried over to our table. Dressed in light blue slacks and a crisp white shirt, she appeared to have come from her client meeting.

"How are you guys doing?" Tiffany asked, with a nervous hitch to her voice. Was she nervous to see Breck or my mother, or was it just her general shyness? Mama was technically her boss at the lodge, which would put even the most confident person on edge. Not that it mattered whether you were on the payroll or not. Mama assumed she was the boss of all of us.

"We're super," Mama said. "How did it go this morning with the bridezilla?"

"Fine. I think, anyway," Tiffany said. "She liked the menu ideas I presented."

"Would you like to sit with us?" I asked. As much as I was enjoying this, someone needed to put Breck out of his misery.

"Thank you, no," Tiffany said. "I have a lot of work to do."

I glanced over at Breck. He was moving a crumb around his plate with great care.

"Dr. Stokes, thank you for walking me home last night and

for the advice about food for Muffy," Tiffany said. "I bought a tin of the brand you suggested, and she ate it all up."

Breck looked up and flashed his warm smile. "Wonderful news about your pooch. She should probably come in for a checkup anyway. Just to make sure she's just a picky eater and not ill. Free of charge."

"How kind of you. Thank you," Tiffany said.

"You're looking quite smart," Mama said to Tiffany. "The new wardrobe pieces are suiting you."

"Thank you, Mrs. Barnes. I feel like a whole new person since you took me shopping."

"We had such fun together, didn't we?" Mama said. "I always wanted a daughter to shop with."

"I was homeschooled, and my mother made all our clothes," Tiffany said, seeming to feel obligated to explain. "All the pieces seemed to resemble one another somehow. Out on the farm we didn't have much need for...what did you call them, Mrs. Barnes?"

"Staple pieces," Mama said.

"Like this blouse. Mrs. Barnes helped me choose my staple pieces when I first came to work here because my clothes were just awful."

"The blouse looks nice on you," Breck said. "A gunnysack would, actually."

Tiffany's eyes widened. Her knuckles went white as she clutched the folder tightly against her chest.

"Whatever a gunnysack is, I don't actually know," Breck said, before turning back to his beloved crumb.

Tiffany brought the folder up toward her chin. "Well, I should go. Like I said, I have a lot of work to do."

"Have a great afternoon," Mama said. "I'll see you tomorrow at the staff meeting."

"Yes, right. See you there." Tiffany did a slight curtsy, blushed red, and fled.

"Dude, a gunnysack?" I asked Breck.

"I don't know why I said that—she's just so pretty that I lost my head."

"I think you scared her to death," I said.

"I've never known you to be interested in a girl," Mama said. "I thought you might be gay."

"What?" Breck and I asked at once.

"Not that anything's wrong with that," Mama said.

"I'm not gay," Breck said. "I'm simply hopeless with women. I'm the one they all want to adopt as their little brother or something."

"I think she likes you," Mama said. "Or she wouldn't have turned so red. I'm feeling a sudden urge to invite Tiffany and Breck for dinner."

"I don't know if I should be terrified or happy," Breck said, chuckling.

"Terrified," I said.

"Happy. Mama Barnes to the rescue." She lifted her gaze upward. "This sky has me worried. I've never seen it this smoky."

"Be ready to evacuate," I said.

Breck's forehead creased. "I need to come up with a plan for the animals at the shelter." He looked at his watch. "I better go, actually. I've got to go out to the Andersons' and check on their mama cow. She's about ready to give birth, and they asked me to come by."

"The life of a country vet," I said. "Your work is never done."

"You got that right," Breck said, standing. "Keep in touch if we end up having to scoot out of here."

"Will do," I said.

He gave us a quick smile and sauntered down the sidewalk to his truck.

"Did you really think he was gay?" I asked.

"He's always been so nicely groomed and well-mannered," Mama said. "Especially compared to you and Huck. It crossed my mind a few times."

"I can assure you he's interested in women. He had a girlfriend during vet school." They'd broken up because she was way too possessive and jealous.

"This gives me a new mission," Mama said. "Operation Tiffany and Breck."

I didn't say anything, grateful to have her focused on them rather than Brandi and me. All I needed was Mama's interfering ways to make a complicated situation worse.

AFTER LUNCH, I DROVE OUT TO SEE GRAMMIE AND PA. THE SMOKY sky had me worried, and I wanted to make sure they had a plan in case the fire jumped the river. I bounced along the dirt road past Camille Stokes's estate and horse pasture. As I drove by, several horses lifted their heads and whinnied at me.

I passed Brandi's parents' driveway next. Their house wasn't visible from the road, tucked behind a thicket of trees. I hadn't been there since high school, but I didn't need to have my memory refreshed to see the cottage where Jasper and his new bride, Lizzie, had moved just before their baby, Florence, arrived.

Other than the acres Alexander bequeathed to his faithful staff back in 1910, the original property remained in our family. For generations, we'd managed to resist developers, choosing the land over money. Every Barnes who wanted one would have a section of land he or she could call their own. My father felt particularly protective of the acreage, seeing it as the most important asset and handed down to sons and daughters. Someday, God willing, I would have children to leave the land, as would my sister.

At the end of the dirt road, I turned right into my grandparents' place. When my father married my mother, Pa had suggested they take the big house. He was tired of the upkeep. My grandmother wanted a country-style cottage. They'd chosen a flat acre with the mineral-rich soil for Grammie's gardens and built one exactly to her specifications.

I parked near the barn, scattering curious and remarkably bold hens as I got out of the truck. A vegetable garden, enclosed behind a fence to keep the deer out, burst with tomato plants, beans, squash, and cucumbers. Painted white with dark blue shutters and front door, the cottage stood between two oaks. Wide flat rocks made a walkway toward the house. Flowers and shrubs grew in clusters around the yard, a little unruly rather than manicured. Climbing roses decorated the white fence and trellis.

I went in without knocking. "Grammie? Pa? You guys home?" The house smelled like freshly baked cookies. The scent seemed to have permanently made its way into the walls. This was one of my favorite places on earth.

Grammie's voice called out from the kitchen. "Back here."

I passed through the living room, decorated in tans and grays, all soft and comfortable like my grandmother herself.

She was barefoot in front of the kitchen sink, dressed in jeans with the cuffs rolled up and a T-shirt from a Bruce Springsteen tour, circa 2003. I spotted a pair of muddy tennis shoes just outside the French doors that led out to the stone patio.

"Trapper, what a nice surprise." She had this way of saying my name that made me feel as if I were the most important person in the world. "Give me a hug."

I wrapped my arms around her small frame. She smelled of dirt and the flower pollen that dusted one shoulder. "What're you up to, Grammie?"

Tucking a bit of her silver hair behind her ears, she grinned up at me. "I've been out in the garden." She pointed to a bin of red tomatoes in the wide ceramic sink. "I'm drowning in these guys, so I'll be canning this afternoon."

"Do you need some help?" I asked.

"I'd love it." She peered at me. "But aren't you busy?"

"Nah. For the first time in my life, I've got nothing but time."

Pa came in from outside and said hello in his soft-spoken way, then patted me on the back. Tall and broad-shouldered, even in his mid-seventies he hadn't slowed down much. Since he and Grammie had retired from running the lodge, he still skied and worked his small farm like a man half his age.

For the next few hours, the three of us worked together. Pa sat at the table, coring the tomatoes. I blanched them in boiling water, then tossed them into an ice bath. Grammie peeled and scooped the seeds out and boiled them once more while Pa sterilized the mason jars. Next, we stuffed jar after jar with the stewed tomatoes. When they were ready, Grammie placed them in the pressure cooker. Steam clouded the windows and made the air thick with moisture. By the end, we had four dozen jars lined up on the kitchen table.

After our work we sat outside under the awning and drank glasses of ice water. Inside, one by one, the lids to the mason jars popped, assuring us they were properly sealed.

"You haven't done much canning since you left, I bet?" Pa slapped me on the knee.

"Not once," I said, laughing. "Hotel rooms weren't too good for canning."

"We're glad you're home," Grammie said. "There was a time we thought you might never be back."

"I promised my dad when I left that I'd be back after hockey was done," I said. "I thought I might have a few years longer than I did, but the old knee didn't agree."

"I worried Brandi might keep you away," Grammie said. "This is a small town. Hard to stay away from anyone you don't want to see."

"I've seen her," I said.

"We heard about the dancing in the middle of the street," Pa said. "Classic Barnes move."

"Who told you?" I asked.

"Your father," Grammie said. "Who heard it from Camille, who heard it from Breck."

"This town," I said.

Pa chuckled. "Some things never change."

"By noon the day after our first date, every person in town knew we'd gone down to the river for a picnic," Grammie said. "Such a scandal back then to be alone in a car with a young man."

"It didn't help that someone saw me kiss her," Pa said.

"On a blanket spread out on the grass," Grammie said. "Very romantic."

"That got back to her father right away. Not good for me. He did not care for the blanket idea."

"Too close to a bed," Grammie said, laughing.

"What did he do?" I asked.

"There were a few threats and a shotgun involved," Pa said.

"My father was absolutely opposed to me marrying Normandy," Grammie said. "We had to elope and beg forgiveness afterward."

"I had to rescue her from lock and key," Pa said. "Quite literally."

"Why did he hate you?" I asked.

"He'd had a disagreement with my father back in the day," Pa said.

"It was more than a disagreement," Harriet said. "George Barnes, your Pa's father, stole my father's girlfriend right out from under him."

"Emma, who turned out to be my mother," Pa said.

"My mother was his second choice, and she knew it every day of her life," Grammie said.

"How sad," I said.

Grammie's bottom lip trembled. "It was. My mother had a sad life."

Pa reached over and took Grammie's hand. "Don't fret, love."

"I know, I know," Grammie said.

"Everything worked out in the end because Harriet agreed to put up with me forever."

"We've had a happy marriage," Grammie said. "That's what we want for you. Whatever you do, don't choose someone as a replacement for Brandi. If you want her and she refuses you, don't do what my father did and marry for spite."

"I wouldn't," I said. "I'm too much of a romantic."

Pa patted my knee again. "That's some Alexander in your blood. We come from a long line of romantics."

"I'm trying not to get ahead of myself, but the magic was still there between us," I said. "But there's something she's not telling me."

"Take it one day at a time," Pa said. "If it's meant to be, then it'll work out."

"Like with us," Grammie said, smiling over at Pa. "As hard as my father tried to keep us apart, true love won in the end."

As my mother had earlier, Grammie peered up at the sky. "Is it me or does it seem smokier than just a few hours ago?"

"The wind picked up this morning," Pa said. "I'm worried."

Grammie wrung her hands. "Fire scares me to death. Those poor people out west who didn't get out in time haunted me for months."

"Same," I said. "I was in LA for the Malibu fires. Some friends of mine lost their homes." I glanced down at my exercise band. "It's getting late. I better get going. I'm supposed to go to Mom's for dinner, and I should get cleaned up first."

They walked me out to my truck. I glanced nervously up at the dull orange sky. "You know, it would ease my mind if you guys had some bags packed in case we have to evacuate."

Pa nodded. "I think you're right."

"I'm going to do the same," I said. "Camping gear plus some essentials."

"I hope it won't come to that," Grammie said. "But we won't hesitate if they tell us to go. As much as I'd hate to leave our home, we know to take it seriously."

I kissed her soft cheek before climbing into my truck, watching in my rearview mirror as they walked toward the house holding hands.

As it turned out, I was not able to ask Brandi to dinner. Mama beat me to it. No sooner had I pulled into my driveway than I received a text from my interfering mother.

Invited the Vargases and Brandi to dinner. Come by at six.

I stared at the message for a good minute. How had this happened? I'd wanted to take Brandi somewhere quiet so we could talk. Having dinner with both sets of parents was not my ideal evening.

Regardless of my apprehensions, I showed up right at six. I parked near the barn and walked around back to the patio. Dad was putting chicken kebabs on the grill as I approached.

"Hey there, son," he said. "Right on time."

"I always have a nose for dinner." A table under the patio awning had been set for six.

Before he could answer, Mama burst out through the French doors carrying a tray of raw vegetables and ranch dressing.

"Good, you're here," Mama said. "Brandi and her parents will be here any minute."

"Mama, what did you do? How did you get them to agree to come to dinner?"

"I went out to their house and just knocked on the door," Mama said. "I told her this was ridiculous and that it was time to forgive each other and be friends again."

"How did she react?" I asked.

"Not well. The woman's so stubborn." Mama smoothed her cotton shirtdress over her hips.

I had to hold back from catching my dad's eye for fear I'd laugh.

"Did you apologize?" Dad asked as he thrust his hands into his cargo shorts.

"Yes, I did." She put her hands on her hips. "I don't know why you had to ask like that. I'm perfectly capable of apologizing. Not that I know what I did, which I'm also perfectly willing to overlook, as this is about my son and the woman he loves, not some petty feud between us. And for your information, she didn't reciprocate. She stood there during my apology like she hadn't been at all in the wrong." She frowned at me. "Don't look at me that way. If you kids are ever going to make this work, that woman has to be on board. Brandi's too sweet to defy her."

"Does Mrs. Vargas hate me?" I asked.

Mama went to the table, straightening forks that were already straight.

"Mama?"

She turned to look at me. "Well, fine. If you want to know the truth, she started going on again about how you ruined her daughter's life instead of recognizing that it was Brandi who broke it off. Can you believe that? After ten years? I swear, she's like a child who doesn't get her way."

"Rose, did you keep your temper?" Dad asked.

"I certainly did. Even though I wanted to let her have it. I mean, the audacity of that woman, blaming my son for something that wasn't his fault."

"I'm not sure what I did to make her hate me," I said. Other than sneaking her daughter out her bedroom window when we were young. I kept that theory to myself. "I'm surprised she agreed to dinner."

"I hope it's not an ambush," Dad said.

Mama didn't say anything, but the look of worry in her eyes told me she had hoped the same thing.

I decided to change the subject. "Dad, did you go see Brandi yesterday?"

He opened a bottle of beer and tossed the cap into the

wastepaper basket just outside the French doors. "I might've dropped in for a sandwich. Why?"

"She told me you did," I said.

He gave me a look of pure innocence. "I was curious about those sandwiches I kept hearing about."

"Really?" I asked. "Just the sandwich."

"I'll be damned if I sit back and let her get away from you a second time," he said. "Anyway, it sounds like you owe me a note of gratitude. I heard you kissed her right in the middle of the street."

I groaned and rubbed my eyes, which were stinging from the smoke. "I did forget how quickly rumors spread here."

The sound of a car pulling into the driveway drew us out of our conversation.

My mother scuttled inside to answer the front door.

I exchanged a look with Dad. "This could be a disaster," I said.

"I know. But you know how she is. Once she gets an idea, she can't let it go." Dad patted my shoulder. "It'll be okay. Just have a nice time. Take Brandi for a walk down to the creek."

Brandi's parents came out to the patio with her right behind them. Malinda and Jack Vargas were as attractive as their only child. Ten years had passed since I last saw them, but they appeared remarkably unchanged. A homemaker, Malinda was small and blond like Brandi. Jack had the lean look of a long-distance runner. He worked as a salesman for a technology company out of Denver, telecommuting when he wasn't on the road.

"How does it feel to be home?" Jack asked as he pumped my hand a little too hard.

"Still getting acclimated, sir," I said.

"A little slower paced than you're used to," Malinda said. She had a flat way of talking that made the most innocuous sentence sound like an insult.

"Yes, ma'am. A little. I've missed the slower pace."

Brandi had drifted over to where my father was opening a bottle of Chablis. Mama asked the Vargases to please sit and if they would like wine. Mr. and Mrs. Vargas sat together on one end of the sectional. I brought them each a glass and sat opposite them. To my surprise, Brandi sat next to me.

Once everyone had their drinks, a long, awkward silence settled between us. I tried desperately to think of something to say. Finally, Dad asked Jack about work. Mom and Malinda started talking about the smoke and how it made their eyes water.

I only half listened, stealing glances at Brandi. She sucked down at least half a glass of wine in the first five minutes.

I whispered in her ear, "You want to take a walk down to the creek?"

She lifted her gaze toward me. "Can I bring my wine?"

"Sure." I stood and offered my hand.

She nodded and allowed me to lift her to her feet, then waited by the steps down to the grass as I topped off her wine. "We're going to take a walk," I said.

"Don't be long," Mama said. "Dinner will be ready in a half hour."

I avoided Mrs. Vargas's glare as I grabbed my beer, and the two of us set out together.

I waited until we were a good distance from the patio before speaking. "Well, this was unexpected," I said.

"Yeah. Mom sprang it on me just as I was getting ready to call you," she said.

"You *were* going to call me? I thought I scared you away with the flowers."

She nudged me with her elbow. "Yes, I was going to call you. I was at work today or I would've earlier. I'm sorry about my reaction toward the flowers. I was embarrassed in front of my customers."

"It's all right. My fault. I should've known better than to

bring a bouquet to your work," I said. "I forgot how gossipy this town is."

We walked over the manicured grass until we reached the fence that enclosed the landscaped part of the yard. A wide, flat meadow led down to the creek bed. During warm months, we mowed the natural grasses to keep them from growing too tall and wild. I held the gate open for her, and she slipped by me.

"The gesture was sweet. A man hasn't brought me flowers in a long time."

I contemplated that for a moment. Did that mean she'd been seeing someone at one point? Had she spent time with anyone in the ten years since I last saw her? The grass made a soft carpet under our feet. A warm wind blew her hair. Wind and fire. I shuddered. Would we be safe? Given the orange sky, I wasn't sure.

She stooped to pick a buttercup from the meadow. "Here's a flower for you," she said.

I rubbed it against her cheek. "Buttercups remind me of you. All sunny and yellow."

She blinked as she looked up at me. "I forgot how tall you are. How big."

"I didn't forget anything about you."

"Is that true?" she asked.

"I never lie to you." I wrapped one arm around her waist, searching her eyes for any hesitation before I kissed her. She responded immediately, wrapping her free arm around my neck and pressing close. The kiss deepened. I drew her close and ran my fingers down her back. God, she felt good. So right. I pulled away. "I have to stop before I throw you down in the grass."

She grinned and tossed her hair behind her shoulders. "That would be like the old days."

I held out my hand. "Let's keep walking before we end up in trouble."

Her face clouded, and she dropped her gaze downward.

What had I said wrong? I didn't ask. Instead, I took her free hand and led her across the meadow.

"The whole town knows about last night," she said after a minute or so.

"I know. Does it bother you?"

She shrugged. "Not really. I don't care what anyone thinks."

We headed down the slope toward the creek bed. This time of year, the water was shallow and warm from the sun. Still, there was a nice pool between two narrowed sections of the creek where we used to fish and swim.

"Give me your glass," I said. To get to the water's edge, we had to climb over a few rocks, and I didn't want her to slip.

She did so, and I watched as she made her way over the uneven rocks to a section of sand. Years ago, I'd dragged a log over as a makeshift bench. She sat, and I handed over her wineglass.

I eased my long body onto the log, wincing when pain shot through my knee.

"Does it hurt?" she asked.

"Every once in a while. I'm going to be one of those old men who can predict the weather by the pain in my knee."

We both slipped off our sandals and put our feet in the creek. After the water settled, minnows drew near, cautiously at first until their curiosity got the better of them. I sipped my beer, conscious of Brandi's body heat and wishing I could take her in my arms and make love to her as I had when we were young.

She giggled as minnows nibbled at her toes.

"You always had the most ticklish feet," I said.

"It's embarrassing when I get my toes done at the salon," she said. "I can't stop laughing."

"I've missed your laugh."

"I missed yours, too," she said. "We might've gotten a little carried away last night."

"How so?"

"I don't know. Maybe dancing in the middle of the street was a little over-the-top?" She smiled, then leaned her head against my shoulder. "You're such a romantic."

"I know it's a little much. I'm sorry."

"Don't apologize. You've said you're sorry too much in the last twenty-four hours. You shouldn't have to say that to me. Not now. Not after all the ways I hurt you."

"How about if we just start fresh? Forgive whatever happened in the past and see what's here?"

She didn't answer for a long moment. "There's something I have to tell you."

"Go ahead."

She didn't speak for a long moment. More minnows came, swarming around our ankles and feet.

"I'm afraid," she whispered. "I don't know if I can tell you."

I chose my words carefully. My gut told me to tread lightly, to make sure she understood that my love was unconditional. "You don't have to tell me now or any time if it's something from your past. I don't care what's happened between now and the last time I saw you. All I care about is the future."

She tossed a stick into the water. "Do you know what I've figured out since then? You're a lot better a person than me."

I lifted a section of her hair, loving the silky texture in my coarse and calloused hands. "That's not true. You're my favorite person in the whole world. And I have extremely good taste."

"You were always my favorite, too," she said. "When you left, it was like part of me disappeared. I was so lost, Trapper. So sad."

"I've been thinking about something I want to tell you. We were always Trapper and Brandi in the same sentence. As painful as it was, maybe breaking up is what we both needed. You deserved to be just Brandi, rock-star businesswoman. I'm sorry I made it all about me back then without considering your feelings. I was so full of myself. It makes me cringe to think about how I acted."

"You weren't. Not to me. You were always generous and kind

and loving. It hurt like hell to watch you leave. There hasn't been a day I haven't thought about you."

My heart soared. "Do you know how much it means to hear you say that?" I smiled at her, then leaned down and kissed her softly.

"That time with you was the best of my life." Her voice wobbled slightly. "The minute you drove out of town, it's like the lights went out."

"Have you been happy, though?" I asked. "When I thought about you, I always hoped you were happy."

She looked at me with eyes that read more sad than happy. "I guess so. What's happy really even mean?"

"Fulfilled might be a better word. Were you fulfilled? Content?"

"I've led a quiet, uncomplicated life, with routines and discipline. My business gives me joy. I never really knew where my place was in the world until I opened the shop."

"I kept waiting for the day the guys called and told me you were married," I said.

"I figured you'd come home with some actress on your arm." She wriggled her toes, and the minnows scattered. Her toenails were painted pink and so cute I wished I were a minnow so I could nibble on them. "Were any of those women you were linked to serious?"

"No, never. Just casual dating."

"So, you had sex with them?" she asked.

"I'm not a saint." I tugged at the collar of my shirt.

"I'm not going to think about that." She set aside her wineglass, then drew her knees to her chest and wrapped her arms around them.

"What about you?" I asked. "Has there been anyone?"

Her shoulders rose and fell as she took in a deep breath. "No. I shut myself down. Closed for business. No one else would ever be you."

"You've not dated at all?"

She uncurled her legs and put her feet back in the water. "I've been too busy with the shop to even think about dating. I work, go home, microwave a frozen dinner, watch TV or read, then go to bed to do it all over again."

"You might be surprised how similar my life was to that," I said. "Work was all I did for the last ten years. I had to be so disciplined about my diet and working out and keeping my nose clean, there wasn't time for much else. It might seem glamorous to other people, but the life of an athlete is more about focus than fun."

"Was it everything you dreamed of when we were small?"

I traced her jawline with my thumb. "Here's what surprised me. After I got everything I wanted—the prestige and the winning seasons and all that money—I still felt the same inside. I never stopped thinking of myself as a boy from Emerson Pass. I'm prouder of being from here than I am about anything else. I'm from the DNA of great men. I'm a loyal friend and good son and grandson. That's who I am. Much more so than playing professional hockey in LA. Nothing changed. At the end of it all, my origins define me, not that game. I didn't know that when we were kids. Does that make sense?"

"I think so. But you made it all come true. Whereas I've just been here."

"There's nothing wrong with that. We've all come back."

"You guys had somewhere to come back from," she said.

"Why didn't you go to college? You'd applied other places, right?" Her mother had made sure of that.

"I didn't get in anywhere."

I drew back, shocked. "What?"

"I couldn't tell you at the time. I was too mortified. Not one of the places I applied would take me. My SAT scores were low, especially in math. I didn't have the college prep courses you guys had. Really, I have no idea why I thought I'd get into the places you and the guys were applying to."

"I had no idea." Had that been why she'd gotten it in her head she wasn't good enough for me?

"No one knew but my parents. I'd wished I didn't have to tell them, either."

"There's nothing wrong with the way you are," I said. "I hope I never made you feel like that."

"Not you. My mother took care of that all by herself."

"I'm sorry I was too wrapped up in my own stuff that I didn't notice something was wrong. I felt you withdrawing, but I thought it was just nerves. I wish I'd known so I could've reassured you. You're perfect just the way you are. A fancy degree doesn't mean crap to me."

She bumped my shoulder with the side of her head. "You always were the sweetest guy in the world."

"You've built a successful business all on your own, from your talent. That's something to be very proud of." I lifted her chin, forcing her to look in my eyes. "Do you hear me?"

"You always built me up, made me feel like I could do anything," she said. "I've missed that."

"I say the truth. That's all."

We sat together with her head on my shoulder, watching the bugs play on the water. Her admission had made so many things fall into place for me. I'd always wondered why she hadn't gone to college. The guys knew better than to mention her to me, but Mom had told me she decided not to attend college and that she'd opened a bakery a few years after high school. I'd been surprised, but I hadn't let myself evaluate it too carefully. She'd always loved to bake. Now that I thought back to school, I remembered how much she'd struggled academically. I suppose if I were to examine it truthfully, I'd have to admit I helped her get through high school. I wrote most of her papers and spent long hours as her math tutor. Her difficulties never made sense to me, because she was one of the brightest people I knew.

"I remember you struggling in school," I said. "But I didn't understand it because you were always so much smarter than me."

"There's an explanation," she said. "I'm dyslexic. I didn't know until a few years after we graduated. A friend suggested I have myself tested, and turns out I'm not actually stupid."

"You're not stupid, Brandi. Don't ever say that."

"I thought I was."

"Why weren't you ever tested when we were kids?" I'd never thought of it before, but it was odd that no one ever questioned why school was so hard for her. My mom would've been all over that had it been my sister or me.

"My mother refused."

"Why the hell would she do that?" I asked, immediately hot.

"I don't know. I've never asked her."

"You should," I said.

"We're not close. I disappointed her by opening the bakery instead of going to community college. It's better when we don't see each other."

"And the business totally took off," I said. "You get the last laugh."

"Not that she would ever acknowledge it. Don't look at me that way." She smiled and kissed my cheek.

"What way?"

"Like you feel sorry for me," she said.

I did feel sorry for her, not because I thought any less of her for her choice of career but because her mother was such a witch. "I admire you. No pity here."

"You know just what to say to a girl." She picked up her wineglass. "We better get back. If we're late for dinner, our mothers might send us to our rooms."

"I don't want to, but you're right," I said as I stood and offered her my hand, then lifted her to her feet.

I took her hand, and we traipsed through the wildflowers and the grasses. Overhead, the sky had a strange orange glow, like the end of the world was near. "I don't like this sky," I said. "It gives me the creeps."

AS WE PASSED THROUGH THE GATE INTO THE YARD, MY DAD MET US on the lawn. "We got a call to evacuate," he said. "The entire southern mountain's on fire, and it jumped the river. With this wind, they're afraid it's moving too fast to contain."

"That's where Garth's house is," I said, thinking out loud.

"And Crystal's," Brandi said.

"Your parents left to grab a few things from their house." Dad took the empty wineglass and bottle from our hands. "We're supposed to head to the high school in Louisville."

"I don't have my car with me," Brandi said.

"Forget the car," I said. "You'll go with me in my truck. I don't want you out of my sight."

"Yeah, okay," she said.

"Don't dawdle," Dad said. "This is no time for sentimentality." The fear in his tone scared me. Dad was not one for the dramatic. If he believed we were in danger, we were. He loved this house and property. All of our family history dwelled in every board and crevice of this house. Leaving it defenseless was the last thing he would ever want to do.

"We'll see you in Louisville," I said.

"Keep your phones," Dad said. "Your mother will be frantic."

"You do the same," I said.

MINUTES LATER, WE ARRIVED AT MY HOUSE. "DO YOU WANT TO come in? I'll be less than two minutes. I already have all the camping gear packed up."

"I'll go in to use the bathroom," she said. "Who knows how long we'll be in the truck."

In the house, I directed her toward the powder room, then ran upstairs. I snagged my toiletry bag from where it hung in the bathroom. From years of travel with the team, I always had it packed. I found a spare toothbrush for Brandi from the bag I'd gotten from the dentist at the last cleaning.

When I came downstairs, Brandi was waiting for me by the powder room. Together, we went to the garage, where I had the camping gear stacked in one corner. I added another sleeping bag to the mix, along with a mat. Everything went into the back of the truck. Then I lugged the plastic container that stored my gas cookstove and some old pots and pans to the corner of the truck bed. I ran back into the garage for my cooler. Fortunately, I had two bags of ice in my garage freezer. I added that along with a huge pack of frozen hot dogs, hamburgers, and buns I'd bought at the Louisville Costco on my way back home from the airport in Denver. My plan had been to have the guys over for a cookout and some beers this weekend, but that wasn't happening now.

I hauled the ice cooler out to the truck and, at the last minute, grabbed three cases of beer and a bottle of whiskey—also for the party that wouldn't happen—and added those to my loot. After dropping those into the truck, I went back one last time for a case of chili and another of baked beans. Survival mode, I guess, had my mind focused on the immediate needs of my friends and family, should this evacuation drag into days and days. I hopped back into the driver's seat and started the engine, breathless by the time I sped out of my driveway.

We hurtled down the road toward town. "There's enough food back there for an army," she said, teasing.

"I don't know what it will be like down there. The stores might not have anything left by the time we get there."

"This is weird," she said. "I'm scared."

"All this is just a precaution," I said, trying to keep my voice light. "Everything will be fine."

I drove us into town. A mushroom of dense black smoke

hovered over the mountain. Red and orange flames shot up from under the cloud in angry bursts.

"Crystal's house is up there somewhere," Brandi murmured.

"Same with Garth's," I said. "If it jumps the river, the rink is in its direct path."

"And the high school."

We were a block from the bakery. "Do you want me to stop so you can grab a few things?"

"Yes. I'll hurry."

I pulled into the alley next to the bakery, and she jumped out, then unlocked her door and disappeared.

I tapped my fingers against the steering wheel. Her compact car was parked behind the building. I didn't want her to separate from me. Could I convince her to stay?

Less than five minutes later, she jumped back in the truck with a duffel bag and a hatbox. "I'm ready."

"You want to stay with me?" I asked. "Or take your car?"

"Stay with you. I'd rather not be alone."

"Good. I want you here." We exchanged a quick smile before I pulled back onto Barnes Avenue. Normally quiet in the evenings, the side of the street that headed toward the highway was packed. We crept along for a good five minutes.

The highway was no better. Cars inched east like ants marching home. We continued at twenty miles an hour as town faded from my rearview mirror. Brandi was on the phone with her dad, assuring him that we were fine. "I'm with Trapper in his truck. We'll see you in Louisville."

"Everything okay with them?" I asked.

"Other than my mother shouting instructions into my dad's ear, yes." She frowned. "I've called and texted Crystal two times already, but there's no answer. Do you think she's all right?"

"If I had my guess, she's driving and can't answer the phone."

My phone chimed with a text, probably from the guys. I slid it across the seat to Brandi. "Can you see what that is?"

She picked it up and squinted at the screen. "What's the pass code?"

I immediately went hot. The pass code was the same as all my passwords—Brandi's birthday. "It's your birthday," I said.

"Trapper, really?"

"I know. Embarrassing," I said.

She set the phone on the dashboard, unbuckled her seat belt, and scooted over to kiss me on the cheek. "I love it."

I love you.

"Get back into your seat belt," I said, gruffly.

She gave me one more kiss before bouncing back to her place and buckling her belt. My phone pinged again.

She grabbed it from the dashboard and looked down at the screen. "There are two messages. One from Breck and another from Huck. They're both asking if you're headed out of town."

"Tell them I'm fine and that you're with me." She clicked away at the phone. A second or two later, it rang again.

"Breck says he's glad we're together. And to take good care of me." She fanned her eyes. "That's really sweet. And makes me want to cry. When you guys left, I didn't think I'd ever have any of you back in my life."

I reached over and took her hand. "We all missed you as much as you missed us."

"Huck says he's staying to cover the fire and not to do anything stupid." She set the phone on the seat. "Like stupid, how? As in, not evacuate?"

"I'm not sure."

"That's a strange thing to say," she said. "You're always the most responsible guy in the room."

"Yeah, but Huck's kind of an old lady that way. Nervous."

"Breck texted again. He's at the shelter," Brandi said. "Picking up all the animals and then he'll head out."

My hands started shaking. Breck would be too close to the fire. I gripped the steering wheel. Should I go back and help him?

As if he read my mind, another text came through. Brandi relayed the information. "He says he's fine and that Tiffany and his mom are with him."

"Tiffany? I wonder how that happened?" I asked.

Brandi bent over the screen. "Another one from Huck. 'And whatever you do, don't sleep with her.'"

I cleared my throat. "Maybe you better give me that."

She slid the phone across the seat without meeting my gaze. I grabbed that sucker and pulled up Breck's number. It rang one time before he picked up. "Are you okay?"

"I'm fine. We're here, loading up the dogs." He grunted, followed by the whine of a dog. "I had to swing by the clinic first. We had a dog in for observation, so he's with us too. We're almost done. Just have a few more cats. They're all in carriers, thank God."

"Why's Tiffany with you?" I asked.

"She was with me at the office with Muffy when we got the call to evacuate. Her car is unreliable, so I convinced her to stay with me." His voice lowered. "She's completely terrified. Muffy's not doing too well, either."

"That makes three of us," I said. "Just get the hell out of there, okay?"

"Roger that," Breck said. "We'll see you in Louisville."

"Why would Huck be concerned if we slept together?" Brandi asked when I hung up.

The muscles in my neck constricted. "He's protective of me, that's all."

"And he hates me for what I did," she said.

"*Hate*'s a strong word."

"Huck never approved of me," Brandi said. "Or liked me."

"I suspect it's the opposite. He always had a thing for you. Breck says Huck felt guilty about being in love with my girl and hid it by being a jerk."

Her eyes widened. "That can't be right."

"Breck's always spot-on about things like this."

"Do you think he'll be upset if we get back together?"

I grinned at her, despite my nervousness over our situation. "Are you asking me to go steady?"

She punched my thigh. "Trapper, I'm serious."

"Yes, I will go steady with you. However, I'm not sure where my varsity jacket is."

She laughed. "No deal unless you have the jacket. I want to wear that thing around town like I used to."

"You were so cute in my jacket."

"I was over the moon the first time you ever asked me to wear it." A sadness in her voice caused my chest to ache.

"What makes you sad about that memory?" I asked.

She hesitated a moment before answering. "I miss feeling that the most important thing in the world was that the boy I loved wanted me to wear his jacket. Being so in love and carefree and ignorant of how life can bring you to your knees in an instant. Back then, I lived totally in the moment without any fear of the consequences of my actions."

"Give me your hand," I said.

She leaned closer and placed her hand on my upper thigh. I brought it to my mouth and kissed her knuckles. "I'm sorry for whatever brought you to your knees. I'd fix everything for you if I could."

"I know, Trap." She withdrew her hand and trailed her fingers down my neck before straightening.

We crawled along, quiet. I glanced nervously into the rearview mirror, hoping each time for a miracle. There was none. The horrifying black cloud remained.

Brandi shifted in her seat. "What if the whole town goes up in flames like the one in California? Those poor people have been displaced ever since. We've always had Emerson Pass to either go home to or stay home in."

"They'll get it contained before that happens," I said.

"Always the optimist."

"You used to like that about me."

"I did. I do. I'm always too afraid to be optimistic. Right now, I'm afraid I'm going to lose the only thing in my life that gives me a purpose."

"They're only buildings. You have insurance, right?"

"Yes, of course."

"If we lose the bakery, we'll rebuild. As long as you're safe. That's all that matters."

"We?"

I laughed and tugged at one ear. "I mean, we as a *community*, not we as a *couple*."

"I kind of like the word *we*," she said. "As in you and me."

"I will find that varsity jacket if it kills me."

A few seconds went by with Brandi staring out her window before she turned back to me. "The equipment alone is worth thousands and thousands of dollars. Who knows how long insurance claims could take?"

"It's going to be all right." I wasn't at all sure if that was true, but I knew how she could worry herself into a frenzy.

Behind us, a car beeped its frustration at the snail's pace. I wanted to answer back with my own frustrated beep, but refrained.

I squeezed her knee. "You know, when Alexander Barnes discovered Emerson Pass it was nothing but a bunch of scarred wood from a fire. The miners had all gone after stripping the mountains of gold and silver, and all that was left were a few bitter men. That's why he rebuilt everything in brick. These buildings are over a hundred years old. They're tough. Like you."

"I'm not sure I'm tough."

"If you could see yourself from my eyes, you'd know I'm right."

She swiped at her phone and made an impatient sound from the back of her throat. "Still no text from Crystal."

"She's probably just driving," I said. Brandi needed a distraction. "Why don't you read one of the letters from the box? I've never heard any of them."

"Are you interested or are you trying to distract me?"

"I love reading the journals from Quinn. I mean, now I do. When we were younger, I couldn't care less."

"It's funny how that changes, isn't it?" she asked as she tugged the top from the hatbox. "I'll just pick a random one."

"Sounds good to me."

She read out loud.

August 3, 1914

Dearest Mummy,

Thank you for your letter with the news from home. I'm sorry to hear of your fall and do hope you've done as the doctor asked and stayed quiet.

You've asked for news of the children to entertain you during your recovery, so I'll do my best to tell you about a few of their antics at Florence's birthday party. For her third birthday, Quinn insisted we throw her a celebration like the Barneses' children have. She's worried Florence will feel sad or disregarded unless she's treated the same. It's so very American of her to be worried about the child's sense of self-worth. You'll find it odd, I'm sure, but things are different here in America, especially in the mountains. Given my daughter's domineering disposition (so much like her father) I can assure you she's fine. She and Addie are fast friends, growing up more like sisters. This house is overrun with the little rascals, all growing up together like wild American flowers.

We had cake and ice cream, and the children played croquet on the lawn. The whole gaggle of children were in attendance: Merry's boy Henry, the Wu children, and the Barnes brood. We're like an orphanage, albeit with enough parents to go around. All of the children played except for Theo. He read a book about anatomy under the shade of an oak tree. He's certain he'll become a doctor and learn how to cure the world of all diseases.

Even Josephine and Poppy, who think of themselves as young ladies these days, joined the fun. I know you enjoy hearing about their dresses and hats so I made sure to take note. Our fair and tall Josephine looked fetching in a pale pink dress with a yellow straw hat. Poppy's dress was light blue with a lace collar, which suited her small frame. She kept removing her hat to get a better view of the ball and had a pink nose by the end of the afternoon. There are no feathers in the hats now, since we've learned they were harming the bird population. (Cymbeline and Flynn fretted for days about the poor birds. They'd live with the animals in the barn if they could.)

Cymbeline grew cross when she didn't win and threw her croquet mallet against a tree. Quinn had to send her inside as punishment. For a girl of only ten, she's quite ferocious when she's angry. Lord Barnes says she will either run the world or rot in prison, and he's terrified of both outcomes. He's joking, of course, but Quinn does worry about our headstrong girl. I figure the more headstrong the better. This world is not for the meek, despite what the Bible tells us. (Sorry, Mummy.)

Flynn is also competitive, although he doesn't have the temper of his little sister. He felt sorry for her, being in trouble more than a few times himself, and asked if he might check on her. Quinn said to wait a few minutes but that, yes, he could talk with her and perhaps suggest better ways to deal with her frustration. Theo, during the kerfuffle, didn't look up from his book.

Fiona, at seven, is like a little mother to Florence and Addie. She's such a sweet thing and never grows impatient with her charges. Addie is kindhearted and gentle like her mother, but I'm afraid Florence is a bit of a handful. Like I said, she's bossy and opinionated and sure of how things should go. She tried to give lessons to Merry's Henry about how to play croquet. He, as usual, laughed at her and went about his own business.

During all this, Quinn, Merry, and I rested in the shade of an oak and watched, fatigued from the heat. Merry let baby Jack play on the blanket with his blocks until he grew tired and fell over and went to sleep. Quinn's feeling better since my last letter. The baby will come in the winter, and the doctor assures us all is well. Given her nausea, we're certain it's another girl. Poor Lord Barnes will continue to be surrounded by females.

To answer your question about another baby. I'd welcome one, of course, but I'm almost forty now. I doubt another one will come. I'm happy to have my Florence and the others to play auntie to, so don't be sad for me. I've a full, happy life.

When it's just the three of us at our cottage, Jasper is loving and tender to both of us. Since the day he finally gave in to his feelings, he's let his heart lead him. His stoic, disciplined ways crumble when in the presence of his daughter. You would not recognize him.

I miss you, Mummy. Please take care and write as soon as you're able.

Love,

Lizzie

Brandi sighed as she put the letter back in its envelope.

"How did Lizzie end up with the letters she sent her mother?" I asked.

"They were sent to her later, I believe."

We drove in silence for a few minutes as the words from all those years ago drifted through my mind. No matter what era one lived in, the center of every life was the people one loved.

She picked up her phone. "I'm going to try calling Crystal again."

I waited, hoping Crystal would pick up.

"Still no answer. I'm really starting to worry," Brandi said.

"It's possible she got out of there without her phone."

"If she had to leave quickly," she said. "Did you see how lit up the mountain was?" She hugged herself. "I feel sick."

"I know. Me too." I reached across the seat and squeezed her knee.

We continued on at twenty miles an hour for another mile.

"Does it eat you up that you never won the Stanley Cup?" she asked.

Surprised by the question, I had to think how to answer. I'd been disappointed. That much was inevitable. A man doesn't spend his life in pursuit of winning and not feel a sense of loss when the pinnacle of his profession is not reached. However, I had a different perspective on things than some might, having worked on myself to become a more enlightened human. "I'd have loved to win the championship. Those years we got close gave me a taste of what it would've been like and I wanted it, trust me. However, how many people are lucky enough to play professional hockey for six years and make that kind of money?"

We'd gone ten miles down by now, dropping in elevation, and no longer able to see the cloud of smoke. The air was less smoky but still hid the blue sky. "Only twenty more to go." I peeked at the gas gauge. We had three-quarters of a tank. No worries there.

"I should have popped into my kitchen. The day-old stuff was all piled in the back."

"What do you do with it?"

"I send it over to the assisted living facility." She curled her hands under her chin. "What about them? How do they evacuate?"

"They have their own bus. They'll get them out. We had plenty of warning. The firefighters know what they're doing."

"You're simply trying to cheer me up," she said.

"Maybe. But that doesn't mean it's not true," I said.

"How about some music?" I asked.

"Sure." She twisted around in her seat, clearly uneasy.

I turned on one of the satellite country stations. The same one I'd played for our dance in the street. We made it another half mile as the radio played a George Strait song.

"What was it like in LA?" she asked.

"Fine. I had a little condo in Santa Monica. The beach was awesome. I learned to surf."

"You did?"

"Not well, but it was fun. A buddy of mine on the team was from out there and spent some time coaching me."

"The guy always on the ice learned to surf?"

"Weird, right?" It occurred to me that to her, surfing was a symbol of my other life. The one away from here. Away from her. I put that aside to think about later.

Speed of traffic increased as we merged onto the four-lane highway toward Louisville. My chest loosened as we hit forty miles per hour. A roadside sign said Louisville was five miles away.

"Thank God," she said. "I thought we'd be at that speed forever."

"You hungry?" I asked. We hadn't had dinner. By now it was almost eight. The strange orange sun had disappeared. "There are some protein bars in the glove compartment."

"Starving." She yanked open the glove box and tossed me a chocolate peanut butter one and took another for herself.

It took us another fifteen minutes before we reached the Louisville high school. A cop stood at the entrance, turning cars away. The lot was obviously full. When it was my turn, I rolled down the window and waited for the bad news.

"Hello, sir," I said. "All full?"

He greeted us warmly but with an edge to his voice. I'm sure he'd gotten a mouthful all night. "Afraid so." He looked into the bed of my truck. "You have camping gear?"

"Yes, sir."

"For anyone with supplies, we're sending them down to the state campground. It's another ten miles down that way," he said, pointing east.

"You sure they have space?" I asked.

"Yes. It's a giant state campground with bathrooms and showers. You'll be safe and comfortable there." He gave us the address, which Brandi typed into her phone.

We thanked him, and I pulled back onto the street. I handed Brandi my phone. "Can you send a group text to Breck and Huck? Tell them to go straight to the campground instead of the high school and pass it on to anyone who's still on the road."

She tapped into my phone, then picked up hers to call her parents. They were still on the road but had decided to stay in a hotel. "No, I'll just stay with Trapper." She fidgeted. "Yes, I'm sure. Mom, I'll be fine. Let's just check in tomorrow morning."

I called my parents next. Mom picked up and said they'd also secured a hotel room and asked if we wanted to meet them there. "No, I'll go to the campground with the other guys. I've got camping gear and food."

"Smart boy," Mom said. "Keep Brandi safe."

"I will."

My dad got on the phone next. "Take this as a sign and don't mess up."

"Yes sir, I'll do my best."

7

B randi

LEAVE IT TO TRAPPER TO MAKE EVACUATING FROM A MASSIVE FIRE that threatened our entire community fun. A few minutes after we arrived, he had the tent up and had placed the cooler and cooking stove on the tailgate of his truck, as if we were getting ready for a party.

The road from the high school had taken us to a lower elevation. The sky here was clear and free of the smell of smoke. It was dark now, and a sprinkling of stars twinkled at us. The campground was flat and grassy, with cement driveways and paths. Campers had erected tents. Children ran and shouted, probably delighted to be free from their cars. The smell of gas grills cooking various types of meat filled the air, like any old night at the campsite.

Trapper turned on two battery-operated lanterns, which shed a surprising amount of light. I paced around the campsite, worried about Crystal. We'd heard from everyone by then except for her. Breck, his mother, and Tiffany had found a place for the shelter animals and were on their way there now. His mother had called a friend in Louisville, and they were going to stay there for the night.

Out of nowhere, I heard someone call my name. "Brandi?" I looked up to see two people, one carrying a lantern, walking toward us. A split second later, I realized it was Garth Welte and Crystal.

"Trapper, it's Crystal and Garth."

He turned from the cookstove, and we both sprinted over to meet them at the edge of our site. Crystal and I hugged as if we'd been separated for years instead of hours. "I've been calling and texting you. When you didn't answer, I thought the worst."

Crystal withdrew from my embrace and swiped under her eyes. Her usual perfectly applied makeup was smeared down her cheeks. "I didn't have the chance to grab anything but my laptop and my purse. I assumed my phone was in there, but I remembered later I'd just put it on the stand to charge. The smoke was so thick I could barely see. If Garth hadn't come for me, I don't know what would've happened."

Garth stood with his hands in the pockets of his jeans, his relaxed demeanor replaced by a haggard weariness. "The damned thing came out of nowhere. I was afraid we'd get trapped up there if we didn't just go."

"We had to leave everything or risk our lives," Crystal said. "All my framed photos were in that house." She wrapped her arms around her middle, shaking. "My wedding album. I was so panicked I just left it all."

Garth gave Crystal's shoulder a quick squeeze. "We're a little shaken up," he said, as if he needed to apologize.

"What else could you be?" Trapper slapped him on the back. "But dude, you were quick on your feet. Well done."

Garth grimaced, shaking his head. "My house is slightly higher elevation than Crystal, so I saw the flames coming down the mountain before she did. I'd packed my car when I got home from the bar last night because I had a bad feeling. Montana boy, so I've been through this before. As I drove down my driveway, I saw Crystal's car parked in front of the house. I scared her half to death by pounding on her door like a lunatic, but there was no way I was leaving without her."

"I was so scared, I just jumped in his car," Crystal said. "There's no way I could've driven."

"The good news is I've got all my camping gear and a bunch of canned goods," Garth said. "I remembered last night that my dad had done that once when we had to evacuate."

"I don't know what made me think to do the same thing," Trapper said. "Instinct maybe."

"Turns out they were able to contain the one we escaped from when I was a kid," Garth said. "We went home the next day. I'm not sure we're going to be so lucky this time."

"I'm glad you got out of there and didn't do anything foolish," Trapper said.

"Thank you for saving my friend," I said to Garth as my voice broke. "I was beside myself."

"He's my hero," Crystal said, wiping her eyes. "And one heck of a good neighbor."

"Come on over to my truck," Trapper said. "We've got drinks and food."

"We have beer," I said. "And hot dogs and hamburgers."

"And whiskey," Trapper said as he opened the cooler.

"I don't think I can eat," Crystal said. "But I'll take a beer."

Trapper opened beers for all of us and handed them around. We all took a grateful sip.

"Where's your car?" Trapper asked Garth.

"That's me over there." He pointed to a black SUV in the row behind us. "We set up a tent before it got too dark."

Trapper held out his hand to Crystal. "I don't know if you remember me, but it's nice to see you again, despite the circumstances."

Crystal gave him a fragile smile. "I remember you, Trapper. How could I forget? You and Brandi were always so nice to me when I was here for summers. Brandi's friendship was one of the main reasons I wanted to come home." She tossed her hair behind her shoulders. "We're pretty sure our homes are gone."

"Damned if I didn't just get the house finished," Garth said, grimacing. "Maybe it's good I never decorated."

Crystal sniffed. "I keep telling myself it's only objects. Just a house. But it represented my fresh start after losing Patrick. My return to my favorite place on earth."

"No matter what happens, we can rebuild," Trapper said. "Even if the buildings in town are damaged, we can restore them. My family will make sure of it."

"If there are families displaced, I want to help," Crystal said. "I can't bear to think of the children without homes."

"We can talk about that once we know the final outcome," Garth said. "As your attorney, that's my official advice."

She smiled at him. "Are you my attorney now?"

"After I saved you, it's only fair," Garth said, teasing. "I'm just a poor country lawyer in need of clients."

"Isn't your specialty divorce law?" Crystal asked, matching his tone, despite her obvious distress.

"We call it family law," Garth said. "But yes."

Their interaction gave me pause. Was it an air of flirtation and intimacy between them? Was that what happened when you escaped a forest fire together? She'd said before that Garth had been friendly, even checking on her a few times without being overbearing.

I pulled hot dogs from the cooler. Trapper found a can of baked beans. Crystal leaned limply against the truck.

"Damn, I forgot a can opener," Trapper said. "And silverware."

"Got you covered," Garth said as he lifted a Swiss Army knife from his pocket. "Give me that." He dug right in, getting the lid off in a matter of seconds, then peeled the wrapper off and stuck the tin container on the stove to heat. "I'll be right back with some forks and plates."

As I grilled dogs and toasted the buns over the flames, I searched on my phone for any updates on the fire but found nothing other than that Emerson Pass had been evacuated. Garth returned with four folding camping chairs and a stack of paper plates and plastic utensils. He and Trapper took the chairs from their casings and set them up in a circle near the tailgate. Crystal and Garth both sat and sipped their beers. Trapper opened a bag of corn chips and salsa. We moved the cooler to use as a table and set one of the lanterns on top. Then we left our friends to relax while we finished making dinner.

Around us, voices punctuated the quiet night as families prepared meals or readied for bed. At the site on one side of us, a couple had erected a small tent and were now making sandwiches from a loaf of bread and lunch meat. On the other side, a man and woman with small children huddled together in the back seat of their car. The kids on their parents' laps wriggled and fussed. They'd pulled in after us and didn't appear to have anything to eat. If they were like the rest of us, they'd left right around dinner. Were they hungry? My heart ached at the thought of those babies going to sleep with empty stomachs.

Trapper stood beside me by the cookstove, so close I could feel the heat from his body. I gestured toward the neighbor's car with the spatula. "Should we see if they need dinner? We have plenty."

He looked over to the car. "Totally. They must not have a tent, either."

"We should offer them ours," I said, no louder than a whisper.

"Where will you sleep? And we only have two sleeping bags."

I drew in a long breath, knowing I was tempting fate. However, these were extreme circumstances. "I'll sleep with you in the truck. We used to share a bag, remember?"

He tensed. His chest rose and fell. "I remember we didn't sleep much back then."

The memory of his hard body on top of mine weakened my knees. "True." I looked up at him.

"I can't be that close to you and control myself." His eyes glittered in the light from the camp stove.

"You won't have to." It was wrong. I knew it was wrong. But in that moment, I no longer cared. I'd take as much as I could of him before he knew what I'd done and left me for good.

He wrapped a big hand around my waist and lifted my blouse to slip a finger along the small of my back. "You sure?"

My breath hitched. Every part of me hummed from that simple touch. "I'm sure."

"Jesus, Brandi," he whispered in my ear. "Do you know how much I want you?"

"I do." I swallowed and glanced over to our friends. They had their heads together, talking softly. Thankfully, they seemed oblivious to us. "But for right now we have company."

"Right, yes." He grinned down at me. "I'll be good for now."

"Will you ask our neighbors if they'd like some hot dogs?" I asked.

Trapper nodded and went over to knock on the window of their car. I couldn't hear the exact exchange but a few minutes later, he returned. "They'd love some food. And our tent."

Our tent. I liked that word *our* a little too much. I set a pile of cooked hot dogs on a paper plate.

"They have blankets and a few sleeping bags," Trapper said. "But that's it." He lowered his voice. "They live not that far from Crystal's place and said they barely got out of there."

Trapper took the sleeping bags and mattress pads out of the tent and arranged them in the bed of the truck. I shivered, imagining what might happen there later.

Together, Garth and Trapper took the stakes out of the ground and lifted the entire tent over to the other campsite. Crystal helped fix plates of food, and we took them over as the guys pounded the stakes back into the ground. The woman, who held the youngest of the two little girls, introduced herself as Rhonda. Her husband was Matt. Neither looked much older than twenty. She wore a waitress uniform like the ones from the local diner. Matt was in coveralls with grease on the front. Their daughters were Mara and Katie, who looked at us with big eyes as they clung to their parents.

"I can't thank you enough," Rhonda said as she adjusted Katie on her skinny hip. "We'd just picked the girls up from day care when we got the news. They'd closed the road to our house, so we couldn't grab anything. We happened to have some blankets in the car from a trip down to the river last week. To make it worse, payday's tomorrow so we're down to nothing in our bank account. I had a little tip money, but it was a slow day. All we could get was a jug of milk and a box of saltines for the girls."

"Hot dog," Katie shouted.

"Yes, yes. Let's get you fed," Rhonda said.

Mara and Katie were given their hot dogs and set on top of the car's trunk to eat. I placed the other two plates on the hood.

"Please let us know if you need anything else," I said.

"Again, thank you," Rhonda said. "I just don't even know what to say."

"We're neighbors," I said. "That's what neighbors do."

Rhonda ran her hand through her ponytail. "We just bought our house out on Harley Road. Put every bit of money we had into the down payment. If we lose it, I don't know what we'll do."

Crystal reached into the pocket of her jeans and pulled out a stack of folded one-hundred-dollar bills. "Take this. It's five hundred."

"No, I couldn't," Rhonda said, pushing away Crystal's outstretched hand.

"Please. In case we're here for a few days. You can get groceries tomorrow. Maybe even a hotel room."

Rhonda shot a nervous glance at her husband, who was talking to the guys over by the tent. "He doesn't like charity."

"You can pay me back once we get home," Crystal said. "Please."

"Okay, yes, then. Thank you."

We left her, agreeing that we both needed the restroom before going back to our site. "How in the heck do you just have five hundred dollars in your pocket?" I asked as we strolled down the cement path toward the nearest bathroom.

"You'll laugh, but I always keep some cash in the inside pocket of my purse in case of an emergency. Like the zombie apocalypse, for example."

I nudged her shoulder with mine. "If that happens, money won't matter."

She chuckled. "I suppose that's true."

"Anyway, that was kind of you," I said. "You're mega rich, yet you haven't forgotten what it's like to be a regular person."

"I'm still a regular person. I just happen to have inherited my husband's money. There's nothing special about me."

"You're special to me."

"Stop it. You're going to get me crying again. Anyway, spill it. How in the world did you end up here with Trapper?"

I explained about dinner at Rose and Fenton's. "Like you, I didn't want to drive by myself, so I agreed to come with Trapper."

I squinted as we walked into the lit bathroom. Several ladies with small children were brushing their teeth at the sinks. We did our business, washed our hands, and went back out into the night.

Trapper had put more dogs on the grill and opened another round of beers. Temperatures had dropped, and I was chilled in my cotton sundress. The four of us filled our plates. I plopped into one of the chairs, grateful to sit and eat. Trapper sat beside me. I gobbled up my dog.

"A little dry without condiments," I said. "But all in all, not bad."

"I'd prefer one of your ham-and-butter baguettes." Garth wiped his hands on a paper towel.

"Let's hope there's a bakery left for me to whip you up one," I said.

Crystal had barely touched her food. "Those poor people. What if they lose their house? What will they do? I mean, it's one thing for you and me, Garth. We can rebuild. But what about the uninsured or underinsured living paycheck to paycheck?"

I thought about how much I owed the bank for the loan I'd taken out to buy new ovens and equipment last year. I'd be in the same situation if the place burned. Homeless, unemployed, and deeply in debt.

"Hey now," Garth said to Crystal. "It'll be okay. Somehow."

"You don't sound convinced." I swallowed the burning sensation at the back of my throat. "I have everything sunk into that bakery. If I lose it, I'm not sure I can recover financially. I took out a massive loan when I expanded the kitchen and remodeled."

"Why didn't you ask me for the money?" Crystal asked.

"Because you're not a bank," I said.

"Exactly my point," she said. "I help my friends if they need it. What good is money if you can't do that? It sure as hell can't keep people alive."

The three of us went still, knocked mute by the pain in Crystal's voice.

She looked upward. The gold ring she wore on a chain around her long neck caught the light. "I'm sorry. I shouldn't have said that."

"Nah," Garth said. "You shouldn't be embarrassed by grief. Hell, I still fall on my knees and pray to God to give me some peace about my little brother. He died when I was ten. I miss him every single day."

"I'm sorry." The pain of my own loss came roaring back, as it did when I heard about others' grief. "That must have been terrible for your entire family."

"Yeah. His death broke up my parents' marriage." Garth's low drawl belied the serious nature of his words. "Losing your eight-year-old son to cancer is hard to get through intact."

"Garth, that's awful," Crystal said. "Your poor parents."

"I can't even imagine how hard that must have been," Trapper said. "You came out pretty awesome despite all that."

"I have my issues," Garth said. "I'm a work in progress."

"Aren't we all?" Trapper asked.

"Some of us might be in stasis," Crystal said in a way that made us all laugh.

"You two stay put while we clean up a bit," I said.

Trapper and I gathered trash and put away the cookstove, then returned to our circle with more beers.

"I think I need a shot of whiskey," I said as soon as I settled back into my chair.

Trapper fetched the bottle. We didn't have any glasses, so he took a swig, then handed it to me. I did the same and passed it over to Crystal. She looked at the bottle for a second before lifting it to her mouth and taking a swig. She coughed and beat her chest. "Holy crap, that's strong. I'm more of a cosmo type of girl." She shoved the bottle at Garth. "Here you go, Ski King. Show me how it's done."

Garth raised his eyebrows. "Ski King?"

"She's the Sugar Queen," Crystal said, pointing at me. "Seems appropriate."

Garth tipped the bottle, then wiped his mouth. "Does that mean Trapper's the Hockey King?"

"No way." Crystal waggled her beer bottle at him. "I mean, come on, the name Trapper says it all."

I laughed. "True."

"I always told my parents they doomed me for any other life," Trapper said. "What else could I be but a hockey player?"

"You need a nickname then," Garth said to Crystal. "City Mouse?"

Crystal placed one hand over her heart, pretending to be hurt. "Is that why you keep stopping by to make sure I haven't frozen to death? You think I'm a city girl?"

Garth put up a hand, laughing. "I saw you trying to chop kindling last winter. I was honestly worried you were going to cut your foot off."

"Wait a second," Crystal said. "You can see me from your house?"

"I have a direct view of your woodshed," Garth said. "Which is why I'm concerned."

"Listen, you." Crystal poked his shoulder with her beer. "You stick to skiing and lawyering and don't worry your pretty-boy head over my ineptitude at country living."

"Nope. That's not how I roll," Garth said. "This *country* boy looks out for his pretty city-girl neighbor."

"Can't blame him for that," Trapper said.

"Don't try to make up now by calling me pretty." Crystal kicked Garth's knee lightly with her foot.

Garth grinned. "I'm not blind, City Mouse."

"Give me that bottle," Crystal said.

Garth handed it to her, and she took another swig. "God, that's terrible." She wiped her mouth with the back of her hand.

"You didn't cough this time," Garth said. "Progress."

Garth had my friend laughing and acting lighter than I'd seen her since we were kids. In fact, she was lit up like a Christmas tree. Was it the booze or the boy?

"I've never been camping before," Crystal said as she handed the bottle to Trapper. "I didn't think I ever would."

"It's the company that makes the difference," Trapper said as he winked at me.

I loved his wink, his attention, the way he looked at me as if he wanted to take me on his lap and kiss me senseless. Trapper's light had always warmed me. He still had the power to fill me up, to make me glow.

"Fleeing for your life isn't the best introduction to one of America's greatest leisure activities," Garth said. "You can't judge all camping from this experience."

"If I did, I would say it's damn fun," Crystal said. "Although I might just be drunk."

We chattered in quiet voices as a half-moon rose in the sky. The campground quieted as people crawled into tents or cars. Occasionally, a laugh punctuated the night. Even at times like this, humans could find something to laugh about. Under the purple ceiling sprinkled with silver stars, it was hard to believe that our town was in jeopardy.

"So, City Mouse, did you ever meet Bill and Melinda Gates?" Garth asked.

"Once, at a charity function. I was so nervous I spilled my cosmo on Melinda's shoes. She was completely gracious. I wanted to fall through the floor."

"I can't imagine meeting those types of people," I said. "Actually, nothing sounds worse."

"I was always nervous, but they're just like us," Crystal said.

"Just like you," I said. "Not me."

"Money doesn't make the person," Crystal said.

"True," Garth said. "But tell that to my ex-wife."

"You have an ex-wife?" Crystal asked.

"Unfortunately, yes," he said. "I married a woman right out of college. Once my ski career was over, she was out of there. She loved those endorsements and the lifestyle. When I told her it was time for me to quit and go to law school, she was no longer interested in this good ol' boy. She moved on to a pro baseball player after she left me. That hurt. I mean, those guys all have beer bellies."

"Even so, you have those medals to remind you of what you accomplished," Trapper said. "No one can ever take those away from you."

"You crushed it at the 2010 Olympics in downhill," I said. "All the girls had your picture on their walls."

"It was fun while it lasted." Garth said, grinning. "But I have a great time no matter where I am or what I'm doing."

"Amen to that," Trapper said as he reached over to clink beer bottles with Garth.

"Living here has been awesome," Garth said. "Other than maybe losing my house. I already lost the first damn one to my ex-wife. Maybe I should rent from now on."

Our beers were empty. It was ten by then. A forest ranger was making rounds, reminding everyone that quiet hours started now.

Garth reached out his hand to Crystal. "What do you say we get a little shut-eye?"

"Shut-eye?" Crystal giggled. "I do love the way you talk, Ski King."

"You want the SUV or the tent?" Garth asked.

"Which will keep me safest from a bear?" Crystal asked.

"I don't think there are any bears in this campground," Trapper said.

"If there are, I'm not worried," Crystal said. "Not with Ski King here to protect me."

They stared at each other, a little too intimately. She'd told me countless times that she had no intention of becoming romantically involved again, and yet here she was all soft and yielding and flirtatious.

For the first time, it occurred to me that Crystal and I could share the tent and Trapper and Garth could sleep in the truck with their sports-guy testosterone to keep them warm. *I should say something to save us all from temptation*, I thought. If I hadn't been so weak, I would have. The idea of Trapper doing anything but sleeping next to me was the last thing I wanted. Given that, I watched as Crystal allowed Garth to help her up from the chair. He took his lantern, and then they walked hand in hand toward their campsite.

"How much you want to bet they both sleep in the tent?" Trapper asked.

Our heads were inches apart as we looked out in front of us and not at each other. I smelled the manly, spicy cologne on his neck and wanted to trace the muscle of his neck with my mouth.

"That's kind of crazy," I said. "Crystal is adamant about not getting involved with anyone. I've never seen her even smile at a man. Her husband's death devastated her."

"Maybe Garth will change her mind," Trapper said. "According to Breck and Huck, he's a great guy who does all kinds of pro bono work for women who need help with custody battles against abusive exes and kisses babies and walks old women across the street. From what I can see, he's all that and more."

"You were always a good judge of character," I said.

He trailed his fingers up my arm. "I'm not interested in what's happening in their tent. I'm more interested in what's going to happen in ours."

"We don't have a tent, remember?"

He chuckled as he kissed my neck. "I'm interested in what's going to happen in my truck. Is that better?"

I throbbed with wanting him. First, however, I needed to brush my teeth and go the restroom one more time. "I have to brush my teeth and pee first. And I'm not walking over to the bathroom all by myself."

"I'll grab our bags."

In the bathroom, I brushed my teeth, scrubbed my face of makeup, and changed from my dress into sweats and a T-shirt. What a long, strange day it had been. There were several other women washing up, so I didn't linger at the mirror wondering what the heck I was doing.

Still, a voice whispered in my ear. *Really? After one day, you're back in Trapper's arms? This must be the fastest reconciliation in the history of romance. What about your secret?*

But this is you and Trapper. Epic love.

Until he knows what you did.

One night. One damn night. After everything, that seemed fair.

Outside, Trapper waited for me under an aspen tree. I swear it felt like the most normal thing in the world to see him there. He held out his hand, and I took it. With his other hand he held his phone out in front of us, producing enough light to see the path back to our site. A cricket chirped, and the scent of grass mingled with fir trees. The campground was quiet now with only a few moving about with flashlights or lanterns.

I trembled when we reached the truck, suddenly nervous. He set our bags in the cab as I climbed into the bed of the truck. I hadn't noticed earlier, but he'd zipped the two bags together. I slipped into the warmth of the sleeping bag and scooted to the left. With the mattresses, it wasn't too hard. He still had the flashlight from his phone on as he moved around. I closed my eyes. The truck bounced slightly as he closed the tailgate. A second later, he climbed over the side. He knelt near the top of the sleeping bag and pulled something from his backpack. "Portable charger," he said, then killed the light. Since it was totally dark, I could only hear his presence—a thud of the backpack, then the crinkly noise of the sleeping bag as he joined me.

"I can't see a thing," he whispered. "I hate the dark."

I smiled to myself. For such a big guy, his fear of the dark was strange. He'd been like that when we were young. I reached out to him, finding his bulk in the dark. "I'm right here."

He slipped in next to me. "There you are."

"Here I am," I whispered. "Waiting for you."

He reached for me, tugging me against his chest, and kissed me. His mouth tasted of mint toothpaste. "Do you want this?" he whispered into my hair.

"Yes, I want this." I wrapped my legs around him.

"God, you feel so good." He groaned when my hands

reached under his shirt to explore his muscular back. "When I think about all the years we've missed…"

"We're here now," I said. "Let's not waste any more time."

He pulled me under him. "I don't plan on it."

I was lost in the moment. Tomorrow, I promised myself, I'd tell him the truth.

I WOKE STIFF AND SORE AS THE SUN ROSE FROM THE EAST. TRAPPER and I had slept like spoons with his arm around my waist. I'd been so tired after our physical antics that I'd fallen into a deep sleep. I wriggled around to get a look at him. He opened one eye, then the other. "Hey, you're not a dream."

I smiled. "I'm not, and I need to pee."

"But you're naked." He drew me closer, sounding sleepy. "Stay a little longer."

"I'm afraid this is a desperate situation. Where are my clothes?" I felt around the sleeping bag and located my sweats. I managed to pull them on without exposing myself to the campground. Further exploration revealed the shirt. This would be harder. "I need your help. Pull this over my head."

"This definitely reminds me of old times. Stay still now. If you wiggle, I can't get it over your head." We both started to laugh as he tugged the shirt over my head.

"Ouch, that's my hair."

"Either you have a big head or this is a particularly small hole."

"I do not have a large head." I giggled as I put my arms into their slots.

"Shhh…you'll wake the whole campground." He trailed his fingers across my stomach and up to my breasts. "Maybe I should do something to quiet you down."

"Don't you start that now. I mean it. I have to pee."

He withdrew his hand. "Fine. I'll go with you." He lifted a

pair of my thong panties from near his head. "You've forgotten something. Which means I'll just carry them around in my pocket for the rest of the day."

"You're a very naughty boy." I shuddered as he sat up and pulled his sweatshirt down over his six-pack stomach. The things the man had done to me in the dark of the night would stay with me a long time. They'd have to.

His phone buzzed. With his long arm, he reached for it and yanked the cord from the charger. "Message from Huck." A small muscle in his cheek twitched. "Crap."

"What is it?" I asked. "What's happened?"

"They put out the fire. They're going to let people back in this afternoon."

"But?" I knew there was a but, given his dour expression.

"The fire tore down the southern mountain, jumped the river, and burned down pretty much everything along River Road. Including my ice rink, Jamie's inn, the high school, and Huck's new house. Garth's and Crystal's homes are gone too."

"How did they get it out?" I asked.

"They brought in some firefighters from Oregon and California and doused everything with chemicals to box the fire in. Once they did that, the fire was contained and burned itself out." He rubbed his eyes. "We have to tell Garth and Crystal."

"Are you okay?" I asked. "I'm so sorry, baby."

He tilted his head and looked right at me. "It's all right. The whole place was going to be gutted anyway. We'll have to start from scratch, but it's not the end of the world. Losing a house or poor Jamie with her newly opened inn—those hurt. Not to mention the school. I'm not going to spend a minute feeling sorry for myself. Our friends are going to need us."

"Where will the kids go to school?" I asked out loud, as if he would know.

"We'll figure out a temporary solution," he said. "My dad will think of something."

"How did Huck sound?" I asked.

"Grim but stoic. He's staying at his parents'."

A flood of memories rushed over me. We'd had many fun times in Huck's parents' kitchen. Garret Clifton, a direct descendant of Josephine Barnes, was the closest we had to celebrity in Emerson Pass before Trapper made the professional hockey team in LA. He wrote a famous mystery series that had been turned into a television series. Huck's mother, a force in her own right, ran one of the local banks. They were opposites: a word person and a math person. Huck took after his father, inheriting the love of writing. Sadly, it had taken him in an opposite direction and to a war across the world. Huck had come home broken. This was the last thing he needed.

"What will everyone do?" I asked.

"Rely on friends," he said. "This is the time to band together. We've always been able to accomplish anything together."

I fidgeted with the sleeve of my sweatshirt, suddenly unsure what to do or what the day might bring. Last night was a cocoon, a sanctuary from the real world. One that consisted of Trapper and me. In the light of day, reality rushed right back in. What we had could never continue.

"Baby, what is it?" He scooted closer and drew me onto his lap.

I buried my nose in his neck. "Nothing. I love you, that's all."

He lifted my face to look me in the eyes. "I've been waiting ten years to hear those words come out of your mouth. I love you too, Brandi Vargas. With everything I am. I'm going to spend the rest of my life showing you how much."

Guilt crushed me. Dread engulfed me. I held on to him as tightly as I could and prayed for a miracle.

8

T rapper

FLOODED WITH SO MANY CONTRARY EMOTIONS, I HARDLY KNEW what to do with myself after I heard the news from Huck. I floated on air after the night I'd spent with Brandi. She loved me. I wanted to declare it from the mountaintops. My girl had come back to me.

Conversely, half my friends had suffered devastating losses. My job now was to help them through.

I made it a life goal to be positive, to uplift however I could, but this was a tough one. Brandi had found some coffee packets, tin cups, and a pan in my camping gear. By the time I returned from the bathroom, she'd boiled water and made us both cups of coffee.

Garth and Crystal were still inside their tent. I imagined waking up hungover to this kind of news. "We better keep that water hot," I said.

Brandi sat huddled in one of the chairs, blowing on her

coffee. I sat next to her. "This isn't fun," she whispered. "They're going to take it so hard."

I nodded, then kissed her on the forehead. She looked so cute with her hair all tangled and her face clean of makeup.

We'd almost finished our coffee when we saw Garth sauntering across the grass toward us, looking rumpled and exhausted.

Brandi had already risen to make him a cup of coffee.

"Morning," Garth said.

"Good morning." Brandi handed him the cup of coffee.

"Thank you, ma'am. You're an angel."

"Sleep all right?" I asked.

He sat across from me and gave me one of those looks men give each other when one of us has scored with a girl but we're sure in the light of day that we've made a terrible mistake. Out loud, he said, "No complaints. Other than this headache, which can only be blamed on overserving myself."

"How's Crystal?" Brandi asked.

"She was still sleeping." Garth's ears pinkened under Brandi's gaze. "In the tent. You know, with me. So I'm not sure."

"Listen, man, take a seat," I said. "We have some news. Huck texted."

"Is it gone?" Garth winced and sucked in a deep breath.

"I'm afraid so," I said. "Crystal's too."

Garth scrubbed his chin with one hand as if there were dirt there. A deep shudder went through him. When he looked up at us, he'd composed himself. "Well, hell. That sucks, but no one got hurt. I need to remember that before I have a pity party. Wait, that's right, isn't it? Firefighters are all okay?"

I nodded and told him about the men and women who had come from California and Oregon to help. "They saved most of our town."

"Those people are my heroes," Garth said. "Even before this."

From across the way, I spotted Crystal falling out of the tent, then righting herself. "Looks like Crystal's headed this way." I said this mostly as a warning for Garth.

He jumped to his feet and sprinted over to her.

"He took it well," Brandi said.

"Like a man. God bless him," I said.

Garth put his arm around Crystal's shoulders as they walked over to us. Brandi made another cup of coffee.

"My head's throbbing." Crystal sank into one of the chairs. "I'm not used to drinking."

"I've got painkillers," Brandi said. "Here's some coffee. We'll go somewhere for breakfast in a minute."

Crystal rested her elbow on the arm of her chair, then plopped one cheek into her hand before looking at me. "Do we have bad news?" Her voice trembled. "I can see in your faces that we do."

Garth knelt near her chair. "Both our houses are gone."

She made a squeak from the back of her throat, like a child trying to be brave. "Oh, oh, okay." Her chest rose and fell as she locked eyes with Garth. "We thought so, of course, so it shouldn't be a shock."

"No, but it still hurts," Garth said.

"We lost the high school and rink too," I said. "And Jamie's inn."

Crystal's eyes glistened with unshed tears as she turned toward me. "We did?"

"But the rest of the town's okay," Garth said. "Your shop's okay. Brandi's, too. The whole downtown area was untouched."

"Thank God," Crystal said.

"I'm so sorry."

"It's all right. I'll be all right." Crystal's complexion had gone almost gray. Her hand shook as she raised the cup to her mouth. "I had all this art. Pieces Patrick had collected. I should've given it to a gallery. I had no idea it wouldn't be safe with me. They were a part of him. A little piece of him to keep for myself, and now I've let them burn."

Garth, still kneeling next to her chair, patted her hand. "I'm sorry, sweetheart."

Sweetheart? Garth's tone sounded so tender and loving. Was it more than just drunken sex between them?

"Where will I go?" Crystal asked, as if speaking to herself and sounding so lost and sad that it pierced my heart.

"You can stay with me," Brandi said.

"No, you'll stay with me," I said. "Both of you. I have plenty of rooms. We can go home today and come up with a plan."

"That's kind of you, brother." Garth straightened, brushing the knees of his jeans, wet from the dew on the grass. "I appreciate it."

"Yes, that's better, Brandi," Crystal said. "Your place is small. We'd be on top of each other."

Brandi sat in the chair next to her and patted Crystal's forearm. "Whatever you want is what I want."

"We can go home today?" Crystal asked, sounding slightly less desolate.

"Yes, they said it's safe now," I said.

Crystal looked up at Garth. "I don't even have a car. I shouldn't have been so cowardly and just followed you out."

"That's what insurance is for," I said. "You can get something brand-new." I felt certain she could buy whatever she wanted without a second thought. With or without insurance.

"I'm sorry for acting like such a baby," Crystal said. "I know I should just be grateful that Garth and I are all right."

"Don't you dare apologize," Brandi said. "You have every right to wallow for as long as you like."

"It's impossible to think of everything being gone." A lone tear trickled down Crystal's cheek. "All my wedding photos."

"They'll be on the cloud." Brandi took Crystal's hand. "We'll get new prints of photos made."

Crystal sniffed and wiped her face with the napkin. "I don't even know where to start. Should I buy a car down here before I go home?"

"I think so," I said. "Get whatever you need before you come back to Emerson Pass."

"I'll have to buy a phone." Crystal's face crumpled. "This is all overwhelming. I'm sorry I sound like such a baby."

Brandi continued to pat her arm. "Sweetie, it is overwhelming. Anyone would feel this way."

"I'll take you wherever you need to go." Garth handed her a napkin. "I need everything too. We can buy some new clothes before we head home."

"I forgot about clothes." Crystal spoke as if she'd forgotten we were there.

I exchanged glances with Brandi, who looked as if she might burst into tears right along with her friend.

"We should eat." Brandi smoothed a wayward strand of hair from Crystal's damp face. "A big breakfast with pancakes and bacon."

"I could eat," Garth said.

"Showers first?" Brandi asked.

"Definitely showers," Crystal said. "And I'll take that painkiller now, too."

THIRTY MINUTES LATER, GARTH AND I HEADED BACK FROM THE showers. The campground had come to life. Like busy bees, people were packing up their cars. At least a fourth of the sites were already empty.

"How you doing?" I asked Garth. He'd been quiet since the ladies had left for the showers.

"I'm fine," he said. "Can't lie, though. I'm bummed about my house."

"I mean it about staying with me for as long as you like. There's plenty of space."

He clapped me on the shoulder. "You don't even know me. It's big of you."

"I'm glad to do it. In Emerson Pass, we stick together."

"I think I may have really messed up with Crystal." Garth massaged the back of his neck with his free hand.

"How so?"

Garth ran a hand through his wet hair. "We were both a little drunk. She hadn't been with anyone since her husband."

"Did she tell you that?" I asked.

"She told me afterward—while crying."

I cringed. "Oh, dude, that's rough."

"I feel like a jerk."

"Were you the pursuer?"

"No, that's just it. She asked me to join her in the tent. Not that I didn't want her. She's about the prettiest thing I've ever seen, and damn if she isn't sweet and smart, too."

"Then you have nothing to apologize for," I said. "You two can write it off as a by-product of a bad situation."

"I'm sure you're right. Still, she's fragile. I feel like a heel. My dad raised me to be respectful to women, not take advantage of them during moments of weakness."

"It takes two," I said.

"I guess so. Bottom line, she's not ready for a relationship, and neither am I. Not to mention she's a freaking billionaire. We have nothing in common."

"Have a talk with her today," I said. "Tell her you're sorry you let things get out of hand. Go back to being buddies."

"Good plan," Garth said.

He didn't sound convinced.

"What about you and Brandi?" Garth asked with a teasing lilt to his voice. "Were you warm enough in the bed of your truck?"

I grinned. "Yes. We were warm enough."

BRANDI AND I ARRIVED BACK HOME THAT AFTERNOON. TRAFFIC HAD been slow, but at least this time it was in the right direction. We gasped at the sight of the southern mountain. The path of the fire had spared some sections of the mountain and scarred others. A patchwork of black and green appeared like a half-shaven face.

Brandi reached for my hand. "It's awful."

I turned in the direction of River Road. As much I dreaded it, I had to see what was left of my rink. However, police cars blocked off the road right before a sharp turn, making it impossible to see the high school or rink. I parked on the side of the road.

"I'm going to ask if we can get closer," I said.

"I'll go with you," Brandi said.

We both hopped out of the truck and walked over to a deputy. I recognized him from high school. Mason Harper. We shook hands. "Mason, it's been a while," I said.

"Hey, Trapper. Did I hear right, you bought the rink?" Mason asked.

"Sure did. I don't suppose you'd let us get a little closer? I'd like to see the damage."

"I can let you in," Mason said. "As the owner, you have a right to see."

"Five minutes," I said. "And then we'll be out of your hair."

We hustled back to my truck. Mason moved aside one of the squad cars so we could pass through. A mile later we arrived at the edge of the fire's destruction. The rink and high school were within a hundred yards of each other. Now they were piles of charred wood and melted steel.

If the mountain was a man's half-shaved face, the high school was a neglected mouth. The scorched walls looked like decayed and broken black teeth. Steel frames remained, like old fillings. Beyond, the grass that had once covered the football field was no more. Our metal bleachers had melted into disfigured shapes.

The ice rink, built in the forties without steel enforcements, was nothing but ashes. "I guess my renovation has turned into a rebuild," I said.

"Maybe it's a blessing in disguise?" Brandi asked.

"I'm going to choose to think of it that way."

At seventeen, I'd sat right here in my old beater of a truck with this same gorgeous girl and told her about my dreams. My truck was new now. My girl older. And all those dreams had already come true.

"Everything I became, all the successes and failures started right there." I pointed to the fallen rink. "We have to build it again. Better this time. For the kids."

She smiled over at me. "It's been a dozen years since we sat in this exact place and you told me your dreams. Now it's time for you to make new dreams come true. If anyone can do this, it's you."

I smiled back at her. "Only in this dream, you're going to be by my side."

Her gaze shifted to her lap. "I hope so."

I tugged on a section of her hair. "I want you more than anything else. This time, I choose you and only you."

She lifted her head and looked into my eyes. "I choose you, too."

9

B randi

TRAPPER AND I LAY ENTANGLED IN BLANKETS AT MY PLACE, breathless and damp. "Thanks for letting me come up." He kissed my neck. "I'm sorry I attacked you instead of giving you a proper tour."

"I'm not." I snuggled closer to him. "We can have a nap before we head out to your place." The late-afternoon light sneaked between the curtains in my bedroom. "Anyway, you saw it all. There's only two rooms."

My one-bedroom apartment above my bakery was seven hundred square feet. Inspired by a painting of daisies, I'd decorated it in whites and yellows. The four-poster bed was a find from a used furniture store in Louisville. Dad had refinished it using a honey-colored stain. The elevated height meant I had to use a child's footstool to get into bed, but I loved it anyway. This bed was my sanctuary.

Sometimes at night I'd listen to the sounds of the walls and ceiling creaking, and I'd think of all the lives that had passed through this building.

"Do you remember how much fun we used to have down at the river?" Trapper asked as he traced his fingers down my arm. "A little country music on the stereo and contraband beer?"

I smiled. "Remember how I had to sneak in and out of my bedroom window?"

We'd had countless days by the river back then with Breck and Huck and whoever else wanted to join us. Whenever we could, during warm summer days, we'd all meet at the river. We'd draped our bodies over the hot rocks that jutted out of the water until we were hot enough to jump in for a swim, then repeat the whole cycle. At night, when we could get away with it, the gang had gathered around a campfire in the sandy area. "What did we find to talk about all night back then?"

"Probably mostly nonsense," Trapper said.

"Breck always liked some girl who didn't like him."

Trapper groaned. "He kept falling for mean girls who were not interested in a guy with the softest heart in the world."

"He was way too nice."

"Why don't girls like nice guys?" Trapper asked.

"We do. Just not in high school," I said. "Except for you and me. You were always nice, and I loved you more than anything."

"When we were apart, I used to search my brain for the memory of how we started dating. All I could remember is always being together."

"Mr. Finley asked if you'd tutor me in geometry during the beginning of sophomore year. He said anyone who could toss a puck around the ice in the exact direction he wanted must be good at geometry. You started coming over on Tuesdays and Thursdays. We'd sit at the kitchen table studying and playing footsie."

"I remember now," he said. "I used to stare at you as you worked through a problem and feel like I was going to die if I never had the chance to kiss you."

"My mother was having none of that," I said. "She had eagle eyes, too."

He shuddered. "Yes, she did. From what I could see yesterday, she still does."

"I don't care what she thinks." I didn't. She'd done enough to control my life.

He caught hold of my waist and hauled me on top of him. My hair spilled over and onto his chest as I looked into his brown eyes. "Are you really here or have I slipped into insanity?"

"I'm here."

"You're beautiful. God help me, I can't keep my hands off you." He rolled us over so that he was on top of me. Instinctually, my legs wrapped around his waist.

"Trapper, we need to talk about something."

His phone buzzed from the bedside table. He groaned. "Damn, it's the insurance people. Can it wait just a moment?"

"Yes, yes. You have to take that."

I sighed as he rolled off me to answer his phone. The old demons snatched and clawed at me, whispering in their insidious voices. *You're not enough. You're a liar. Tell him.*

AFTER TRAPPER LEFT, I PUT IN A LOAD OF LAUNDRY AND RAN THE vacuum, even though I was tired. A knock on the door surprised me. I didn't often have guests.

My dad stood on the cement steps with his hands in his pockets. Sunlight highlighted the strands of silver in his hair.

"Dad, is everything all right?" He rarely visited.

"Yes, I wanted to come by and see you."

"Come on up. You want tea or coffee?"

"No, thank you. I just had a few things to talk with you about." He followed me up the stairs. When we reached my living room, he went to the window and stood there with his hands still in his pockets and his shoulders hunched.

"Something's wrong. What is it?" I asked.

"Your mother sent me. She wanted me to talk to you about Trapper."

I sank onto the couch. "Okay."

"How serious is this getting?"

"He wants it to be serious," I said.

"And you?"

"I want more than anything to be with him. But I know that once he finds out I've lied to him about something so important, it'll be over."

"We assumed you hadn't told him."

"I would've let you know if I had." I fiddled with the necklace I wore around my neck. "It's our secret, after all." This came out bitter, as dry as a winter leaf.

"We did the right thing back then."

"Did we? Or did we do the thing that brought Mom less shame?"

"You were a child. A scared kid. Your mother's decision was the right one."

"I think about the kind of people Fenton and Rose are, and I can't understand why we didn't just tell them the truth."

"What difference would it have made? She died."

I flinched as though he'd smacked me.

"Honey, I'm sorry. Your mother feels that you and Trapper getting back together resurrected a lot of problems. You've been fragile all these years. Do you think bringing up all this old trauma is the best thing for you?"

I scooted into the corner of the couch and brought my knees to my chest. "I love him, Dad."

"And when he finds out what you kept from him, everything's going to blow up. I'm worried you're not strong enough to deal with the repercussions. I can't watch you have your heart broken again." He paced by the window. "Why couldn't you just stay away from him?"

"Because this is Trapper and me, Dad. We're like two magnets. Nothing's changed between us."

"Other than you kept a secret from him ten years ago."

"Don't you think I know that?" My voice raised an octave. "I'm on borrowed time. I missed him so much, and I had the chance for a few more days. I can't seem to let go. I know I need to tell him, but the words won't come."

Dad sat next to me on the couch and spoke to me as if I were still ten years old. "You have to find a way, honey. It's not fair to either of you to carry on as if you're still carefree teenagers. Isn't that what got you into this mess in the first place?"

I buried my face in my knees as the tears came.

"I'm sorry," he said. "You're my little girl, and I'm worried about you."

"Please leave." I didn't look up, listening to his footsteps cross the creaky floor and go down the stairs.

AN HOUR AFTER MY FATHER'S VISIT, I PULLED OUT LIZZIE'S LETTERS. There was one in particular I wanted to read, dated in 1915.

Dearest Mummy,

I'm sorry it's been such a while since you've heard from me. I was unable to find the strength to write until now. The baby due last month did not survive. If it hadn't been for Dr. Neal's skills, I would not have survived either. There was a problem during birth and by the time they got him out, he wasn't breathing. I'd lost a great deal of blood, but the doctor was able to patch up the problem and saved my life.

Since then, I've been focused on grieving and taking care of Florence. Quinn and Merry have been a great comfort to me, although I can see the guilt in their eyes. Their second babies were born without complications. Both Jack and Delphia are thriving. I couldn't possibly resent them simply because they were fortunate enough to have a second child. Instead, I'm glad they don't have to experience the anguish of losing a child.

Jasper has been stoic through it all and so very kind to me. He won't say much to me about his grief. I think he believes it will cause me more pain if he confesses to his. Men always think they have to protect us, even when it might help me to grieve with him. However, I witnessed him and Lord Barnes in the garden the other day. They sat on a bench that overlooks the field of wildflowers. Jasper slumped over his knees. From the window I could see how his shoulders heaved from sobbing. Lord Barnes patted his back and let him cry. I suppose it's all we can do when a friend is grieving. Be there for them and do not offer words but merely comfort.

We named him Joseph Edward Strom, after Father. We buried our little boy on the piece of land that Lord Barnes deemed for our town cemetery. After the burial, I sent everyone away, even Jasper and Quinn, so that I might have a moment to weep for my boy. I fell to my knees and cried unashamed, knowing God was there to catch my tears. After a few minutes, the song of a bird filled the air. I rose up, searching for the source of the sweet sound. A small sparrow perched on the branch of a pine. When I lifted my damp face to him, he sang louder. I knew, Mummy, it was a message from my little boy. He sings with the angels now. I felt great peace. Someday I'll meet him in heaven. For now, I have my Florence and Jasper and the Barneses and Depauls, more like family than employers or neighbors.

A month has passed since then, and I've finally been able to write these words to you. In my darkest moments, I thought of what it felt like to be in your warm embrace when I was a child. I've lain awake nights remembering all the ways you cared for and loved me. Even though we're far away, I remember it all, Mummy. The memories of my childhood give me such joy and peace. I hope someday they will do the same for Florence. Until I was a mother myself, I didn't know exactly how much you loved me or how painful it must have been when I left for America.

Jasper and I have talked. We have more than enough for your fare if *you'd come. You can live with us in your retirement and see Florence grow up. Please, think about it. Much love, Lizzie*

I set the letter aside and stared out the window, thinking about Lizzie and her little boy. In all the ways the world was different, some things never changed, including grief.

My mother's voice called up the stairs, bringing me back to the present. "Brandi, are you there?"

"Yes." I closed my eyes for a moment to gather strength. "Come on up." A visit from both my parents in one day was never a good sign of things to come.

I gathered up the scattering of letters on the coffee table and put them back in the box. It was almost five. I was supposed to leave for Trapper's in a few minutes.

Mom appeared at the top of the stairs. "Why are you dressed up?"

I glanced down at my dress, a white halter with a flared skirt that I thought showed off my shoulders, and strappy sandals. I'd put my hair up in a messy bun at the nape of my neck. Wide hoop earrings completed the outfit. It had been longer than I could remember since I'd paid this much attention to my appearance. It felt good. I pushed aside the thought that it might be the last time.

"I'm going out to Trapper's for dinner."

"Isn't he too busy saving the town to make you dinner?"

"Mom, don't be like that. The Barnes family is completely generous. Why can't you cut them some slack?"

"Because it bugs me how everyone bows down to them in this town."

"Why're you here?" I clenched my stomach muscles, ready for a fight.

"I talked to your father. He obviously made no progress with you."

"His point was well taken," I said. "I know I have to tell him the truth. I'm going to."

"How he reacts will tell you everything you need to know," Mom said.

I didn't respond, taking the hatbox to the closet instead.

"Are you really picking up with him where you left off?" she asked.

I turned to look at her. "Why do you care?"

"He's not right for you. And he ruined your life."

"He didn't make me pregnant all by himself," I said.

"Oh, I remember how it is to be a teenager. If I'd held back instead of giving in to my immediate desires, things would've been a lot different."

"Has it ever occurred to you that when you say things like that, it's hurtful to me? You're basically saying that if you could, you'd erase me."

The muscles in her face twitched, as if she'd bitten into foul meat. "Brandi, not everything's about you."

"I know that. But this is. I wrecked your life—all your plans. You've said it over and over."

"It's not so simple. I can love you and still have regrets about my life. They're not the same."

"How come you didn't have an abortion?" I asked.

She froze. The blood rushed between my ears, keeping time with the beating of my heart. There were one, two, three, four, five thumps before she spoke. "My mother and father wouldn't allow it. I couldn't go against them."

"Would you have done it if they'd not stood in your way?"

"You can't think of it that way. It's not what happened. I had you. There's no good in thinking about different scenarios and what I would or wouldn't have done. Your father stepped up and married me even though we were both children. He brought me here to this place he loved so much. That was his only request. Could we go home where he had family? I guess I had the last laugh on my mother. Once we moved out here, we barely saw them."

"The last laugh. Because they made you have me. See, there it is again."

"Brandi, honestly. Don't twist my words. Life went a certain direction for me. Do I wish I could've gone to college and had a career? Yes. But that's not mutually exclusive from how I feel about you." She gestured toward the closet where I'd just put away Lizzie's hatbox. "I've always felt like an outsider here. Like I was some kind of desperate mail-order bride sent out west."

"Did you know Lizzie lost a baby too?"

"Which one's Lizzie?"

"Never mind." I collapsed into the easy chair and hugged a throw pillow to my chest.

Still holding her purse, Mom walked over to the bank of windows that looked out to Puck's and the southern slope. "If you get back with Trapper, he'll leave you one day. You'll see. He's interested in rekindling something with you out of nostalgia. Once it comes down to day-to-day living, he's going to see how unsuited you two are."

"What's unsuited about us?"

"He's wealthy and famous and is friends with rich actors and athletes. Someday he'll inherit half this town. Do you really think he's going to stay interested in you?"

I crossed my arms over my stomach and rubbed my elbows with my fingers. I would not cry in front of her and allow her to see how weak I still was, how her opinion of me still hurt. I clenched my teeth and turned myself to stone. She was right. Why would someone like Trapper Barnes pick me? I didn't fit with him. In high school it had been all right because I was pretty and a cheerleader. Now, in this grown-up world, it was obvious that we no longer belonged together. I was uneducated and unsophisticated, and always had a dusting of flour on my hands. My mother was right. We didn't fit.

And there was the baby. The truth that would send him away forever.

"I'm not saying this to hurt you," Mom said. "I want to protect you."

"Why didn't you get me tested for learning disabilities when I was a kid?"

She went rigid, then clutched at her throat with her fingertips. "Why would I?"

"I'm dyslexic."

"No, you're not."

"I am. I had myself tested. That's why reading was so hard for me. It's not that I'm dumb."

She pulled her purse against her chest and looked at me with slightly bulging eyes. "When did you get tested?"

"A few years after high school. Crystal suggested it. Do you know what a relief it was to learn that I have a legitimate problem? If you hadn't been so prideful, so sure it was just laziness on my part, my whole experience at school could've been different."

"Different how?"

"Like I wouldn't have thought I was stupid. I wouldn't have had to ask Trapper for help all the time. Doing so made me feel like I wasn't good enough for him. I already knew I wasn't good enough for you."

"Are you saying that if you'd had better self-esteem you wouldn't have gotten pregnant?"

I groaned in frustration. "No. You're missing the point. If I'd had help when I needed it, I would've done better in school, which could have changed the trajectory of my life."

"I thought you loved running the bakery." She elongated the word *love*. "Haven't you and your father shoved that in my face enough times?"

"I do love my bakery. Maybe I would've chosen to do exactly what I'm doing. But knowing that I wasn't dumb would've helped me feel a little better about myself."

"I'm the bad guy? Isn't that convenient?"

"You're not bad. It's just that you wanted me to be like you, and I'm not. It was always about achievement, but I couldn't keep up, Mom. You could never see me as I was. Having me tested would've proved to you that I was flawed. You can never tolerate any weakness."

"That's not true. I wanted more for you than I had, and you turned around and did the exact same thing I did."

"Only we didn't give Trapper a chance to step up like Dad did."

"What if we had? It wouldn't have made any difference in the end. The baby died."

A dart of pain shot through me. "At least I wouldn't have lied to him. Now there's no hope for us to ever be together. He'll never forgive me."

"You loved him when you were seventeen years old," Mom said. "It was a lifetime ago. Don't you see that? This is some fantasy you two have cooked up in your heads. In the end, you'll see. Neither of you is the same person you were back then."

"Did you not love Dad after ten years? Is that what this is about?"

"I was in lust with him when we were young. But were we suited? Not really. He's just a boy from a small town with no ambition. I wanted more. Is that so wrong?"

"What're you saying?" I whispered.

"I'm saying that you'll see, later, that this thing between you and Trapper is just a passing fancy, an attempt to hold on to your youth. He's not the boy you remember."

"I think he is, Mom. It feels the same between us. I wasn't wrong about him then, and I'm not now. He's the great love of my life. Not that it matters. Once he knows what we kept from him, he won't want anything to do with me."

"I know you blame me for keeping it from Trapper and think I ruined things for you."

"I blame myself. I should've stood up to you. He deserved to know. He deserved a chance to step up."

"So that you could both be miserable in this godforsaken town?" she asked.

"Like you?"

She hurled her purse across the room and shouted, "Yes, like me."

The purse hit the wall and fell to the floor. A lipstick rolled across the hardwood and stopped just before the stairs.

"You could go, Mom," I said softly. "Go find that life you think you're missing. If you're really so unhappy with Dad."

She smoothed her blouse with her hands and spoke in a clipped, fatalistic tone. "I'm trapped here. You know it as well as I."

"You're only forty-five," I said. "There's a lot of your life left. At least one of us in this family should be happy."

She sighed and crossed over to her purse. "I should go now. I've errands to run. You know your father. He likes his family's recipe of chicken stew on Tuesdays. Always the same, day after day." She knelt to gather her purse, then reached for the wayward lipstick at the head of the stairs. Before she headed down, she turned back to me. "No matter what you think, your sadness did not kill that baby. You have nothing to feel guilty about."

She didn't stay to hear my answer, but I said it to the empty room anyway. "I'm not sure that's true, but we'll never know."

10

T rapper

IN MY HOME OFFICE, I STRETCHED MY ARMS OVERHEAD AND YAWNED, hungry and ready for a beer. I'd had to leave Brandi at her apartment to return home to get my papers together for the insurance company. I spent the rest of the day on the phone.

A call came in from Garth. "Hey, how's it going?" I asked.

"Decent. We got Crystal a new car and bought some clothes. The authorities wouldn't let us go up to see our houses. I'm minutes away from your house. I imagine Crystal's not far behind."

"Great. I'll cook us some steaks."

"Supper would be awesome," he said. "I'm starving."

"Supper? Or do you mean dinner?" I asked.

"Whatever you call it, we'll be there," he said.

For the next few minutes, I hustled around the kitchen. My main floor was designed in an open concept with no delineation between kitchen, dining room, and sitting area. The office and master bedroom were also on the first floor, with four bedrooms upstairs.

Mom had come by earlier to make up the spare beds upstairs with fresh linens and had dropped off groceries. She'd left a bouquet of fresh lilies on my rustic dining room table that filled the room with their sweet fragrance.

I took steaks out of the fridge to bring them up to room temperature. I clicked my flat-screen television onto a national news channel, interested to see if Emerson Pass's fire had received any attention. The story of the day was about the upcoming election. I hit Mute.

I opened the doors to the patio. Now that the smoke had dissipated, the Rocky Mountain air sweetened the rooms.

Garth arrived first, looking a little haggard and in need of a shave. "Hey, man," I said as we shook hands. "Come on in." He carried a department store bag as well as a few others. "Sorry about the roads being closed. It must be killing you not to see what's left."

"The authorities posted pictures on the website. I found my house. What was left of it, anyway. Which wasn't much."

"Crystal's too?" I asked.

"Yeah. They're both gone." He shook his head. "Same with all the luxury homes up there. Crystal says most of them are not permanent residences, so I guess that's good news. There aren't any displaced families."

"That's a blessing," I said. "Still, I know it must hurt to have to see your home gone."

"It's surreal. I don't think it's really sunk in yet."

"Let's get you settled in," I said.

I led him upstairs to one of the guest rooms. "Your private bathroom is through that door," I said.

"I'd rather have you give Crystal the better room," he said. "She'll want her own bathroom."

"Got you covered," I said. "Her room is across the hall and has its own bathroom."

"Great. Okay. I just don't want her to be uncomfortable, you know, about me being here." He set his packages on the easy chair in the corner.

"You guys talk about it today?" I asked.

"Yeah. The elephant in the room had to be addressed. She was cool. Actually, took all the blame onto herself. We agreed to be friends."

"You able to transition back?" I asked.

"Yeah, man. I'm not interested in a girl in love with a ghost."

"Can't blame you for that," I said. "Take your time to unpack. Have a shower if you want. I'll be downstairs with a beer."

"Thanks, man. Seriously, I can't thank you enough for this."

I brushed him off and went back downstairs just as the doorbell rang. It was Crystal, with twice as many shopping bags as Garth.

I took a quick assessment—dark circles under her eyes, hair loose from her bun. "Come in," I said. "Welcome to your temporary home."

She stepped through the door. "Thanks for having me."

I took her bags. "How would you feel about a rest before dinner?"

"That sounds pretty good," she said.

She complimented my house as we climbed the stairs to the second floor, then commented on the framed photographs on the wall of me in various stages of my hockey career.

"Thanks. My mom did all this. Not sure why she thought I'd want a bunch of photos of myself."

"She's proud of you," Crystal said.

I ushered her into the bedroom. It was decorated in soft greens, and the view faced the back of the house into a thicket of trees. "This is a beautiful piece of property," she said. "I always thought so when we were kids, but I didn't realize all this land was your family's."

"It's weird to think how long our families have been here, isn't it?" I placed her packages on the bed.

"I loved staying with my grandmother and grandfather here," Crystal said. "Those were the happiest times of my childhood. I wish my mother hadn't sold the horse farm when my grandparents died."

"My dad wasn't too happy about that, either. That cottage and the five acres of land were a gift to Harley and Merry from Lord Barnes for their dedicated service."

"I'd heard that from my grandparents, but I wasn't sure it was true."

"I know it's true," I said. "My dad has all that documented, plus letters and a bunch of other papers if you ever want to talk to him about it. He loves a new victim."

"I tried to buy it from the new owners when I moved back here but they weren't interested. It makes me sick to think it's out of the family."

"You never know," I said. "Things change."

I left her to get settled in and take a nap, letting her know that dinner would be around seven.

Despite the circumstances, my heart was light as I charged down the stairs to the first floor. On the counter, my phone vibrated with a message. I glanced at it, hoping it was Brandi. Instead, the message was from my new money manager, Keith Shepard. *Call me. Urgent. I've found a problem in your books.*

I'd hired Keith last month to do long-term financial planning and to help me decide if it was prudent to buy the ice rink. His determination was that the rink was unlikely to bring a profit but if I could stomach breaking even, then I had his blessing. I'd explained it was my passion project. He'd said in his usual dry manner, "Most guys as rich as you buy sports cars, not ice rinks."

"I'm not most guys," I'd said.

I called him, worried. I didn't exactly keep a close watch on finances. I spent little and had more money than I would need for the rest of my life if I was frugal.

"Hey, Keith. What's up?"

"Listen, this is weird, but I've found a discrepancy in your accounts. You might want to sit down for this."

"Go ahead."

"Your former assistant had been embezzling money from your accounts for years. She stole a little at a time so you wouldn't notice. It's upward of two million dollars."

My mind numbed. A high-pitched buzz filled the space between my ears. Tara Talley was like family to me. I'd trusted her with my entire life, including managing my accounts. When I retired, I'd given her a huge severance package and thrown her a party.

I leaned against the counter, taking deep breaths. I'd trusted her.

"I'd recommend filing charges," Keith said. "I have enough evidence here to make an easy case for them."

"I can't believe this."

"From what I know about employees who do this kind of thing, they feel entitled to the money. You have so much, she has so little, that kind of thing."

"I paid her a great salary."

"I know, man. This isn't logical, but stuff happens."

"I have other news," I said. "The rink I bought burned to the ground."

"What the hell's going on out there?"

I explained about the fire.

"Don't sweat the rink. You knew going in it wasn't a money-maker. I'll get a little more aggressive with some of your invest-ments but seriously, with the way you live, you'll be fine. And we'll get the money back."

"I trusted her with everything. All I asked is that she never lie to me."

"I know."

"Thanks for finding it."

"Not to brag, but it wasn't easy. She's smart, like one of those hacker geniuses."

"Yeah, she went to MIT." In hindsight, that might have been a poor hiring decision on my part.

I hung up, reeling. Tara Talley stealing from me. This was not something I would have seen coming in a million years. It wasn't the money, really. I'd thought of her as a dear friend. I'd hired her right out of college. Quiet and nerdy but with a quick wit and uncanny ability to multitask. After only a few months, she'd taken over my schedule, managed my public appearances, and worked closely with my publicist to arrange endorsement opportunities. Truthfully, her savvy skills had increased my wealth. Maybe that's what made her think she was entitled to some of it. Was she?

I shook my head, trying to clear my thoughts. The guilt that so often plagued me crept into my consciousness. Why had I been given so much? Should I have paid her better and this wouldn't have happened?

I texted Huck and Breck with the facts, then called my dad's cell phone.

Mama answered. "Hi, honey. Everything all right?"

"Not really." I told her what I'd just learned.

"I can't believe it," Mama said. "She was your right hand for so long."

"I know. She had my total trust."

"You and your dad always believe the best in people, and it bites you sometimes."

I sighed. "I guess so. But I swear, I didn't see this coming." I ran my hand through my hair. "Keith thinks I should press charges."

"Why wouldn't you?"

Because she's a human being who clearly needed the money more than I did? Two million when I was worth fifty? Was there really a reason to pursue it? She'd grown up poor and had worked her way into a scholarship at MIT.

"What if she needed the money for a sick relative or something?" I asked.

"For heaven's sake, Trapper. That's your money, not hers. You were a good employer."

"Can I talk to Dad?"

"Hang on."

A few minutes later my dad got on the phone, which told me that Mama had filled him in already.

"Mama told you?"

"Yeah, son. This is a hard blow, especially now."

"I never would've seen this coming."

"Me either, to be honest. She always seemed like a nice girl. A little strange, but a lot of supersmart people are."

"Right."

"You'll have to press charges, even if you don't want to," Dad said. "What she did was a crime."

"I know. I need a second, that's all."

"I get it," Dad said. "In other news, what's going on with Brandi?"

Brandi. My heart surged with joy. She was back in my arms. "We're good, Dad. Really good."

"Has she filled you in on the missing piece yet?"

I hesitated. Should I tell him the truth? I didn't want anything to taint his feelings for her. "She said there's something she wants to talk about when she's ready. I'm not pushing, Dad. I can't lose her again."

"That's probably wise. Pushing could backfire."

I hung up feeling better. Huck and Breck had texted while I was on the phone.

Breck: *I'm on my way over.*

Huck: *I'm going to look into her further.*

By the time I hung up, Brandi was at my door. She smiled up at me, holding out a loaf of bread that would normally have made my mouth water. "I brought you a loaf of fresh sourdough."

I slumped in the doorway. "Thanks, baby."

Her smile faded. "What's happened?"

"Nothing to worry about. Come on in and I'll tell you all about it."

I SAT ACROSS FROM HER AT MY DINING ROOM TABLE AND TOLD HER what I knew. She sat motionless, watching me, as my story unfolded. "I swear to you, I would never have seen this coming."

"You trusted her. There was no reason not to. You always assume everyone's as good as you. They're not, obviously, but it's not something you should feel bad about."

"I keep thinking I should've seen something that would've clued me in, but she was a model employee and a good person. Or so I thought."

She moved my pepper shaker a few inches to the left. "Sometimes good people do bad things because they have to. Or think they have to."

"That's what I was thinking. What if she needed it for some reason? She never talked too much about her personal life, so I'm not sure. What if her mom was sick or something?"

She tilted her head as she gazed at me. "You don't have to press charges if you don't want to."

"How did you know I was thinking that?"

"Because I know your heart." She moved around to where I sat slumped over the table. I pushed the chair out and gathered her onto my lap. "Whatever you decide, I'll stand by you," she said.

"Compared to my worth, two million is kind of a drop in the bucket."

"I figured."

I buried my face in her sweet-smelling hair. "Is that weird to you?"

She shifted and took her face in her hands. "Money doesn't play into how I feel about you in either direction. Your wealth isn't really news to me. Your face was everywhere for a while. I figured you didn't do all those endorsements for free."

"What did you want to tell me earlier when we were interrupted by the phone?" I asked.

A flicker of apprehension passed over her features. "Yes, there is something."

The front door opened and slammed shut. Seconds later, Huck appeared in the doorway, looking like hell. He hadn't shaved in days and wore the same rumpled shirt, untucked, and jeans from a few days ago. A baseball hat covered his wavy hair. He'd lost everything in the fire and yet here he was, showing up for me when I needed him.

"Brandi?" Huck said. "I didn't know you'd be here." Translation: *I didn't know you two were back together, and I don't like it.*

"Hey." She scooted off my lap and sat next to me.

"I didn't know you had company," Huck said.

I'd figured my reconciliation with Brandi would bother him. I'd hoped to tell him about it alone, not like this. With all that had happened, I'd forgotten my plan. I lifted a shoulder and gave him a look that hopefully conveyed my feelings on the matter. Which were—*it's none of your damn business and I don't really want to take any crap from you right now.*

He took the hint. Although if I knew Huck, he'd come back around to it later.

I stood and gave Huck a guy hug—more of a back-patting with no contact between chests. "I'm sorry about your house, man."

"Yeah, it sucks. But like my dad said, I wasn't in the house when it burned." Huck's bungalow had been built in the fifties near the riverbank. It had been on the market when he decided to move home. Handy with a hammer and nails, Huck had remodeled the place himself. Like Crystal and Garth, he was now without a home.

He leaned against the counter. "I did some digging on your

former assistant. Tara Talley recently bought a house in Arizona and a brand-new sports car."

"Okay, well, that answers the question about whether or not she has a sick mother." My heart sank. I'd wanted an excuse for her. Any sob story would have worked.

"How do you know all this?" Brandi asked.

"I have friends in the right places," Huck said. "I've been digging up dirt for a living for a long time."

"I think it's called investigative journalism," I said.

Huck tugged on the brim of his cap. "She played this well, trickling little by little out of your accounts until you retired, hoping you wouldn't ever notice the missing money."

"Which I didn't," I said. "I'm an idiot."

"Not an idiot," Brandi said.

"You bring in the police yet?" Huck asked.

"Not yet."

Breck came in through the patio doors. He grinned the moment he saw Brandi. "Hey there."

"Hey, Breck." She smiled back at him.

"I've come from the shelter. I got all the pooches settled in, so I thought I'd come see how things were shaking over here." He clapped Huck on the shoulder. "How are you, man?"

"I'll live," Huck said. "I've seen worse."

"Mom made up a room for you at the house," Breck said.

"You're staying with Breck instead of your parents?" I asked.

"Yeah, my folks have their routine, and I'd just be in the way," Huck said. "Breck and his mom have enough room for me. Anyway, it was either that or kick Stormi out of the apartment above the newspaper office. She already hates me. I don't need her making a voodoo doll in my image and poking me to death."

"I don't think she makes voodoo dolls," Brandi said in a serious tone.

Huck raised an eyebrow. "You know her?"

"She took all the photos for my website. I really like her."

"You don't find her irritating?" Huck asked. "With her New York accent? She's pretentious as hell."

"I think she's sophisticated and witty," Brandi said. "She's obviously not from here."

"What's the matter with being from here?" Huck's thick eyebrows came together, making him look like a grumpy old man.

"Nothing," Brandi said. "I'm just saying that no one would ever call me sophisticated."

"Come on now," Breck said, with a friendly tap on her head as he passed around the table toward the island. "You're still the prettiest girl in town and you know it."

"That's categorically not true," Brandi said. "Anyway, I'm talking about being interesting and worldly. Not a person who can make a great sweet roll."

"Don't underestimate the power of those sweet rolls," Breck said as he opened the refrigerator door and leaned in to check out the goods.

"You're perfect the way you are," I said to Brandi as I kissed the top of her head.

"Anyone want a beer?" Breck asked from the refrigerator.

Huck declined, but Brandi and I agreed to one.

Breck set the beers on the kitchen island and simultaneously moved a stool out with his foot, then sat. He sniffed the air. "Is that bread up for grabs?" he asked, pointing to the loaf of fresh bread Brandi had brought.

"Yes, but it needs butter." Brandi got up from the table to fetch the butter dish I kept by the toaster.

"I'll get a knife and cutting board," I said, temporarily forgetting about Tara Talley and the two million dollars. Brandi's sourdough could cure most problems.

"Why are you hesitating about involving the police?" Huck asked. "Were you sleeping with her?"

"What? No way," I said. "I don't sleep with employees."

"Dude, what's wrong with you?" Breck asked Huck. "That's not how we roll."

Huck lifted his shoulders in a cantankerous shrug. "It happens."

"Not with me," I said, with a nervous glance at Brandi.

She was busy cutting the sourdough and seemed unbothered by this line of questioning.

"Good, because that muddies the water," Huck said.

"She was a great assistant. That's all," I said.

I wasn't sure why Huck would even need to ask. The three of us had remained close after we went our separate ways, talking or texting most days even when we were separated by miles. We knew the details of one another's relationships, just as we did our professional enterprises. During veterinarian school, Breck had dated a few women but no one seriously. Huck had spent time with a reporter friend on and off over the years. Not a relationship exactly, but more like casual sex when they happened to be in the same place at the same time. Since he'd come home, he hadn't mentioned women at all. Whatever had happened to him over there, he didn't talk about it, even with us. Breck and I knew he'd talk to us when he was ready. I had a feeling that once he worked through whatever it was that ate him up, a relationship with a woman might be a possibility. Until then, he seemed chained to the demons of his past, unwilling to allow joy into his life. Which made him difficult to be around. I loved him like a brother, but lately I didn't like him much.

We were quiet as we dug into the pieces of fresh bread slathered with butter. "God, this is good," Breck said. "Brandi, you're a genius. It's good to have the band back together. We have some good times coming our way. I can feel it."

"I and others are homeless," Huck said. "Trapper's been stolen from. The town has no place for our kids to attend high school. A historic ice rink is charred rubble. We're hardly ready for a party."

"Don't be such a grouchy bear," Breck said. "We're going to

take care of all these problems, and then we'll be living large in Emerson Pass like the old days." He winked at Brandi. "And now we have our girl back."

"She's my girl," I said, tossing a beer cap in his direction.

"And grumpy over there owes me ten bucks," Breck said.

"You're a bastard." Huck grimaced as he fetched his wallet from his pocket and slapped a ten-dollar bill on the table.

"What was the bet?" I asked.

"How long it would take for you to win Brandi back." Breck held the bill in front of him and grinned. "I said two days. It's truly hard to be this smart."

11

B randi

THE NEXT MORNING, TRAPPER'S FATHER STOOD BEHIND A LECTERN set up in the lobby of the lodge. My staff and I had shut down the bakery and were serving people scones and muffins. By the time Fenton started to speak, the platters were empty.

I already knew the content of Fenton's speech and would have to fight the lump that had already developed in my throat.

Twenty-one families had lost their homes. The Barneses had decided that for anyone who had not been able to find family or friends to stay with, there would be rooms at the lodge for however long they needed them. After news of the fire, most tourists had canceled their plans, leaving more rooms empty than they'd normally have, even in the off-season. Trapper had told me that morning it would mean a huge financial loss for the year but that his father didn't care. If there were people in town who needed housing, he would provide it.

The lodge had remained mostly the same for decades, with

stone fireplaces and picture windows that looked out to the slopes. The crowd gathered, taking up all the seating and the rest standing.

Fenton tapped the microphone that staff had set up for him. "Is this thing working?"

The crowd answered yes.

"Thanks for coming this morning," Fenton said. "I know it's been a frightening few days, and I'm thankful we didn't lose any people or animals in the fire. Our firefighters and police officers did a heck of a job getting us all out of here in a safe and timely way. For those of you who've lost homes, my sincerest sympathies. My wife and I would like to offer rooms here at the lodge for anyone without family or friends they can stay with. This morning, I received a wonderful call from the good people from Wolf Enterprises. For those of you not familiar with them, they were the firm that refurbished Jamie Wattson's inn these last few months as well as built Garth Welte's home. They've offered their architect, interior designer, and contractor at half their normal fees. They recently had a fire in their own town and know how deeply disruptive it can be. We're getting bids and plans from several firms in Denver to rebuild the high school. I'm not going to lie to you. It's going to be a long haul before we get our kids back in an environment designed for learning. Given that, we're offering the lodge here as a temporary high school. It's going to be challenging for teachers to plan lessons in an open environment such as the lobby, but we also have conference rooms and other locations. We're working with the principal and school board on details and will get back to you. To rebuild a new high school for our four hundred kids will be close to thirty million dollars. While some of that cost will be covered from insurance, we're still on the hook for a great deal."

"How will we pay for it?" someone from the audience called out.

"We can't afford another school levy," another voice shouted out from the audience.

"On that note, I'd like to introduce my son, Trapper. He has some good news to share about funding."

Trapper took his father's place. "Hey, everyone. Thanks again for coming. We have a long road ahead of us, but as Pastor Lund reminds us every Sunday, the good Lord provides. Along with the offer from Wolf Enterprises, a good friend of mine from my sports days called this morning. Not only is he a famous retired quarterback and color commentator, he's a resident of Cliffside Bay and good friends with Wolf Enterprises. A few of you may have heard of him. Brody Mullen has offered a significant donation to help us rebuild the school and homes of those who were underinsured."

A murmur went through the crowd. Apparently, I was the only one in town who didn't know about the famous quarterback.

"Brody has friends in high places, so to speak," Trapper said. "Including actresses Lisa Perry, Pepper Griffin, Genevieve Banks, and her husband, Stefan Spencer, who have also offered two million dollars each. In addition, an anonymous man or woman has donated ten million dollars to help rebuild the high school, as well as another ten million to help the uninsured or underinsured rebuild their homes. The details about how to apply for money will be held at a separate meeting this afternoon in conference room B."

A cheer went through the crowd.

I smiled to myself, pretty sure Crystal was the anonymous donor.

"In other news," Trapper said, "as some of you may have heard, I purchased the ice rink just before it was burned in the fire. Fortunately, I'll have the funds to rebuild, but that will be put on hold until after the other construction is completed. Instead, we're going to get it cleaned up and put in an outdoor rink by the time tourist season starts this winter. All proceeds from this endeavor will be given back to the rebuilding funds."

More cheers as he changed places with his dad.

"I'm sure most of you know our town's history. Over one hundred years ago, Alexander Barnes hired a schoolteacher from the east to teach at our very first school. It was a one-room school with a potbelly stove built by the volunteers, all with the sole purpose of educating the town's children. The first class roster recorded by Quinn Cooper listed less than a dozen children. We have more students than in those days, but the spirit of this town remains the same. In the words of Quinn Cooper Barnes, 'Be curious, be kind, protect one another.' Those words still have meaning today, perhaps more than ever. We embody the spirit of those first townspeople. We believe in community and taking care of one another in times of difficulty. Alexander Barnes told his children that to be of service to another human being was the greatest way to find meaning in your life. Seek out your neighbor, ask them how you can be of service. We will rebuild this town together, one brick and board at a time, just as our forefathers did before us."

"And foremothers," someone shouted.

Fenton grinned, then tented his hands under his chin. "I apologize. Yes, ma'am. Foremothers."

At this point, I caught a glimpse of my parents out of the corner of my eye. I hadn't realized they were here. Dad listened to Fenton's speech with his head bowed. Mom, however, was fixed on the lectern. Her expression of pure hatred sent a cold shiver down the back of my spine.

In Trapper's kitchen, my hands flew as I mixed butter into flour for biscuits. As if they hadn't just gobbled down a loaf of bread, the guys were outside after begging me for a batch of biscuits. Trapper's kitchen was stocked with all the right things, including an expensive set of pans and a state-of-the-art cooktop.

I did a quick knead of the biscuits and flattened the dough, then used the rim of a wide glass to cut out circles. I was lifting them onto a cooking sheet when Crystal came downstairs. She looked so much better than when I'd left her this morning. Hair newly washed and blown out, makeup applied, she looked as put together as she always did. She wore a new pair of loose-fitting jeans rolled up at the bottom and a yellow cotton T-shirt. I admired her slender frame. T-shirts didn't look like that on my curves. If I ate fewer biscuits, I might have a smooth stomach like hers. However, I really enjoyed biscuits.

"You look rested," I said.

"I needed that nap." She looked around the kitchen. I'd been in the process of making a salad. A stack of peeled carrots and a bunch of green onions waited to be chopped. "What can I do?"

I asked her to finish the salad. "The guys are making steaks to go with the salad and biscuits."

"It sounds like a party out there." With the expert moves of a professionally trained chef, Crystal chopped the carrots into tiny slivers.

"That's how they are," I said. "Like an ongoing party."

Crystal scooped carrot slivers into the salad bowl. "What's your plan?"

I leaned into the counter. "I'm going to tell him tomorrow. I just wanted one more night before he hates me forever."

"He's not going to hate you."

"You don't know that," I said.

"Just tell him exactly what happened. He's going to understand."

I turned toward the window. Trapper was at the grill, his broad shoulders shaking with laughter. God, how I wanted this to be my life.

Crystal came around the island and drew me into an embrace. "You're going to be all right. What happened hurt you more than anyone else. Don't forget that. You're the one who had to bury that baby by yourself."

I closed my eyes, soaking up this love from my dear friend. "I'm scared."

"I know, sweetie. I know."

We moved out of the embrace. I pushed my hands against the edge of the countertop. "I don't know how to find the words."

"My grandmother always used to say, plain talk is the best," Crystal said.

"Yes, plain talk." I could do it. I'd have to dig into that place of great love. The same place I'd had when I let him go when I needed him the most.

We returned to our tasks. I put the biscuits in the oven and set the timer.

"How are you doing about the other night?" I asked gently.

"I don't know what I was thinking." Crystal stopped chopping the onions and hung her head. "I'm such an idiot."

"Why would you say that?"

"Because I wasn't ready. He's a lovely man—kind and thoughtful. I shouldn't have led him on like that when I have no business being involved with anyone."

"Could it just be what it was? A fling?" I asked.

"I'm not the fling type."

"I don't think he is either," I said. "How was it?"

"You mean the sex? Hot. While we were in the throes, so to speak, I completely forgot anything else. Then, when it was done, I got emotional and basically ruined everything."

"Emotional?"

"I cried and started talking about Patrick," Crystal said, flushing.

"Oh God."

"I know. I'm such a mess." She paused, knife in midair, and looked out the window. Garth was standing next to the outside refrigerator with a beer in his hand. "I'm strangely drawn to him in a different way than I was Patrick. For one thing, Garth's not my type. At all. This feeling is purely physical, almost primal. He makes me laugh and feel lighthearted, which, as you know, I'm not. I love his country-boy vibe."

"That sounds pretty good. Maybe you could just keep it casual? Have some fun?"

"Like a booty call type of thing?"

"Why not?"

She tapped the knife against the cutting board. "Because it feels like cheating."

"He's been gone for two years," I said.

"I know. But Patrick was my person. My one and only. Moving on with someone else feels like our love story has to end. I don't want to stop feeling married to him, because then I have to accept that he's never coming back." Her voice broke. She took in a shaky breath. "Anyway, it doesn't matter. Garth apologized and agreed it was a mistake. He's such a gentle soul and so decent that it felt instantly fine between us."

"Good, since you'll be living in the same house with him for a few months."

"Right. All the more reason to remain friends, not a booty call."

I kept further thoughts to myself. I had a feeling that whatever was between them couldn't be so easily dismissed. I'd seen my friend sparkle for the first time since she'd moved to Emerson Pass. Garth Welte was one of the good guys. I wanted my friend to find love again, but it wouldn't happen until she was ready to accept that her life should go on, even without Patrick.

As for me? I couldn't help but assume I was screwed. Pain was coming my way. It was only a matter of time.

THAT EVENING FELT LIKE THE OLD DAYS. BRECK AND HUCK STAYED for dinner, and with the added bonus of Garth and Crystal, it was a lively group. Breck kept the conversation going, asking Garth and Crystal questions about themselves. Breck had a way of leaning into a conversation, making eye contact and nodding

as if whatever someone was saying had to be the most interesting thing he'd ever heard. This same quality made him good
with animals, I supposed. He met a creature exactly where they
were. I'd missed him. Being with Trapper's friends had seemed
like an impossibility. Too painful. Too many memories. Tonight,
though? It was as if no time had passed.

"So, you're in Montana," Breck said to Garth. "And your
parents split after your little brother's death."

"That's right." Garth pinched the bridge of his nose between
his thumb and index finger. "Like I told these guys, they
couldn't get through it together." He cleared his throat. "My
mom fell completely apart. She was not a Montana native and
decided to move back to Denver. I spent summers with her, but
for the most part my dad raised me. When I was fifteen, we
moved to Salt Lake so I could train."

"Is your mother still in Denver?" Crystal asked.

His features softened when he looked over at her. "Yeah. She
remarried and had another family. I have three half sisters.
They're a lot younger than me."

"Do you see them much?" I asked.

"Not a lot. But one of the reasons I wanted to move here was
to be closer to them. I'd like to have more of a relationship with
them."

"What about your dad?" Crystal asked.

Garth chuckled. "My dad's what you'd call a character. He
packs more into a week than most do their whole lives. Plays
hard—booze and women; a little gambling for good measure.
He's currently on his fourth wife, a wealthy Italian woman he
met on the slopes in Switzerland. All of his wives, he met
through my skiing career, in one way or another. They all have
one thing in common. They're all independently wealthy."

"They're not dead, are they?" Huck asked.

Breck shot him a look.

"No, he doesn't kill them," Garth said, good-humoredly.
"They simply grow tired of him and kick him to the curb. He

lands on his feet, like a damned cat, every time. Each time with a woman younger and better-looking than the last one."

"Does it bother you that he's so irresponsible?" Huck asked. I could easily imagine him interviewing the enemy during the war.

Garth tipped back his beer for a long drink before answering. "Truth is, I'm conflicted. My dad's probably the most fun person you'd ever meet. People love him. He's this combination of a man's man with his cowboy boots, yet completely charming to the female persuasion. And, man, can he tell a story like nobody's business. 'Course he has a lot of them. Most of them begin with, 'One night in this bar in—' fill in the blank."

"Isn't that the beginning of all great stories?" Breck asked.

"At least for us," Trapper said.

"When you're twenty-five it's a lot different than fifty-five," Huck said.

"I agree," Garth said. "Do I approve of his lifestyle? It's not really for me to say. His life, his rules. Would I want to be like him? Never. In fact, I've spent most of my life trying to be exactly the opposite, even though I love him to death." He drew in a deep breath. "Well, shoot, I didn't mean to talk the horns off a billy goat."

Crystal laughed. That same spark that had come to her eyes from the other night had returned.

"We love it," I said.

Trapper lifted his glass. "To new beginnings and new friendships."

"Absolutely," Garth said. "And thanks again for having me here. I'm starting to think Emerson Pass is my kind of town."

"Amen to that, brother," Breck said.

Huck and I did the dishes while Trapper gave Garth and Crystal a tour around the garden and property.

"So, here we are," Huck said. "Kind of like old times."

"Only we can legally drink now," I said, flashing him a grin.

"What are your intentions with our Trap?" His eyes narrowed. A pulse in his cheek twitched.

My stomach dropped. "Intentions? What do you mean?"

"Like what's your plan?"

"There's no plan. We're getting to know each other again. The feelings we had for each other back then are still there."

"You seem pretty cozy, pretty fast." Huck crossed his arms as he leaned against the counter.

"We were together for three years during formative years. We know each other pretty well."

"Do you have any idea how broken he was after you sent him away with no explanation?" Huck didn't take his eyes from me.

"I can imagine. Ten years later and I wasn't over him. I can't remember a time when I didn't love him. So yes, I can imagine."

"You sent him away, Brandi. Remember that? Your decision, not his."

"It was for the best," I said.

"He leaps before he looks," Huck said. "If you're planning on suddenly yanking the rug out from under him again, I'd think twice."

"You have no idea what you're talking about," I said. "Not that that's ever stopped you from running your mouth."

He shrugged. Huck didn't care what I or anyone else thought about him. "I can read people better than anyone. In a million years, I wouldn't have predicted you'd break up with him before senior prom. I mean, who does that after all you'd been through together?"

I flushed with heat. Anger and guilt warred for the lead. "I don't owe you an explanation."

"Is that right?" He raised both dark eyebrows and glowered at me. "How about to Trapper? Do you owe him one?"

"What happened is between him and me," I said. "It's none of your damn business."

"How is it that you never left this place? Were you too afraid?"

"God, you can be a prick sometimes. You came back here, so what's the difference?"

"I came back. You never left," he said.

"I wanted to stay because I love it here. How dare you judge me. Why'd you come back here if you hate it so much?"

"My reasons for returning are complicated." He looked down at his shoes and stuffed his hands in the pockets of his jeans. "I wouldn't expect you to understand."

"Why not? Because I'm not smart enough?"

"Intelligence has nothing to do with it," Huck said. "But I can hardly explain to a woman who's never left her mommy about what it was like in Afghanistan."

Stunned, I gaped at him. "What the hell happened to you? You used to be a nice person."

"When it comes to Trapper's well-being, I won't play nice."

My voice shook. "No one cares about Trapper more than I do. No one."

"You had a strange way of showing it."

"There were things out of my control that forced me to make the decision I did."

"You told him you didn't love him and sent him away with a broken heart." He snarled like an angry wolf. "Those are the facts. Isn't that right?"

"Yes. But it wasn't true. I loved him. I loved him enough to let him go. He didn't need my deadweight pulling him down." I sputtered with anger, fighting tears.

Silently, he watched me through narrowed eyes, as if trying to decide how much further to push. "Word around town was that you disappeared for like a year. No one saw you come or go from your mommy's house. Why was that?"

My stomach dropped. "I don't know what you're talking about."

"You do know. I know, too."

"What exactly do you think you know?" My chest was so tight I could barely breathe. Did he dig up something on me? Could he possibly have figured out my secret? He was an investigative reporter. There were ways to get medical records if you knew the right hackers.

He moved across the kitchen and got right up next to my face. His voice was low enough that only I would hear him. "You were pregnant, weren't you? Was it Trapper's or someone else's?"

"You're out of line," I said. "Get away from me."

"I'm going to find out, and when I do, you can bet your ass Trapper will too."

I moved away from him and smacked into the back of the sink. Was he guessing or did he know? He must not know that the baby hadn't lived, or he would have said so.

"Hey, what's going on?" Trapper asked from the doorway that led out to the patio. Given his gruff tone, he understood the dynamic.

"Not much," Huck said. "Other than I'm trying to figure out Brandi's angle."

"I don't have an angle," I said.

Trapper strode over to where I was standing by the sink and wrapped his arm around my shoulders. "What the hell, Huck? Just because you're miserable, everyone else has to be?"

Breck entered, smiling, but abruptly stopped when he saw our faces. "Okay now, what's happened?"

"Huck's acting like an ass, that's what," Trapper said. "What happens between Brandi and me is none of your business."

"Dude, really?" Breck asked Huck. "Can't you leave well enough alone?"

"If you've forgotten, we're family," Huck said. "Barnes people take care of our own."

"I hardly think he needs protection from Brandi," Breck said.

At this point I wanted to sob into Trapper's chest. Was Huck about to spill my secret right here in front of everyone?

"Listen, Huck, you know I love you, but this is not cool," Trapper said. "You need to leave before I punch you."

Huck uncrossed his arms. "Roger that. You always did drop everything when she called."

"You're damn right I did," Trapper said. "I'm not stupid."

Huck nodded. "When it comes to her, you just might be. You better tell him the truth, Brandi, or I will." With that, he turned on his heel and walked out of the kitchen.

Trapper removed his arm from around my shoulder. "What the hell is wrong with him?"

I flinched as the front door slammed.

Breck rested both hands on the granite island. "See, here's the thing. Huck was always in love with you, Brandi. Which, strangely, leads to hostility. Even anger."

"No, he never liked me. Not even in elementary school." A memory of him tossing balls at me during recess flashed before my mind. "He was mean to me."

"That's how he showed his feelings," Breck said. "I'm not saying the male gender is intelligent in any way."

I smiled as tears gathered in my eyes. "Breck, you've always been the kindest person I've ever known. Thank you for believing in me and trying to make me feel better. But in this case, there's more to it than Huck's misguided feelings."

"What's going on?" Trapper asked.

"I need to talk to you upstairs," I said. "Will you excuse us, Breck?"

"Yes. Go. I should be on my way home anyway," Breck said. He shot me one last kind smile and headed for the door.

T rapper

Brandi closed the door of my bedroom and sank into one of the easy chairs by the open window. Her shoulders curved inward as she tented her hands and placed them between her knees. A breeze passed through the screen and ruffled the curtains.

"Hey now. It can't be that bad," I said.

She gestured toward the other chair. "Come sit."

I perched on the edge of the cushion and leaned across the space between us to caress her cheek. "You're scaring me," I said.

"My parents came to see me. Separately."

"What did they want?"

"To find out whether or not we were back together. I told them we were." Her bottom lip quivered. She looked down at her hands.

"I can only guess what your mother thinks," I said.

"She feels trapped here. Stuck with my dad and this town.

Because of me." The words were delivered in a pained staccato, punctuated by gulps of air in between.

I ached for her. Damn her mother. The woman should leave if she was so unhappy here. "What does her dissatisfaction have to do with us? We love each other. We both want to be here."

"Because her unhappiness has been the biggest influence in my life." The corner of her mouth twitched. "This thing I have to tell you—I don't know how to say the words."

"Just say it."

A long pause ensued. The muscles of her thighs tensed as she pushed against her still-folded hands. "I got pregnant the spring of our senior year."

My mind blanked, as if a cloud had taken the place of coherent thought. "What?"

"The baby didn't live. She was stillborn."

I jerked away, as if a snake had bitten my hand. "That's impossible. Why are you saying this?" I pressed the palms of my hands into my knees as spots swam before my eyes. A baby. Stillborn.

"She died in my womb a few days before she was delivered." Brandi removed her hands from between her legs and wrapped her arms around her stomach.

"No. You would've told me." I blinked, trying to focus on her face, but her features swam before me like an abstract painting in watercolor. "That's not how we were. We told each other everything."

"My parents said they'd disown me if I told you," Brandi said. "They wanted me to get an abortion and I refused. We made a deal. I could have the baby as long as I gave her up and agreed to keep it a secret."

"Adoption? You were going to give our baby away?"

She shook her head. "At first I was too afraid to think clearly. All I knew is that I didn't want your life ruined because of my mistake. Later, I came up with a plan."

"Your mistake? What're you talking about?" I spread my

hands out over my knees and took in a deep breath. "I don't understand what you're saying."

"I forgot to take my pill two nights in a row. I should've told you so we could take precautions."

"Is that why you broke up with me?" Now the thoughts came so fast I couldn't keep up with them. "Is that the real reason? You didn't want me to know about the baby?"

"I didn't want a baby to ruin your life," Brandi said. "Like I wrecked my parents' lives. I didn't want you to be bitter and angry like my mom. I couldn't wreck another life."

"I don't know what to say." Or feel. I realized my cheeks were damp. *A baby. A little girl.* My gaze darted around the room. "You were going to give her up?" Had I already asked her that?

"I thought at first I might, but as the pregnancy went on, I knew I couldn't. I had a plan to run away. Crystal's mother in Seattle had agreed to take me and help me get on my feet."

My stomach hardened into a boulder. I fixed my gaze on her, wondering how it was possible that she'd kept this from me. "You were going to keep her and not tell me?"

"I—I…I didn't think you'd want her…us."

"She was my baby. How could you think I'd reject her? Or you? I loved you. Did you know me at all?" I swiped away the tears that had filled my eyes.

"I was trying to protect you. Do you really think you'd have wanted to be saddled with a worthless wife and needy baby? If I wrecked your chances of a hockey career, I would never have forgiven myself. The truth is—I was alone. Crystal was the only one I could turn to."

"You should have given me the chance. I loved you more than anything."

"Except you didn't. When I asked you—you chose hockey." Tears fell down her cheeks and onto her arms, which continued to hold her middle. "It doesn't matter anyway. Our baby didn't live long enough for me to know what came next."

For the first time in my life, I couldn't soften toward Brandi.

The betrayal cut like a sword through my gut. A baby. A baby I never got to hold or see or grieve for.

Hot tears fell from my own eyes. "How could you lie to me?"

"I'm sorry," she whispered. "I didn't know what to do."

"I have to get out of here. I have to think." This was like learning half the things they taught in history class were untrue, and here was the real version of events. I needed to talk to Breck.

"I understand." She'd drawn her legs up and rocked back and forth on the chair.

"Why didn't you tell me this sooner? We've been together for days. How could you let me back into your life—back in your bed—and not tell me about our baby? Jesus, Brandi."

"Because I knew you'd leave me once you learned the truth. After ten years of missing you, I just wanted a few days. I'm sorry." She hid her face in her hands.

"I have to go." I lumbered to my feet and lurched toward the door. The last thing I heard before I entered the hallway was her sobs. I couldn't go back. Not like this. I had to sort through this new reality before I could be there for her. We'd had a baby that she'd planned to keep and not tell me about. How could this be the girl I'd trusted with my whole heart? My whole big stupid heart.

13

B randi

I WRAPPED MY ARMS AROUND MY MIDDLE AND ROCKED BACK AND forth as I sobbed. He was gone. This was too big a lie to recover from. The desolation and loneliness washed over me in wave after wave of darkness. There had been a small part of me that hoped he'd understand. Hope had set me up for this mighty fall into despair.

After a few minutes, I got it together enough to think through the next steps. Rose and Fenton. I wanted to tell them myself before Trapper could. It was the least I could do. Once they knew, then they could look after Trapper.

I called the house. Rose answered. I asked if I could come out to see them.

"Now? It's late," Rose said.

"I'm sorry, but it has to be tonight."

"Are you okay? You sound strange."

"I need to talk to you."

"Yes, come. We'll be on the patio."

"I'll be there in a few minutes."

THEY WERE SITTING TOGETHER ON THE LOVE SEAT WHEN I CAME around the corner of the house. Lamps brought enough light to the patio that I could see them clearly.

"What's going on?" Rose asked as she stood. "Something's happened. Is Trapper all right?"

"Trapper's fine," I said. "I mean, physically."

"What about you?" Fenton asked.

I sat across from them. "I have something I need to tell you. It's going to be hard to hear, so brace yourselves."

They nodded.

"I got pregnant the spring of our senior year. The baby didn't live. She was stillborn at nine months."

They both stared at me as if they'd heard me wrong. Rose rubbed her collarbone as the color drained from her face. Fenton swayed slightly.

"My parents made me keep it a secret. They wanted me to put her up for adoption, but I had other plans. She died a few days before my due date. I didn't know, of course, until they induced me."

"Did Trapper know?" Fenton asked.

"No, no. He knew nothing. I didn't want him to give up his plans." I stood on shaking legs. "I just wanted you to hear it from me. Trapper knows now. I told him tonight. He didn't take it well—not that he should. He left very upset. I wanted you to know that too, so you can look after him. He won't want anything to do with me after this. Also, her name was Ava Elizabeth, and I buried her in our family plot. I'm very sorry." I lunged forward and stumbled in my sandals, falling and scraping my knees.

Rose sat behind me on the hard stone and wrapped her arms

around me. "You poor little girl," she whispered as she held me against her chest and rocked me like a baby.

I sobbed and sobbed until there was nothing left. Finally, I allowed Fenton to help me into the house. We went to the family room with the large windows and rows and rows of books and where great love stories had played out between the dark walls a century ago. He led me to the plush couch, and Fenton and Rose sat with me between them. They each took a hand.

"Sweetheart, we're sorry we never knew," Fenton said. "If we had, we would've helped."

"I'm sorry," I whispered. "I've no excuse, other than my parents said they would kick me out of the house if I told anyone. They wanted me to abort but I just couldn't, so that was our compromise." Hot tears slid from the corners of my eyes. "If I'd told Trap, he would've given up everything. I didn't know what else to do."

"You did the right thing with what you knew at the time," Rose said.

"Do you hate me?"

"We could never hate you," Fenton said.

"Trapper might never forgive me," I said.

"He's just in shock," Rose said. "He loves you. When he calms down, he'll think of it from your perspective and come to understand why you did what you did."

Fenton drew my head to his shoulder. "You were very brave."

I shuddered, remembering how they'd had to tear her lifeless angelic body from my arms. "My mother let me bring her home and bury my baby in the family plot. She wouldn't let me put her name on the gravestone." I sobbed through my words but continued, wanting desperately for them to understand. "No one but the three of us, Crystal and her mother ever knew she existed. It was wrong and cruel. Her name should be there, marking the fact that she lived inside me for nine months. But *I* know. I know her name. I wrote her name and dates in my Bible.

Ava Elizabeth. God and I know her name. She was a person. I loved her so much."

"Oh, sweetheart," Fenton said, pulling me close. "We're sorry you had to do this all alone."

I leaned into Fenton, giving him my body weight and my burden. I was not alone. Not now.

"Losing a child is a pain no one should have to suffer," Rose said. "We're here for you. Whatever you need."

I looked into Rose's sympathetic eyes and understood what it was like to be loved unconditionally, without judgments or expectations. This, I thought, is why Trapper's such a fine man.

"My mother kept saying to forget it and pretend the whole thing hadn't happened. But it was impossible. How could I forget my own child? The only thing that helped was working so hard I was too tired at night to do anything but fall into bed. And seeing Trapper's dreams come true. At least I'd been able to give him that. My mother was angry and bitter because of me. She had to give up her dreams. I didn't want that for Trapper. He was always good and honorable, and I was such a drain on him."

"That's simply not true," Fenton said. "You gave him joy."

"You're not responsible for your mother's happiness or sadness," Rose said. "The only one who can control that is her. It's time to let yourself off the hook. If she's too selfish to see what a gift you are, then she doesn't deserve to have you in her life."

"No matter what I do, it's not enough," I said.

"You're enough, just as you are," Rose said.

"I've been afraid and ashamed," I said. "Carrying around this secret has made me tired and old."

"Now that your secret is out, you don't have to be afraid or ashamed any longer," Fenton said.

"Goodness, your knees are bleeding," Rose said. "Hang on. I'll get some bandages." Her sandals clicked on the hardwood floors as she crossed the room.

"What do I do?" I asked Fenton. "What now?"

Fenton squeezed me with his strong arm. "Give Trapper a little time. He'll come around. I can imagine he's in shock."

I leaned my cheek against his chest. "I think about Lizzie and Jasper sometimes. How long it took for her to finally win his heart."

"Too long," Fen said. "But Jasper was a stubborn fool. Trapper takes after Alexander—a romantic who knew who he wanted from the moment he met her."

Rose returned with bandages and hydrogen peroxide and knelt on the floor next to me.

Fenton loosened his arm from around me and rose from the couch. As Rose cleaned my wounds with a cotton ball, he went to the desk.

When he returned to us, he had a Bible in his hands. "Will you take us out to the cemetery?" Fenton asked. "I'd like to welcome her to the family. You can bet that Rose and I will say her name out loud." He patted the leather cover of the good book. "I'll put her in our family Bible."

I closed my eyes against the tears that had come once more. "No one but me has ever been there. I go every Sunday after church."

"I'll be damned if we don't put her name on that gravestone," Fenton said.

Rose secured two bandages on each knee, then sat back on her heels. "There you go. All fixed up."

This is what it's like to have a mom.

"I'm sorry," I whispered. "I didn't mean for her to die. I wanted to be a mom like you, Rose."

"What happened was not your fault," Rose said. "It was simply a tragedy."

"Maybe my broken heart made it so she couldn't thrive," I said. "I've always been so weak."

Rose wrapped her small, warm hands over mine. "Listen to me, little girl. What you endured all by yourself would've have been too much for a lot of people. You kept going. You made a life for yourself. That's the definition of strength."

"Love yourself as much as you have Trapper and Ava Elizabeth," Fenton said.

He'd said her name out loud. I started to cry again, this time covering my face with my hands and sobbing as Trapper's parents patted my back. When I finished, I accepted a tissue from Rose and wiped my face. Exhausted, I rested my head against the back of the couch.

"Where do you think Trapper went?" I asked.

Fenton walked to the bar and poured himself a whiskey. "If I have my guess, he called Breck. They'll talk it through like they do most things. Later tonight, you'll get a phone call. You two will talk. You will tell him absolutely everything, just as you have us. When he's ready, take him out to the cemetery. You'll cry over what you lost. And then, by the grace of God, you'll both finally start the life you're meant to have. Together."

14

T rapper

DRIVING TOO FAST, I BARRELED DOWN THE GRAVEL ROAD TO BRECK'S house. Tears blurred my vision. The sun had set by then, and the muted light made it even harder to see. Huck was right. I was too trusting. I'd believed Tara to be my most trusted employee and friend, and look what she'd done. Two million dollars right out from under my nose. Now, this.

I thought back to that night she'd ended things. How had I not questioned her motives? We'd been in love. Her bullshit explanation that she didn't love me enough to go with me had been a blatant lie. What was wrong with me? How could I be this blind? Was I just such a romantic and so desperate for love that I'd missed all the signs?

Other than my mother, Brandi and Tara had been the only women I'd ever trusted. I hadn't thought either of them capable of this kind of deception. A baby. A secret pregnancy. What kind of people made their teenage daughter do that?

I reached Breck's driveway. The gate was open, and I drove through. The fenced fields on either side of the long driveway were trimmed short by the horses. Lights from Breck's house were warm and inviting. They called to me like old friends. How many times had we spent together in Breck's mother's farmhouse kitchen that smelled of maple syrup? Brandi and me. Huck and Breck. We'd all been carefree then. Our whole lives ahead of us. I'd thought the world was out there for me to take. Nothing could stop me.

Their gray barn was all shut up for the night. An image of the hayloft floated through my mind. Brandi and I had spent a night there the March before graduation. We'd made love twice on a blanket spread out over bundled stacks of hay. That was the night. I knew it in my bones. The night we'd made a baby.

My stomach churned. Bile rose to my throat. I pulled to the side of the road and vomited into the tall, dry grass. When I was done, I leaned against the side of my truck to catch my breath. A wail came from deep inside me. I did this with my arrogance and carelessness. Not Brandi's mother, but me. I'd made her pregnant. I'd made her feel as if she couldn't come to me. I'd left for the world I wanted. For years she'd had to see me in magazines with other women. Meanwhile, she'd been here trying to salvage a life after burying our baby.

I was a selfish boy. And now? Was I a selfish man? I'd left her tonight to cry alone as I did all those years ago. She'd been so small and sad in that chair, and I'd left her. She was right. Once again, I wasn't there for her. It was all about me.

"I didn't know," I whispered to the grasses. "I didn't know."

The dry grass rustled in the breeze and seemed to say, "You do now. What are you going to do about it?"

BRECK SAT AT THE ISLAND IN HIS MOTHER'S WHITE KITCHEN AS I paced and spilled Brandi's secret. When I finished, he poured us both a tumbler of whiskey.

"Well, this explains a lot about how she's acted over the years." He handed me the glass.

"What do you mean?" I threw back the drink in one gulp.

"Kind of like a baking robot." Breck leaned his back against the kitchen sink. "You know what she told me once? Senior year, we were out by the river having a bonfire during one of the October harvest moons. You'd gone off with Huck to get beer or something and it was just the two of us. I asked her if she ever thought about the future. What do you want if you could have anything? She said, and this is a direct quote, 'All I want is to be Trapper Barnes's best friend and the mother of his children and be able to bake bread on Sunday afternoons. I know women are supposed to want more, but I don't.' She went on to say how much pressure she felt to do all the things her mother hadn't been able to do. 'But I can't do them. I'm a mistake. A person who should never have been born.' That's another direct quote." He reached for his glass of whiskey. His brows came together. "It's the saddest thing I've ever heard anyone say."

I pressed a napkin against my wet eyes. Brandi had thought she was a mistake. "How could she think that when I loved her so much?"

"The wounds are deep," Breck said. "Deeper than even your love could fix. Brandi feels like she ruined her mother's life. That belief has colored absolutely everything. When you said you'd choose hockey over her, your answer reinforced what she felt she deserved. She took the burden of the baby on herself. She was conditioned to make the choice she did. And man, it's cost her."

"I'm just so angry," I said. "At her mother."

"She's made some poor choices," Breck said. "Especially when it comes to Brandi. But I guess that's the way it is when everything you ever wanted feels as if it was taken from you.

That loss has a way of shrinking you—making you mean and small."

"It's no excuse," I said. "Plenty of people have had babies at seventeen and go on to become whatever they wanted to be. Sure, it's harder, but women do it all the time."

"The past is the past," Breck said. "You two have found your way back to each other. It's a beautiful thing. Don't let her mother ruin one more day. The best girl in the world wants you. You are someone's dream. Think about that. You know what I would've given to be Brandi's dream?"

"I thought Huck was the one who loved her?"

He chuckled. "Nah. Not the only one. I loved her too. I was just smart enough to know from the beginning she only had eyes for you. You lucky bastard."

"I *am* lucky. I'm mad at myself, too. I should've figured it out and been there for her."

"My dad always said people do the best they can with what they know at the time. You were a kid. If you'd known, you would've been there. You didn't. But you are now, and Brandi still needs you. She's hurting, and you're the only remedy. Text her. Tell her that everything's going to be all right between you."

I took my phone from my back pocket.

I'm sorry for leaving when you needed me most. Everything's going to be all right. Please know that I love you. That will never change.

Seconds later, one came in from her.

Meet me at the cemetery tomorrow at ten.

THE NEXT MORNING, I FOUND BRANDI SITTING BY A SMALL tombstone in the Strom family lot. She rose to greet me. We stared at each other for a moment before her face crumpled into tears. I pulled her into my arms and held her close. "It's okay." I rested my chin on the top of her head. "I'm here now."

"Thank you for meeting me here," she whispered against my chest.

"I'm glad you texted."

The cemetery was made up of green grass and old oaks. Our family plot was at the center with a wrought iron gate around the circumference. For generations, we'd been laid to rest there. Brandi's family plot was similar, with generations of Stroms and Vargases buried side by side.

She withdrew from me and gestured toward a small gravestone, unmarked other than an etching of a bird. Together we walked over and sat on the grass.

"My mother wouldn't let me put her name or dates on here. Her name was Ava Elizabeth. Ava means bird."

"Did the doctors know why she died?" I had to ask, even though I feared it would hurt Brandi to have to recount the details.

She shook her head. "Twenty-five percent of stillborn deaths are unexplained." She drew her knees to her chest and rested her chin on them. "At the time, I thought it was my fault."

"How could it be your fault?"

"Because I didn't want her. I didn't want to be pregnant." Her chin trembled. "I missed you so much that I thought I must have given her my pain. My disinterest in living."

"You didn't want to live?" A heaviness settled over me. I dropped my chin to my chest. I'd done this to her.

She shuddered, drawing in a deep breath. "I didn't. I'd never felt so alone."

"I'm sorry, baby." A sob came from deep within my tight stomach. "If I'd known. If I'd only known." I lifted my face toward her. My breath hitched at the pain in her eyes. "I was a selfish kid who didn't see what was right in front of me. I was too into conquering the world to notice something was wrong. I let you down, and I'm sorry."

"None of this was your fault," she said.

I wrapped an arm around her shoulder and held her tight

against my chest, stroking her hair. "When did you decide you wanted to keep her?" I asked.

"The first time I had an ultrasound. I could see her tiny body and her face. She was real. I couldn't give her to strangers. I called Crystal and told her everything. Her mother said I could stay with them until I could get on my feet. She said she'd come get the baby and me at the hospital in Denver. My mom made me have her there so no one here in town would know."

Brandi scooted away from me to brush a leaf from the gravestone. "When I got to the hospital the day she was to be induced, I was naively unaware that anything was wrong. It wasn't until I saw the nurse's face that I suspected something was wrong. In a split second, everything changed from peaceful to chaotic. There were all these nurses and machines and bright lights. No one would tell me what was going on. I was terrified. The doctor came and looked at the monitor and examined me. His expression was like the grim reaper. He said, 'I'm not getting a heartbeat.' Then I knew."

I tried to steady myself with calming breaths, but the pain in my chest made it impossible. "I can't imagine how awful that must have been."

"A part of me died right there. I had to go through labor knowing the outcome. She was already gone, and I knew it. But it had to be done, so I did it. They gave me Pitocin and an epidural for the pain. I cried through most of the next few hours. She finally came. Still and quiet. So quiet."

"Did they let you hold her?"

"Yes, they were very nice to me. Everyone felt terrible." Brandi sighed and looked up at the sky. "She had these perfect miniature fingers and toes. All these questions ran through my mind. How could she be so perfect but not survive? Why had God taken her? Why hadn't I felt her soul leave me? How could I not have known that she'd already gone to heaven before she even left my body? What had I done wrong?"

"You didn't do anything wrong." Tears flowed hot and wet down my cheeks.

"My mother had chosen this couple to adopt her. They were kind to me. Kinder than my own mother. They brought flowers and told me how sorry they were. I could tell that she'd been crying. It was a loss for them, too. I couldn't even look them in the eye because I knew I'd been planning on running away before they could take her."

"Would you have been able to?" I asked. "Or would your mother have interfered somehow?"

Her expression turned hard and resolute. "Up to the last minute, it's up to the birth mother to change her mind. Crystal and her mom were already on their way to Denver to take me home with them. My mother had given me no choice. I had to choose the baby over them."

"Did that plan include me?"

"I'm not sure," she said. "I wasn't thinking about you right then. I was in survival mode."

"And in the end, you never had to make the decision," I said.

"My little bird flew away from me, up to heaven. I came home and buried her here with Lizzie and Jasper and the rest of the family. My mother made me do it in the middle of the night so no one would know. A tiny coffin in a tiny grave and only me to grieve her."

"God, I hate your mother," I said. "I'm sorry, but I don't think I can ever get past this."

"I've never been able to." The corners of her mouth lifted in a sad smile. "I could see you in Ava's face. She looked like you. I'm sorry I deprived you of a chance to see her."

"If I'd treated you with more care, you would've felt safe to tell me. You deserved better than my self-centeredness and surety that I was the town hero bound for glory. In fact, I was the opposite. When the person I loved the most in the world needed me, I couldn't see it. I was too busy being Trapper Barnes, hockey star. My only excuse is that I was a boy. I'm a man now,

Brandi. If you'll give me the chance, I'll spend all my waking moments trying to make it up to you."

"By asking you to choose between me or hockey, I set you up." Her face scrunched in obvious pain. "If I'd told you the truth, maybe everything would've been different." She let out a long sigh. "I was a girl. A scared, insecure kid. I wanted you to have it all, even if that meant losing you."

I brushed my mouth against hers. "There is nothing in this world I'd choose over you. Not now. Not ever. Your pain is my pain. Your joys are my joys. After all this, can you believe in me? In us?"

"I've always believed in you," she said. "And I'm ready to believe in us."

We kissed. A new kind of tears sprang to my eyes. The truth had led us to a deeper love than I thought possible.

She rested her face in my lap. I stroked her hair as she spoke softly. "I promised Ava I'd never forget her. And that someday we'd be together in heaven. That belief has sustained me through a lot of long nights." She wiped her eyes with the back of her hand. "The nights are the worst."

"Yes, they are." How many had I thought about Brandi until the wee hours of the morning, praying that God would grant me the peace of sleep?

"I come out here on Sundays to talk to her," she said. "I've told her all about you. About how happy we were together and how much I loved you."

"Why didn't you tell me the first night we were together at the campground? Didn't you trust me?"

"Every day I told myself I would, but I just couldn't find the words. I thought I'd lose you again. I wanted as much time with you as I could get before you left for good." Her voice broke. "I needed just a few more memories to get me through the rest of my life. Can you understand that?"

I leaned over to press my mouth against her silky hair. "I do.

But I'm not leaving. I'm here for good. Our little bird made sure we found our way back to each other."

"Our own little angel." She lifted her head from my lap and folded her legs under her to face me.

I wrapped my arm around her shoulder. Golden beams of sunlight glinted through the trees.

"I want to get married," I said.

"Trapper, really?"

"I don't want to wait any longer. I'm ready." I turned to her. "What do you say?"

She smiled as the rays of sunlight glittered in her eyes. "I'm ready too."

I got to my feet and offered her my hand. "Let's go home."

15

B randi

THE NEXT MORNING WAS MY SCHEDULED DAY OFF. I WOKE UP EARLY as usual, but went back to sleep, snuggling close to Trapper's warm body. He slept on his side, curled up like a kid. The next time I opened my eyes it was after eight. Trapper was still snoring softly, so I crept out of bed as quietly as I could. I dressed in shorts and one of Trapper's Michigan sweatshirts and headed toward the kitchen.

I hadn't expected anyone else to be up yet, but the smell of coffee told me differently. Crystal was there, chopping a green pepper. Ramekins filled with diced ham and shredded cheese were next to a bowl with whipped eggs.

She looked up when I came in and smiled. "Good morning."

"Good morning."

When we arrived home yesterday after the visit to the cemetery, neither Garth nor Crystal had been there. Only one of their cars was missing, so we assumed they were together. A note on the kitchen table said they'd gone into Louisville to do more shopping. I'd then texted her that all was well with Trapper and me and that I'd fill her in later. We'd gone to bed before they'd gotten home.

"Tell me everything." She tossed the onions and green peppers into the melting butter and moved them around with a spatula.

I shared with her the extent of our conversation. "It was hard but good in the end. I feel like a thousand-pound weight has lifted from my shoulders."

"I'm so glad," Crystal said. "I knew he would understand when you explained it all to him."

"I'm glad to say you were right. Also, we're getting married. Sooner rather than later."

"Married?"

I nodded and grinned. "You can't talk me out of it, so don't even try."

"I wouldn't think of it." She clasped her hands under her chin. "This is wonderful." She came around the island to hug me. "I couldn't be more delighted for you."

We embraced, holding on a little too long. There was so much between us, so many shared experiences and pain from our lives that we'd supported each other through. "You've always been here for me."

"I always will be." She withdrew. "You know what we should do later? Call my mom. She'll be over the moon."

I smiled. "She was kind to me when I was beyond lost. I'll never forget it."

"Will you want a big wedding?" Crystal asked. "Like the kind where you invite the whole town?"

I shook my head. "Nothing sounds worse. I'd prefer just to elope. Something casual. Maybe here at the house. The sooner the better."

"Since Patrick and I got married after being together a month, I can't say a word. We couldn't stand to wait a minute longer. In hindsight, I'm so glad because that was just that many more months that I was his wife. However, I still had enough time to find a dress and organize a small wedding." She stuck out her bottom lip. "I hate to think of you not having a celebration. Let me throw something together. We can do it here or at Trapper's parents'. If my stupid house hadn't burned down, we could've done it there."

"Let me think about it."

"Fine." She poured the eggs into the pan. They popped and sizzled. After a minute, she tossed the ham and veggies in, then folded it over and plopped it on a plate.

I poured myself a cup of coffee and watched her move around the kitchen. Something was different. Was it a glow? Or the way she carried herself? She wore a loose-fitting cotton T-shirt dress. Her hair was wrapped in a knot on top of her head, and there was a healthy color to her cheeks. "You're looking relaxed."

She didn't make eye contact, focused still on the peppers. "Thanks. I had…a good night."

"How come you were so late getting home?" I asked.

"We had dinner at Puck's after shopping. We had a feeling you two might need some alone time."

"I appreciate that," I said. "Did you sleep well?"

"Sure, yes. Just fine." Her neck pinkened to the same color as her cheeks.

I drew closer. Was that a mark on her neck? "Is that a hickey?"

Her hand flew to her neck. "Um. No. I mean, yes."

"Oh my God, did you sleep with him again?"

She looked up, then put both hands on the counter, her voice lowering. "It was just this one last time." She leaped around the island and grabbed my hand. "Outside. Now."

I giggled as she dragged me outside to the patio.

"We made a pact," she said after closing the French doors behind us.

"A pact?"

"Yes. This would absolutely be the last time."

"How did it happen?"

"I couldn't sleep, so I came down here around midnight to make a cup of chamomile tea. He was down here too, working on his laptop." She pointed toward the kitchen as if he were still there. "The house was so quiet and still and the light in here was...so dim and intimate, like the rest of the world had disappeared." She paced from one end of the patio to the other as she talked. "I just stood there, watching him. I couldn't seem to take my eyes off him. He looked up at me and we stared at each other like we were glued together. Then, all of a sudden, he scooped me up and pressed me against the wall, and kissed the daylights out of me." She lowered her voice to just above a whisper. "I swear I couldn't stop myself. It was so hot. He's so hot. He wrapped me around his waist and carried me upstairs like it was nothing. I got the feeling of his athletic prowess—the guy didn't even breathe heavy." She stopped near a flowerpot and fanned herself. "I'm getting hot thinking about it."

"Did he take you into his bedroom?" I asked, hanging on every word. "I didn't hear a thing."

"No. My room. Since his room is right above yours, we were afraid we might wake you guys, which would have been completely mortifying."

"Were you loud?" I laughed as she covered her face with her hands.

"I plead the Fifth," she said through her fingers.

I settled down on one of the chairs and held the steaming cup of coffee in front of me. "You're so dirty. Go on."

She lowered her hands. "It was good. No, great. Kind of mind-blowingly fantastic. Completely different than the first time. For one thing, I didn't cry afterward." She let out a long sigh. "I can't believe the poor guy would even consider doing it again after how I botched it the first time. That said, we both understand that neither one of us wants a relationship. I mean, he's still reeling from his divorce, and I'm in love with my husband."

"Your late husband," I said softly.

She plopped down in the chair next to mine. "I know I must seem silly to you—loving a man who's been dead for two years."

"Not at all. I've loved Trapper all my life, even when I didn't think there was any chance that we'd ever get back together."

"When I *can* sleep, which isn't often, I still dream about Patrick every night," she said. "And every morning I have to remember all over again that he's gone."

"I know you do." I could see the way his death had taken a toll on her sleep by the dark smudges under her eyes.

She tilted her head to the sky and winced. "Except last night, I didn't dream of Patrick. I slept like a log." She smiled and flushed red again. "Well, other than the time Garth woke me up for seconds."

"I can't believe this."

"I know. This fire has made me into some new person. Some slutty person." Her fingers grasped at the chain around her neck. "I wear his ring. I mean, what's the matter with me? It's not fair to Garth to just fall into bed with him when I have no intention of this going anywhere. I mean, he's like the best guy and old-fashioned, which I know must be making him feel weird, too."

"But you said you made a pact."

"Right. Of course. I shouldn't be worried. He said he's not ready for anything serious either. I mean, we talked about it last night afterward. That's when we agreed that this was the last time."

"And then you did it again?"

"This is not funny," Crystal said.

I covered my mouth and tried to sober up, but the expression on her face was too much. "Crystal, you're not a kid. You're two consenting adults having fun. It's not hurting anyone if you guys have a fun, casual relationship. I mean, what's wrong with just dating and having hot sex as long as you both know it's just for amusement?"

"Okay, yes, when you say it like that, it doesn't sound as sordid."

I laughed again. "It's hardly sordid. When did you become such a prude?"

"I'm not a prude," Crystal said. "But I'm not used to just falling into a stranger's bed on a whim. It's like this fire bonded us somehow."

"What happened when you woke up this morning? Was it awkward?" I asked.

"He wasn't there. Thank God. I forgot how bad morning breath is. It's been so long since I shared a bed with someone. And you should've seen my hair. It looked like I'd been in a tornado."

"A tornado named Garth."

"Again, not funny."

"I'm sorry, but this is way too much fun."

"Oh, Brandi, he's so beautiful. Patrick was handsome, in a geeky type of way. I adored the way he looked, but he wasn't exactly the hard-body type. Garth's got this country-boy vibe going on and his body...is hard...everywhere. But anyway, it doesn't matter. It was just one night of fun. Like I said, we made a pact."

"That seems like a hard one to keep, given that your rooms are next door."

"God, I know. It's going to be so tempting. Honestly, he's such a great guy—funny and thoughtful. Smart, in a quiet way. He loves to read, too, so we've talked about all these books we both like. Anyway, we both agreed that we can't let this get out of hand or one or both of us could get hurt. Friends from here on out." She made a movement with her hands like she was shutting a door.

Good luck with that, I thought.

"Let's go inside," she said. "I promised Garth a Denver omelet. That's his favorite."

I followed her inside to the kitchen, unconvinced about their future. She was cooking for him, hot for his body, and they had many shared interests. Sure, this was going nowhere.

"The kitchen smells just like my dad's," Garth said from the doorway. "I almost thought I was home for a minute there."

Crystal beamed at him. "I hope it's not cold." She pushed the plate with the food across the island toward him.

"It's like living at the finest hotel around here." He rummaged in the drawer for a fork. "I mentioned in passing that a Denver omelet was my favorite breakfast."

Did these two really think they were going to be able to go back to a casual friendship? My prediction? They were back in bed together by the time the sun went down.

"I never forget any detail that has to do with food," Crystal said.

"Me either," I said. "That's one of the reasons we're best friends."

"I'd say it's quite advantageous to have you two around," Garth said. "I may decide never to rebuild my house."

Crystal laughed. "At some point Brandi and Trapper will want their privacy."

I poured him a cup of coffee.

"Coffee, too? I love the service around here."

"What's this?" Trapper's voice drew my attention to where he stood in the doorway. "Have I woken in someone else's house?"

"Would you like an omelet?" Crystal asked.

"Yes, please." He marched over to me and lifted me up in his arms and planted a kiss on my mouth. "Did you tell them?" He set me back on my feet.

"Not Garth," I said. "But Crystal knows."

"Knows what?" Garth poured another cup of coffee and handed it to Trapper.

"We're getting engaged today," Trapper said.

"Well, hot damn. I love weddings," Garth said.

"You do?" Crystal asked. "A divorce attorney who loves weddings?"

"A divorce attorney who's divorced, no less," Garth said. "Call me crazy. I'm a romantic. It takes more than a money-hungry ex-wife to beat it out of this country boy."

Crystal poured another batch of eggs into the skillet. "That does make you a little crazy."

Garth cut up his omelet with his fork. "I'm either delusional or hopeful, depending on how you look at it." He shoved a forkful of his breakfast into his mouth and made an appreciative grunt. "City Mouse, this is awesome."

"Thank you. I'm a trained professional," Crystal said.

"You know what?" Trapper grabbed me and twirled me around in a circle. "Let's get married tomorrow. We can call Pastor Lund and have him marry us at the church, then have a party here afterward."

"Tomorrow?" I squealed as he placed me on a stool.

"I've waited ten years for you," Trapper said. "I don't want to wait another minute to make you my wife."

"What about your mom and dad?" Brandi asked.

"They'll be all for it," Trapper said. "As long as we're married in the church."

"I can throw some side dishes together," Crystal said. "If Garth can barbecue."

"Hell yeah," Garth said.

"However, there's something missing," Crystal said. "I don't see a ring on my best friend's finger."

"I can take care of that this morning." Trapper grinned.

"Fine, but what about a dress?" Crystal asked.

"There's that fancy store in town," Garth said. "Maybe you could find a pretty dress in there." He raised his eyebrows and laughed as we all looked at him. "What? My office is right next door. They have dresses in the window display right now. I see a lot of ladies come out of there with big old shopping bags. I mean, if money's no object."

"Money's no object," Crystal said. "Because I'm paying for it."

"You don't have to do that," I said.

"I know, I know," she said. "But just this once, let me have my way. I want you to have a pretty dress on when you marry this guy." She pointed at Trapper. "And you better dress in the nicest suit you have. I'll call Stormi to take photographs."

I opened my mouth to protest, but she put her hands up. "No arguments. You'll thank me later. Everyone needs a photograph from their wedding day. I promise to keep it simple."

"We better invite the guys too," Trapper said. "Otherwise, I'll never hear the end of it."

"All right, fine," I said. "As long as you two will be our witnesses, I'm in."

"We're going to witness the crap out of it." Garth smacked the counter with his hand. "This is going to be one heck of an awesome wedding."

"I'll call Pastor Lund from my office," Trapper said. "And see if he can marry us sometime tomorrow." He walked across the kitchen toward the office.

Garth frowned. "I sure wish my wedding cowboy boots hadn't burned up in the fire."

"You have special boots just for weddings?" Crystal asked.

"Doesn't everyone?" Garth asked, deadpan.

"No, not everyone," I said. "But we should, of course."

"I wear them to christenings and graduations, too," Garth said. "Any special occasion, really. I mean, that would just be weird to keep them for weddings only." He patted his stomach. "That was some good grub, Crystal. Thank you."

"You're welcome," Crystal said, rolling her eyes and laughing at the same time. "Grub is my specialty."

Trapper returned to the kitchen, wearing a triumphant

expression. "Pastor Lund is in. He says to be at the church at five tomorrow and he'll marry us."

"Eat up," Crystal said as she slid a plate across to me. "Dress shopping is hard work."

"What should I do?" Garth asked. "I want to do something."

"You're in charge of the reception," Trapper said. "Get a hold of some stuff to grill and a bunch of booze."

"I'm on it like a bee to honey," Garth said as he rinsed his plate and put it in the dishwasher. "City Mouse, can you make me a list? I'll go to the store while you guys are at the dress shop."

She nodded. "Yes. I'm thinking light appetizers and a salad or two, plus a couple of skirt steaks."

"I'll call my parents, Breck, and Huck on my way to Louisville," Trapper said as he stuffed his phone in his pocket. "And I'll tell my mom to make sure Tiffany comes."

"Why?" I asked.

"Because Breck has a huge crush on her, and what works better to get a girl in the mood for love than a wedding?" Trapper kissed the top of my head. "I'm out of here. I've got a ring to find."

"Don't forget about one for yourself," Crystal said.

"Will do," Trapper said as he headed out the patio door.

16

T rapper

I pulled up in front of Breck's house in great spirits. I'd enlisted him for my special errand in Louisville. I didn't tell him why, figuring I could fill him in on the way there.

"What's the big secret project?" he asked as he hopped into the truck.

"I need to see a guy about a ring."

He smacked my shoulder. "No way. You guys obviously talked everything through."

"We did. Thanks for being there for me."

"I'm glad, man."

"Brandi and I have been apart long enough." I backed the truck up and turned to head down the driveway. "We're getting married tomorrow."

He did a double take. "For real?"

"For real."

"How is she?" he asked. "I couldn't stop thinking about her after you left."

"She's good. I mean, it's not something she'll ever get over, but she's strong. Together, we're stronger."

"No doubt."

"I'm going to spend the rest of my life making up for all the times I've let her down," I said.

"Good man."

We avoided going into town and headed straight for the highway. I used the voice control to call my parents. "Dad?"

"Trapper, everything all right?"

"Yes, sir. I'm calling to tell you that Brandi and I are getting married at the church tomorrow at five."

"Tomorrow?"

"Yes, sir," I said. "We're having a reception at my house afterward."

"Well, all right. I'll let your mother know."

"Can you tell her to invite Tiffany?" I asked.

Breck shoved my shoulder and made a face.

"Sure thing. Why don't you and Brandi come by tonight? We'll have a drink and officially give our blessing."

"Sounds good. See you then."

I called Grammie and Pa next. She answered, sounding a little breathless. "Hello, honey. How are you?"

"I'm getting married tomorrow."

"Tomorrow?" Grammie asked. "To whom?"

"Brandi."

"Your high school sweetheart?"

"Yes, ma'am."

"Isn't this kind of sudden?" she asked.

"Yes, but I've loved her forever and we're back together, and I don't want to waste any more time."

"Well, then, I guess it's meant to be. Will she want a bouquet? I can put one together from the garden."

"She would love it, Grammie. Can you come to the church tomorrow around four thirty?"

"Your Pa and I will be there in our Sunday best."

After I hung up, I sighed. "I need to invite Huck. I haven't talked to him since the blowup the other night."

"Maybe go by and see him later?" Breck said.

"Good idea."

Breck scratched his neck. "I haven't wanted to make a big deal, and we've had a lot of other stuff going on, but I'm seriously worried about Huck. Ever since he came home from being over there, he's been quick to anger and, honestly, kind of paranoid."

Last night, after we'd returned from the cemetery, Brandi had told me what Huck had threatened. I wasn't convinced he knew the full story. I thought he might have been bluffing to get her to confess. Whatever it was, I aimed to find out and clear the air.

"What did he say about Brandi to you?" I asked.

"Nothing, actually. I haven't talked to him since the other night either. I've left a few messages, but he doesn't return my calls or texts."

I told him about his threat to Brandi. "He basically threatened to out her if she didn't tell me. Do you think he actually knew anything or was he just fishing?"

"I'd guess fishing," Breck said. "I've never heard anyone talk about her disappearance after high school. I wonder who he heard that from?"

"I don't know, but I wouldn't put it past him to dig around in any records he could find. That's his job, after all."

"You'll have to talk to him," Breck said. "I think he'll say he was concerned about you and wanted to make sure you knew what you were getting into. Whatever it was, he's going to have to apologize to Brandi."

"Agreed."

We drove a few miles in silence. I turned on the radio. Breck relaxed with his head resting against the back of the seat with his eyes closed. I figured he was asleep. The guy could fall asleep anywhere.

He startled me when he jerked upright. "How do you think her parents are going to take this?"

I shrugged. "Not well, would be my guess. Neither of us cares."

"I feel bad," Breck said. "Can you imagine what it would feel like to have a mother like that?"

"I can't."

"She'll have your parents now," Breck said. "They're the best."

"They are. Your mom's pretty special, too."

"That she is. She's going to want to be at the wedding," he said. "Is it okay if I bring her?"

"Yes, please do. I can bet she's on the phone right now with my mother anyway. Mama's going to invite her friends, if I have my guess."

———

THE JEWELER SHOWED US VARIOUS STYLES OF RINGS, SO MANY MY eyes started to cross. If Breck hadn't been with me, I might never have chosen. My desire for the perfect ring had caused paralysis of the mind.

"This one here," Breck said finally. He held up the princess-cut solitaire to the light. "And this band for her wedding ring." He pointed to a one with a row of diamonds across the top. "She needs a lot of sparkles."

I laughed. "Done."

Next, I chose a thick platinum band for me. "Let's get out of here so I can propose to my girl."

"I'm afraid to hear the total," Breck said. "I might pass out."

"Don't be such a cheapskate," I said. "You'll never get a girl."

He sighed. "I don't think that's my only problem."

I DROPPED BRECK AT HIS CLINIC AND HEADED THE OTHER DIRECTION. Huck would be at the newspaper office this time of day, and I needed to talk to him. The way we'd left it between us was terrible. As bewildered as I'd been over his behavior the other night, I couldn't get married without him there. We needed to clear the air.

I parked in front of the newspaper office. A few blocks to the south of Barnes Avenue, the building was like Brandi's, with the office on the ground floor and an apartment above. The windows of the apartment were open and as I exited my truck, Stormi stuck her head out and yelled down to me. "Hey, Trapper. Congratulations on your wedding. I'll be there to take photographs."

I cupped my hand over my eyes to shield them from the sun. "Great news. Be sure to leave me a bill."

"I'd do it pro bono, but I need the cash," she said. "A girl has to eat."

"I wouldn't have it any other way," I said. "You'll come to the reception as a guest, I hope?"

"Totally. I'm psyched to be included. It's really cool you're back together. Epic, dude. Epic."

"I'll see you tomorrow."

"Sounds good." Her head disappeared inside the window.

The door to the newspaper office needed a good shot of oil. At the sound of the creak, Huck looked up from where he'd been slouched over a laptop at the back of the room. His thick brows came together. He rose from the creaky chair, which looked as if it had been there since the early 1970s. "What're you doing here?"

I walked past the empty reception desk. The room smelled of burned coffee from the pot that had clearly been left on all day. Several more desks, all piled with papers, took up a large portion of the workspace.

"Brandi and I are getting married tomorrow, and we'd like you to come."

He clicked his tongue against the roof of his mouth. "You've got to be kidding me."

"Brandi told me about the baby," I said. "You can take the threat off the table."

He crossed his arms. "I was right, then? She had a baby?"

"You didn't actually know? Why would you do that, man? You hurt her. What reason would you possibly have to attack her?"

"I was trying to protect you."

"Brandi is hardly someone to protect me from. I just don't get it," I said. "Why would you threaten to tell me? What the hell kind of friend does that?"

"She's been lying to you. I'd think you'd want to know that."

"You forced her to have to tell me before she was ready."

"You're welcome."

"It's not something to be proud of," I said.

"When I moved back here, I heard rumors about how she disappeared after high school for like a year. No one knew where she went."

"She didn't go anywhere. Her mother basically locked her inside for the whole time she was pregnant."

"Whose baby was it?"

"What do you mean? The baby was mine. Who else's would it have been?"

"I don't know." A corner of his mouth lifted in a sneer. "You tell me. Why else wouldn't she tell you back then?"

"It's complicated. But basically, she didn't want me to give up hockey."

"How can you marry her with such a big lie between you? She gave away your baby."

"She didn't, actually," I said.

"What're you talking about? Where's the baby?"

I flinched. "She's in the town cemetery."

He paled. "What?"

"She was stillborn," I said. "Her parents wanted her to put her up for adoption, but she'd been planning on running away with the baby."

"To where and with what money?"

"Do you always have to be the investigative reporter?" I asked. "It's really none of your freaking business. She planned on going to Crystal's mom's in Seattle. She was going to live with them until she could figure out what to do. But Ava didn't live."

For once, Huck didn't seem to have one of his sardonic responses.

"She went through hell, all alone," I said. "We were kids, and she did the best she could."

"I don't understand how you can feel okay about her having your child without you knowing. She clearly didn't trust you to take care of things. Is that really the woman you should marry? She lied to you. Broke your heart. She doesn't deserve you. But go ahead. Get married to a woman who lied to your face while sleeping with you over the last few days. She's not a kid now, Trapper. She's a full-grown adult. You want to see what your future is? Take a look at her manipulative mother. The apple doesn't fall far from the tree."

I shoved him against the counter. "Shut your damn mouth."

He rammed both hands into my chest. "This is a free country. I can say whatever I want. Brandi is a liar."

I took a swing at him and caught him on the jaw. He yelped in pain. His hand flew to his face. "What the hell is wrong with you?"

"What the hell is wrong with *you*?" I shouted back at him.

"You hit me," he said quietly. His dark, intense eyes glittered as he glared at me. "You hit me."

I got inches from his face and spoke through gritted teeth. "If you say anything else against her, you're out of my life. Do you hear me?"

"Screw you, Trapper." He came for me, butting into my stomach with his head. I lost my footing and fell backward into the window, which shattered into tiny squares. Safety glass. I had that going for me, at least.

I lunged for him, and we both fell to the floor. I had my hands around the collar of his shirt but he was surprisingly strong, despite being a few inches shorter and weighing a good thirty pounds less, and flipped me over. He raised his hand to punch me. I shoved him with both hands. He flew across the room and landed against the wall.

He slumped over his knees. "Fine, you win. Just get out."

"Trapper? Huck?" A female voice. Stormi burst into the office. "What in God's name is going on?"

"Nothing," Huck said.

"Are you all right?" She knelt by him.

He slapped her hand away. "I'm fine."

She stood and glanced my way. "Trapper, your arms."

I looked down. A few pieces of glass had stuck into my skin and caused minor bleeding. "Nothing to be concerned over." My voice was hoarse and dry.

She brought her hand to her mouth. "You guys were fighting like two middle schoolers? I thought you were cousins and best friends."

"Distant cousins," I said, bitterly. "And *former* friends."

Huck had his knees bent with his head between them. "Get out before I call the police."

"No problem," I said. "Sorry, Stormi, that you had to see us acting like idiots." I left through the front door and got into my truck, completely shaken.

How could a twenty-eight-year friendship end like this? What had happened to the friend I'd known? What had they done to him over there?

17

B randi

AFTER BREAKFAST, CRYSTAL AND I HEADED INTO TOWN TO THE DRESS shop. "Something sweet," she said. "So at least you have a photograph to show your children. And God knows I have nothing to wear, either."

The upscale boutique catered mostly to our wealthy visitors who came in the winters to ski. I'd hardly ever shopped there, preferring the department stores in Louisville where you could get items on sale. The place was owned and run by Mallory Fox, an elegant woman in her sixties with silver hair and sharp eyes. She'd never come into my bakery, her thin frame evidence of her discipline.

She greeted Crystal the moment we entered. "Dear, I was so sorry to hear about your home. Please let me know if there's anything you'd like me to order for you."

"Thank you, Mallory," Crystal said. "Today we're looking for something pretty for Brandi. She's getting married tomorrow. I also need a dress suitable for a wedding."

Mallory didn't blink an eye. "Are we thinking cocktail dress or something of a more romantic style?"

Crystal, clearly in charge, had walked over to a rack of dresses. "For Brandi, something on the sweeter side."

"I *am* the Sugar Queen." I smiled and resisted the urge to twirl about the store like a dancing fairy. I was getting married to Trapper Barnes. I didn't care what I wore.

I tried on a few gowns, most of them too fussy for my small frame. The sixth dress was a white off-the-shoulder silk sheath with an asymmetrical skirt and a flounce sewn into the neckline. "I think this is it," I said from inside the dressing room.

"Let's see," Crystal said.

I walked out. Crystal put her hands over her heart and beamed at me. "Yes, this is the one."

Mallory nodded. "Yes, dear. That's just right."

Crystal chose a sleeveless sheath in a light green that draped over her slender frame.

"What about an understated tiara for your hair?" Mallory asked. "It's not every day one gets married. Perfect excuse for a little bling." She went to a glass display case. "We have several styles."

I peered through the glass. A simple band with sparkles caught my eye. "How about that one?"

Next to me, Crystal nodded. "With your hair up it will look so pretty."

Mallory sold us new sandals. A strappy low-heeled pair for Crystal and a three-inch one for me. "To show off those legs," Crystal said.

"And give me a little height next to my giant groom," I said.

"You'll both be beautiful," Mallory said as she rang us up. "Don't hesitate to come back if you need anything else."

We thanked her and took our packages out to the car. On the way home, we passed the newspaper office. Huck was sitting on the front steps holding an ice pack to his chin. One of the windows was shattered. I pointed them out to Crystal.

"You don't think he and Trapper got into it?" I asked.

"Like a fistfight? No way."

I didn't say anything further, but I had a bad feeling they hadn't worked out their disagreements. As stubborn as they were, who knew how long it would take?

By the time we got back to Trapper's, Garth had come home with the groceries and greeted us at the door with a worried furrow to his brow. "We've forgotten about a cake."

Crystal gasped. "How could we forget a cake?"

"I could make one," I said. "But it'll have to be something simple."

"No, no. You have enough to do," Crystal said. "They're not my expertise, but I can make one in a pinch."

"I'll help," Garth said.

"Excellent. I'll grab my laptop and we can pick out a recipe," Crystal said. "What kind do you want?"

"A white cake," I said. "With raspberry filling and cream cheese frosting."

"Leave it to the baker to have a precise request," Crystal said.

I left them to it and drove out to my parents' house. It was inevitable. I had to tell them. If they didn't want to come to the wedding, that was fine, but I had to give them the opportunity.

My parents lived in the same cottage that Lizzie and Jasper had built over a hundred years ago. Small for modern times, but charming. A white picket fence enclosed the yard. Hydrangeas with fat purple blossoms and white peonies contrasted with my father's perfectly kept green lawn. The sweet scent of the climbing pink roses that clung to the trellis filled my nose as I let myself in through the gate.

I was surprised to see my dad's car parked by the garage. He often traveled during the middle of the week.

I didn't knock before stepping inside the house. The sound of angry voices coming from the kitchen greeted me.

I couldn't make out what they were saying. Regardless, given the tone, there was no doubt that my parents were arguing. I froze, unsure of what to do. They would be embarrassed to have me overhear anything. I decided to open and shut the door, louder this time, to clue them in on my arrival. I did so. The voices stopped.

"Mom? Dad? Are you here?"

"Yes, in the kitchen," my father called.

I scurried down the narrow hallway to the kitchen. Mom stood with her back to the kitchen sink. Her arms were folded over her chest. Dad was by the sliding glass doors with a red face.

"What're you doing here in the middle of the day?" Mom asked. "Why aren't you at work?"

"It's my day off," I said.

"Are you sick, honey?" Dad asked, moving toward me.

"No, not sick. I just had some things to do." *Rip the bandage off*, I thought. *Just tell them and get it over with.* "I told Trapper about Ava. After talking it through, he understands why I did what I did and your part in it. We're in love, and we're getting married tomorrow."

They both stared at me. My mother's eyes blinked rapidly. Dad's mouth hung slightly open.

"Please tell me this is a joke," Mom said.

"It's not a joke. We want to get married but not make a big fuss. With everything going on in our community, it doesn't feel right to have a big wedding. We don't want to wait any longer."

"You've only been back with him a few days," Dad said.

"This is insanity," Mom said. "You can't tell me it isn't."

"I'm a grown woman," I said. "You don't get to tell me what to do any longer. You've already done enough to keep us apart."

"To keep you apart?" Mom asked. "He's been gone for ten years. How's that our fault?"

I simply looked at her. If she didn't understand how she'd contributed to the demise of our relationship, I certainly couldn't explain it to her.

"After what he did to you?" Mom asked. "Are you completely stupid? He showed who he was the first time around."

"I'm going now," I said. "The wedding will be at five tomorrow afternoon at our church. There'll be food and drinks at Trapper's afterward. I'd like you to be there."

"This is a mistake," Mom said. "You'll regret this. I'm not going to stand and watch you marry the man who ruined your life."

I glanced at my father. Dad shoved his hands in the pockets of his khakis and hung his head.

"For the record, my life was not ruined by Trapper. My heart was broken when I lost a child. If you're asking me to choose between a relationship with you and marrying Trapper, then my choice is him. I'm sorry."

When I got in my car and drove down the gravel driveway toward the road, I let the tears fall. I'd hoped their reaction would be different even though I knew better. Still, I'd wanted them to embrace my choices and to be a part of my life. I had a feeling they wouldn't be after this. They couldn't accept Trapper. Doing things for my mother's approval had never gotten me far. From now on, I would live my life on my own terms. If she didn't like it, then it was her loss.

18

Trapper

THAT EVENING, WE HEADED TO MY PARENTS' FOR DINNER TO celebrate our engagement and talk over a few details about the wedding. As we pulled in the driveway, Brandi let out a gasp. "That's my parents' car."

"What are they doing here?" I asked.

"I've no idea. When I left them this afternoon, they seemed adamant about not attending the wedding."

"Maybe they've changed their minds," I said.

She smiled at me and then leaned close to kiss me. "Always the optimist."

We walked around to the back of the house hand in hand. My parents and the Vargases were on the patio.

"Hello, kids," Dad said, standing when he saw us.

"Is it official?" Mama asked.

Brandi held up her hand. The diamond caught the light and made a pattern on her neck. "It's official."

Mama gave me a hug, then one to Brandi. "We're so happy."

Dad patted me on the back before pulling me into an embrace. "Good work," Dad said. He opened his arms to Brandi. "Welcome to the family."

Mr. Vargas stood to shake my hand. He kissed Brandi on the cheek, then shuffled his feet looking uncertain. Mrs. Vargas remained seated.

An awkward silence followed, broken by my father asking if he could get everyone something to drink. When no one answered, he said, "I'll open some wine then."

He disappeared inside the house as Brandi and I settled into the love seat. I put my arm around her shoulder and pulled her against my side. She was trembling. Damn her mother.

"Mom, what are you guys doing here?" Brandi asked.

"I invited them," Rose said. "I thought it was time we reconciled. Especially since our children are marrying tomorrow."

"And you know how it is," Mrs. Vargas said. "When Rose says jump, we all say how high?" She sounded pleasant enough, but the venom behind her light tone came through loud and clear. That's what jealousy and bitterness did to a person, I thought. The object of your envy wasn't hurt. Only you.

Dad returned with a bottle of wine. Mama fetched glasses from the outside table, which had been set for dinner. No one spoke as Dad opened and poured the wine. I grabbed glasses for Brandi and me.

Dad crossed one leg over the other, then reversed them. "Is everything set for the big day?"

"Yes, we're all ready," I said. "Even the church is booked."

"I'm happy you decided on a wedding at the church," Mama said. "It'll be lovely."

"You're really going through with this?" Mrs. Vargas said. "If so, you can consider this the last time you'll ever see us."

Mama blanched. "Malinda, don't be like this. The kids are in love."

"You expect us to accept him into our family?" Mrs. Vargas asked. "After all that happened?"

"They've been through enough." Mama's voice had gone from pleading to angry in a heartbeat. "It's time we come together and support them."

"You're wasting your breath, Rose. She won't." Brandi's tone was resolute and distant. She was done, I thought. Her mother couldn't hurt her any longer.

"What did you think would happen, Rose?" Mrs. Vargas said. "Your son got Brandi pregnant and then left. We took care of things while the perfect Trapper Barnes became a hockey star." She whipped her head around to look at me. "While you joined a fraternity, the girl you left behind gave birth to a dead baby."

Mama gasped as her face drained of color. "Malinda, stop."

Dad's eyebrows knit together. "What in God's name is wrong with you?"

"If I'd known, I would've been here," I said.

"I highly doubt that," Mrs. Vargas said.

My entire body tensed. "What gave you the right to decide what I would or wouldn't do?" I asked through gritted teeth. "You lied to me about my own baby."

"I'm her mother," Mrs. Vargas said. "You were a spoiled brat who took advantage of a girl like Brandi."

"A girl like Brandi?" I unwrapped my arm from around Brandi's shoulders and scooted forward, leaning over my knees with my fingers laced. "What does that mean?"

"She could barely read," Mrs. Vargas said. "If it wasn't for you, she wouldn't have graduated from high school."

Next to me, Brandi shook, silently sobbing. *There it is,* I thought. Mrs. Vargas had found another way to hurt Brandi. *Evoke her insecurities. Call her stupid.*

"Don't ever say that again. Do you understand me?" I squinted, trying to focus, but it was as if the blood in my body had rushed to my eyes, splashing the world with red. "There's nothing wrong with Brandi. Other than you never supported her."

"Screw you," Mrs. Vargas said. "You have no idea how I've sacrificed for her. I gave up my entire life for this girl, and this is how she repays me."

Mr. Vargas touched his wife's thigh. "Malinda, we should go. You've said enough."

"What about you?" Mrs. Vargas asked. "Why do you never say anything, Jack? You hang me out to dry every single time. The nice one. The silent father."

"We encouraged her to go the adoption route," Mr. Vargas said slowly as he placed his hands on his knees. "We all just wanted to put this behind us and move forward. And that's what we should do now. The past is the past."

"If we'd known," Mama said to him, "we would've helped."

"The great Barnes family swoops in for the rescue," Mrs. Vargas said before her husband could answer. "Isn't that how the story always goes in this godforsaken town?"

"Is that what it was about?" Dad asked. "You wanted to keep us out of it?"

"You bet I did," Mrs. Vargas said. "If I'd allowed you in on the decision, it would have been all about another Barnes child coming into the world. Let's all throw a parade."

"It wasn't your right to keep it from Trapper," Mama said.

"Neither was ready to be a parent," Mrs. Vargas said. "All Brandi knew how to do was bake cookies. Your son was too busy chasing a puck to care about anyone but himself. Someone had to be the adult and make the decision. You two would've just made things worse."

Mama had risen from her chair. She pushed the sleeves of her linen shirt up to her elbows. "Malinda, you need to leave my house."

I took in a deep breath as I looked at Brandi. "These toxic people do not deserve to be in your life." I pointed at Mrs. Vargas. "Go home. Brandi's part of my family now."

Mrs. Vargas stayed where she was, glaring at me with hatred in her eyes. "Over my dead body does she become a Barnes."

"Malinda, enough." Mr. Vargas scooted forward in his chair. "You've done enough. I've let you hurt our little girl for too long. You're really mad at me, not Trapper. Yes, I got you pregnant. We moved here to be with my family instead of doing what you wanted. I've been punished ever since. No amount of couples therapy seems to make a difference." He said the last part as if he were talking only to himself. He lifted his chin and set his gaze on his wife. "I know you've already been to an attorney." He drew in a deep breath, then let it out slowly. "After all these years and all the discussions we've had about whether or not to stay together, you owed me more than to be blindsided with papers."

We all stared at him. No one made a sound. Even Brandi had stopped crying.

"Unlike you, I'm tired of being in limbo," Mrs. Vargas said. "You're right, no amount of counseling can fix us."

"Daddy, what's she saying?" Brandi asked.

"What I'm saying is that your father and I are separating," Mrs. Vargas said. "The details haven't been worked out yet, obviously. This may come as a shock, but we've been discussing it for a long time."

"Separating isn't the right word," Mr. Vargas said. "We're divorcing."

"Finally? You're giving in?" Mrs. Vargas asked.

"You've won, yes," Mr. Vargas said. "I won't fight you if this is what you want. But I'll be damned if I give you my family's house."

Mrs. Vargas rose to her feet and barked out a bitter laugh. "That's all you have to say? You want your precious Emerson Pass house? Your little part of history. This was always part of the problem. You chose this town and a bunch of ghosts over what was best for our family."

"Raising our daughter in Emerson Pass was the best thing we

ever gave her," Mr. Vargas said. "God knows we haven't done much else right."

Mrs. Vargas opened her mouth as if to blast him but seemed to change her mind at the last second. Exposing their marital troubles in front of us had to be the last thing she'd wanted from this evening. I almost felt sorry for her. She was alone and angry by choice. Brandi and Mr. Vargas loved her, but it wasn't enough. Instead, she clung to her rage and resentment. They would not keep her warm at night.

"Thank you for your hospitality, Rose," Mrs. Vargas said. "Brandi, you've clearly made your decision. I hope you'll be happy a year from now when it's sunk in how hard it is to extricate yourself from a bad marriage."

I stole a glance at Mr. Vargas. His head hung low. Clenched jaw muscles hinted at the amount of effort it took to keep from losing control of his emotions. He was hurting and probably would be for a long time.

Next to me, Brandi was trembling. "Yes, Mom, I've made my decision."

"Goodbye, then," Mrs. Vargas said.

Dad stood, his good manners still prevalent even in a time like this.

"No need to walk me out, Fenton," Mrs. Vargas said. "Jack, don't come home tonight. I'll be gone by morning. You can have your beloved house all to yourself. Brandi, I'll call and let you know where I've landed."

Brandi didn't answer, other than to place her hand on my knee.

Mrs. Vargas walked across the patio with her head held high and her back straight. I suspected she was holding her breath. When she reached the French doors, her shoulders shuddered, so quickly I might have imagined it.

19

B randi

LATER, TRAPPER DROVE DAD AND ME TO MY APARTMENT. WE'D
agreed that Dad would stay tonight in my bedroom. I'd drive
out to Trapper's after I got Dad settled.

"Would you like something to drink or some of the dinner?" I
asked as we climbed the stairs. "I'll need to change the sheets on
my bed, but that'll only take a minute. We can talk after, if you'd
like." After Mom had left, the five of us had sat awkwardly until
Trapper suggested we take Dad to my place. Rose packaged
some of her delicious lasagna up for us before we left.

"I'm not too hungry." He raked his fingers through his
sandy-colored hair and lowered himself onto the couch. "I don't
suppose you have any scotch?"

"I don't. Wine or beer?"

"Beer."

I fetched it from the refrigerator and then handed it to him.

"I'm going to heat up the lasagna. You should eat something, even if you don't feel hungry."

He nodded before taking a sip of the beer. I set the plastic bin Rose had sent home on the table. After scooping a few squares onto plates, I microwaved them. The scent of Rose's homemade tomato sauce filled the room as the meal warmed.

I set a plate of steaming lasagna on the coffee table in front of him. He didn't even glance in that direction. Instead, he stared into space with blank eyes. I'd not seen him like this often. Once, when I was a child after his mother died, I'd found him sitting with his knees pulled to his chest on the kitchen floor. We'd been to the funeral and wake that afternoon, and he still wore his black suit. I was only eight and frightened to see my usually peppy father completely gutted.

I'd stood before him and whispered, "Dad?"

His eyes had raised to look into mine. "Brandi? What're you doing?"

"Looking for you."

He'd opened his arms and I'd gone to him, sitting on his lap as he buried his face in my hair. "You're my whole life, baby girl. Don't ever forget that or how much I love you."

"Dad?" I asked now. "What can I do?"

His gaze flickered my way. "We've had problems for a long time."

"You and Mom?"

"Yes. Really, since the beginning."

"I never saw you fighting."

"We didn't fight. Ours was more a war of silences."

I knelt on the soft rug with my hands clasped and stayed quiet, hoping he would tell me more, even as it made me cringe to hear.

"She blamed me...*blames* me for how her life turned out. She'd wanted to be a doctor. Did she ever tell you that?"

"No. Only that she'd wanted to attend college and have a career."

"Here's the thing about life, Brandi. You can spend it making excuses for all the ways you didn't get what you want, or you can adjust and find new ways. After we had you, I went to college. I knew I needed a degree or I'd never be able to take care of you and your mother the way I should. My mother offered to take care of you so that Malinda could go too. But she refused. She said there was no way she would ever make it into medical school while raising a family. So she gave up. It was almost an active, aggressive decision to stop trying. Her misery was a punishment to me."

"Were you ever in love? I mean, before me?"

He scrubbed a hand over his face. "I'd like to say yes, Brandi. Doesn't every little girl want to have come into the world because of a great love story?"

"But you weren't? You married only because of me?"

"I loved her. She never felt the same way I did. I was a summer fling, I guess. The city girl plays camp counselor and has an affair with the small-town boy. It was never supposed to be more than that. I mean, it's hard to know what you feel when you're eighteen years old and scared out of your mind."

"True. But I knew I loved Trapper. I knew I wanted to keep our baby."

He gave me a sad smile. "You've always been so sure of your feelings and never one to keep them to yourself. I've always admired how you love with your whole heart. How unafraid you are to let people know how you love them. That's what broke my heart the most about what happened. After the baby died, it was like all the life went out of you. You shuttered your heart."

"Losing Trapper and the baby broke me. But I've been put back together since he came back to me. There's a part of me that will always grieve my child. That never goes away."

"I've always felt bad about what happened. I mean, the way we handled things. I tried to fight your mother on the adoption route. We went round and round about what we should or should not do about the baby. She was adamant that your life shouldn't be stunted because of a baby, especially if you had to raise her on your own. If I'd fought her on it, she would most certainly have kicked you out of the house. I knew I'd lose you forever if that happened."

"Why didn't you leave her?" I asked. "If you were both miserable, why stay?"

"I didn't want to break up our family. Her motivations are more complicated, I think. What her family thought of her always influenced her decisions."

"What do you mean?"

"She never wanted them to think she'd failed at anything. That's why she was supermom even though she would've been happier as a career woman—a working mother."

It was true. I'd had every lesson imaginable: piano, karate, swimming, ice-skating, skiing. Lunches were packed in perfect, shiny tin boxes with all the food groups covered. A calendar with all my activities was color-coded and hung in the kitchen. She spent hours with me after dinner guiding my homework. Endless flash cards and study techniques. Despite all that, all I ever wanted or excelled at was baking and being Trapper's best friend. "I've been a terrible disappointment to her."

"We let you down. As far as the dyslexia, I should've known something was wrong. Denial's a strange thing, isn't it? I've always been so conflict-averse that I've walked away from too many fights. I should've fought for you." His chin dropped to stare into the beer bottle between his legs. "It was always easier to focus on work. I asked for as much travel as I could get, just to get away. I'm sorry, Brandi. I should've done better by you. We were so young. I didn't know anything, especially about how to be a good father."

"You were a good father," I said. "No one is perfect. Mom presented special challenges for both of us. I just remember thinking if I could be a good girl or a better girl, she would be happy. Nothing I did changed the bitter way she moved through the world. And then to get pregnant. The very thing she'd warned me about every day of my life. I can only imagine how awful that must have been for her. I can't help but feel like bringing this whole thing back into our lives has caused you so many problems. I'm sorry, Dad."

"You haven't caused this," he said. "I've been sleeping in the den since Easter."

"Why haven't you moved out? You could've stayed with me."

"I guess I've held out hope that we could work through our issues. That's been an error on my part. For many, many years."

"Will she be all right? I mean, financially?"

"I've been smart with money. Inheriting the house and property has made it easy to save. I'll be generous in the financial agreement. She'll be fine."

I hesitated for a moment, getting up from the floor to sit next to him on the couch. "It would mean a lot to me to have your blessing on my marriage. Can you forgive the past and embrace Trapper as part of the family?"

"Honey, you have it. I've always liked him. I could hardly hate him for doing the very thing I did at that age. And anyway, he makes you happy, so I'm happy. From the moment I held you in my arms, I've wanted only for you to be content and loved."

"Thank you, Dad." I leaned my head against his shoulder.

"I want you to know that the best thing that ever happened to me was you. I'm proud of you and always have been."

"A fresh start will be good for you, Dad."

"If I may, I'd love to walk you down the aisle tomorrow."

"Really? I would love that." I threw my arms around him, and he hugged me close.

"Promise me one thing," he said.

I pulled away, sitting next to him on the couch. "What is it?"

"That when your mother cools off and reaches out to you, you'll answer. Don't let her latest actions define your entire relationship."

"I'm not sure I can promise you that. Not right now, anyway." Her words had been too hurtful. A period of time would have to pass first. "But I'll work on forgiveness."

"That's all I can ask."

"Good. Now, you need to eat some of Rose's lasagna. You're going to need your strength if you're going to walk me down the aisle."

T rapper

I CRIED WHEN I SAW MY BRIDE WALKING DOWN THE AISLE ON THE arm of her father. She didn't take her eyes off me as she made her way toward me. The asymmetrical dress showed off one of her gorgeous legs and fluttered when she walked. Her hair was twisted into a knot at the back of her neck, set off with a sparkly headband. Her strong, tan shoulders looked amazing in the sleeveless gown.

But it was her eyes that drew me in and didn't let go. Those eyes that I'd stared into a thousand times told me everything I needed to know. She loved me. She was pledging her love to me forever.

They reached us and Mr. Vargas kissed his daughter's cheek and took his place next to my parents.

We stood before Pastor Lund holding hands. The doors of the church opened, drawing everyone's attention, including ours.

It was Huck, wearing a suit that for once didn't look rumpled. He slipped into the back row.

He'd come after all. Despite our fight, he'd come to be here for me. I smiled and nodded at him. He nodded back at me.

Brandi and I turned back to Pastor Lund. "Dearly beloved," Pastor Lund said. "We're gathered here today to witness the matrimony of these two beautiful young people."

Brandi hadn't wanted to write our own vows, because she was afraid to speak in front of everyone. Instead, we'd asked the pastor to take us through the traditional vows. We were nearing the end, and I'd managed to keep it together. Until the pastor asked the last question of me.

"I remember when you two were children attending Sunday school," Pastor Lund said. "Even back then, it was obvious that Trapper Barnes had eyes for only one girl. All these years later, I can see that it's still true. The road to this day has been a long one but here we are, finally. Timing is everything, as they say. For whatever reason, it wasn't yet your time to be together. The good Lord works in mysterious ways. In the years to come, remember to cherish each other and celebrate the miracle of your love. What was lost has now been found again. During squabbles or misunderstandings, try to remember what it was like before you made your way back to each other. As you grow older, keep the passionate teenagers you once were alive. Sneak down to the river together. Kiss in your truck. Dance barefoot in the kitchen. Lie in the summer grass and watch a cloud float by while holding hands. Revel in the small, simple moments of life, knowing how blessed you are to have found true love. Can you do this?"

"Yes, sir," I said.

"Yes," Brandi said.

"Do you take this woman to be your lawfully wedded wife, for better or worse, through sickness and health?"

"I do." My voice cracked. Better or worse. She'd already been through the worst, and without me. I would never allow that to happen again.

He asked the same of Brandi and she said, "I do."

Both our hands shook as we exchanged rings.

Pastor Lund smiled. "Now, look out at the people in the pews."

We turned to look out to the church.

"Friends and family," Pastor Lund said. "There will be times when this couple will need your support. Life can be hard, tragic even, as you already know. During times of need, will you commit to supporting this couple?"

Both my parents nodded, smiling through their tears. Grammie and Pa were holding hands, beaming at us. Breck and Garth sat together with Crystal between them.

Crystal wiped her eyes and nodded. "Yes."

Garth gave the thumbs-up.

"Amen," Breck called out.

"I need an amen from each of you," Pastor Lund said. "Otherwise we might have to call this whole thing off."

I turned to look at Huck. Would he join them? We locked eyes as a chorus of amens echoed through the church, his included.

"Excellent. This has been a long time coming," Pastor Lund said. "I pronounce you husband and wife. You may kiss the bride."

I wrapped one arm around her waist and pulled her close, then kissed my bride.

Our friends and family erupted into cheers and clapping.

We walked down the aisle holding hands. Breck had run ahead to open the doors of the church. As we exited, a sparrow arrived and perched on the railing. She let out a sweet chirp, followed by a flutter of her tiny wings.

"It's Ava," Brandi whispered. "Coming to give her blessing." Tears spilled from her eyes as she looked up at me. "I'm sure of it."

The sparrow hopped along the railing, chirping, then lifted into the air.

We stood with our arms wrapped around each other as we watched the sparrow until she was merely a fleck against the blue sky.

B randi

A MONTH AFTER OUR WEDDING, I NOTICED THAT I'D MISSED A period. I didn't think much of it, figuring with all the excitement my cycle was off. Another week went by before I decided to take a test. I sneaked into the drugstore one afternoon after I left work. Although I was a grown, married woman, unlike the last time I'd had to buy one in this drugstore, I blushed as I set it on the counter. The clerk, bless her, didn't comment.

I drove home with the air-conditioning blasting my face. The weather wasn't that hot, hovering in the low eighties, but I'd been a hot mess all day. My breasts hurt, too. It was either that my period was really late, which was messing with me, or I was pregnant. I couldn't decide which I wanted.

Days after the wedding, I'd moved my things into Trapper's house, leaving the apartment available for a temporary home for Crystal. She thought it best to live there, given her insane attraction to our favorite attorney. "I don't trust myself to stay out of his bed," she'd said to me.

I was disappointed she chose to leave. I'd hoped they would fall in love if they continued to spend nights together. Apart, I feared they'd never realize how good they were together. However, her decision didn't keep me from adding them to my prayers at night. If it was in his plan, then somehow, they would find their way to each other.

He didn't say, but I had a feeling Garth hated to see her go. The first few days after she left, he moped around like a sad puppy. Being a man, he wouldn't say what troubled him, not even to Trapper. I knew. He missed Crystal.

Neither of the men were there when I arrived back at the house. Garth spent long days at his office and often ate out for dinner. "I don't want to be in the way of the honeymooners," he'd said.

As much as we liked him, it was nice to spend the evenings making dinner together and eating on the patio as the light dimmed. By the time Garth came home at night, we were already in bed doing what newlyweds do.

Holding the bag with the pregnancy test against my side, as if it were contraband cigars, I went to our master bathroom and shut the door. I peed on the stick, shook it dry, and tossed it onto the counter. The directions said to wait two minutes before looking to see if there was one line or two. I set the alarm on my phone.

I looked at myself in the mirror. My cheeks were red, as if I'd just run a few miles. I needed to talk to Trapper about turning the thermostat down in the house. I placed my hands over my belly. It did seem swollen, but that could just be from my premenstrual syndrome.

What did I want? Could I handle a pregnancy without living every moment of it in fear? Was this the right time? Trapper and I were having so much fun together. We were still learning how to be a married couple. Did we need more time?

Seconds seemed like minutes as I waited. Finally, the alarm went off. I took in a deep breath and reached for the stick. Two pink lines. In fact, bright pink.

I sat on the edge of the soaking tub. Pregnant. Right at this minute, a baby was forming inside me. A person that Trapper and I had made because we loved each other so much. Time had tried to trick us into believing there was no chance for our reunion. But here we were. Together. Happy. And now a baby would come.

I dropped to my knees on the soft bath mat and started to pray. Right then I knew how much I wanted this baby. Even though I was frightened to lose her or him, the longing for a child outweighed that terror.

Please, God, protect this child.

That's how Trapper found me. On my knees in front of the tub and talking out loud to God.

"Brandi?" He rushed to me and fell to his knees. "What is it?" He placed his hand on my upper back. "Are you sick?"

I lifted my damp face to look at him. "No, Trap. I'm pregnant."

He rocked back on his heels. For a second, shock froze his features. In the next moment, his eyes lit up and filled with tears. He started to laugh and cry at the same time. "Pregnant? Oh my God, Brandi? Really?"

I nodded and pointed to the test by my feet. "I just took it. Two lines."

He picked it up with his long fingers and squinted at the small screen. "Yes, those are two lines. No question. They're so vivid, right? So there's no way it's not true?"

"These sticks are very accurate."

"These are the two best lines I've ever seen." He grinned as he set the test on the edge of the tub. "We're going to have a baby."

Still on our knees, we clasped hands. "You've given me

everything I could ever want and now this, too," he said. "Are you scared?"

"Terrified. But I can't do that to him or her. I have to believe that everything's going to be all right." My voice broke. "I have to."

"I'm scared, too," he said. "But I agree. We have to remember what a miracle it is that we found our way back together."

"Yes," I whispered.

Trapper leaned close and kissed me. "I'm here this time. I won't let you down. Put your burdens on me."

I wrapped my arms around his neck and let him lift us both to our feet.

He placed his hand over my stomach. "I have something I want you to see. Will you take a drive with me?"

"I'd go anywhere with you."

FIFTEEN MINUTES LATER, WE PULLED INTO THE CEMETERY. HE TOOK my hand and led me over to Ava's gravestone. Only it wasn't the one that had left her unnamed. Instead, a new one with her name and dates etched into the stone read:

Ava Elizabeth Vargas Barnes

January 10, 2010 – January 10, 2010

Precious daughter. Guardian angel.

I burst into tears. "Oh, Trap. It's perfect." Trapper wrapped his arms around me and held me close.

"I thought it was about time she had my name," Trapper said. "I'm sorry it took so long. I'm sorry I was gone so long."

I rested my cheek against his chest. "You're here now. That's all that matters."

The September light faded and turned the sky a brilliant pink. We clung to each other, neither of us inclined to leave just yet. I thought about all the men and women who had come before us. Every generation had loved and lost and persevered, just as Trapper and I had.

Standing there as the sky grew crimson, the space between this life and the hereafter didn't seem so far away. Those whose blood ran through our veins were here in the breeze that smelled of wildflowers and the rustle of the wild grasses that grew just beyond the fence.

Fight for love, they seemed to whisper.

And then, clear and sweet, came the sound of a sparrow. This song was just for me. I knew every word, every note. *Be brave, dear Mama. Be brave.*

I will, baby girl. I will.

I looked up into the eyes of the man I'd loved all my life. "Let's go home, Trap."

He took my hand, and we walked across the grass, listening to the music of the sparrow. My two great loves no longer haunted me. They were here with me, as they'd always been. A peace settled over me as I stopped and took one last glance back, searching for the bird. I could not see her, yet I knew she was there.

I moved my gaze to Trapper.

"You ready?" He smiled down at me. "For the next chapter in our love story?"

The next chapter. We had no road map or guidebook. Courage was our only map. This was the way of love.

I simply nodded and gave him my hand.

Be brave, Mama. Be brave.

A note from Tess…

The Patron is now available. Grab it to see what happens between Garth and Crystal!

Pre-order The Pet Doctor for Breck and Tiffany's story releasing February 15, 2022, which is my birthday! Woot.

For more Emerson Pass, download the historical books in the series. Travel back in time to meet the original residents of Emerson Pass, starring the Barnes family.
The School Mistress
The Spinster
The Scholar

Sign up for my newsletter over at my website at www.tess-writes.com and never miss a sale or new release, plus you'll get a free ebook copy of The Santa Trial. You can also join my Facebook group Patio Chat with Tess Thompson for fun giveaways and sneak peeks.

If you loved Emerson Pass, you will also fall in love with my Blue Mountain Series. One click the first installment in this romantic mystery series Blue Midnight for FREE.

Love small town romance with dreamy heroes and smart heroines and a beach setting? Check out my Cliffside Bay Series. The first in the series is FREE! Get Traded here.

I appreciate you helping to spread the word about my books. Thank you for sharing a recommendation with friends and please leave a review on the retailer of your choice.

Sending love from my home to yours, Tess XO

ALSO BY TESS THOMPSON

CLIFFSIDE BAY

Traded: Brody and Kara

Deleted: Jackson and Maggie

Jaded: Zane and Honor

Marred: Kyle and Violet

Tainted: Lance and Mary

Cliffside Bay Christmas, The Season of Cats and Babies (Cliffside Bay Novella to be read after Tainted)

Missed: Rafael and Lisa

Cliffside Bay Christmas Wedding (Cliffside Bay Novella to be read after Missed)

Healed: Stone and Pepper

Chateau Wedding (Cliffside Bay Novella to be read after Healed)

Scarred: Trey and Autumn

Jilted: Nico and Sophie

Kissed (Cliffside Bay Novella to be read after Jilted)

Departed: David and Sara

Cliffside Bay Bundle, Books 1,2,3

BLUE MOUNTAIN SERIES

Blue Mountain Bundle, Books 1,2,3

Blue Midnight

Blue Moon

Blue Ink

Blue String

ABOUT THE AUTHOR

Tess Thompson is the USA Today Bestselling and award-winning author of contemporary and historical Romantic Women's Fiction with over 40 published titles. When asked to describe her books, she could never figure out what to say that would perfectly sum them up until she landed on...Hometowns and Heartstrings.

She's married to her prince, Best Husband Ever, and is the mother of their blended family of four kids and five cats. Best Husband Ever is seventeen months younger, which qualifies Tess as a Cougar, a title she wears proudly. Her Bonus Sons are young adults with pretty hair and big brains like their dad. Daughters, better known as Princess One and Two, are teenagers who make their mama proud because they're kind. They're also smart, but a mother shouldn't brag.

Tess loves lazy afternoons watching football, hanging out on the back patio with Best Husband Ever, reading in bed, binge-watching television series, red wine, strong coffee and walks on crisp autumn days. She laughs a little too loudly, never knows what to make for dinner, looks ridiculous kickboxing in an attempt to combat her muffin top, and always complains about the rain even though she *chose* to live in Seattle.

She's proud to have grown up in a small town like the ones in her novels. After graduating from the University of Southern

California Drama School, she had hopes of becoming an actress but was called instead to writing fiction. She's grateful to spend most days in her office matchmaking her characters while her favorite cat Mittens (shhh…don't tell the others) sleeps on the desk.

She adores hearing from readers, so don't hesitate to say hello or sign up for her newsletter: http://tesswrites.com/. You'll receive an ebook copy of her novella, The Santa Trial, for your efforts.

Made in the USA
Middletown, DE
21 November 2021

53083591R00150